PRAISE FOR SIX

"What if you had to solve your own murder? The brilliant Catherine McKenzie has crafted a twisty and toxic psychological deep dive into mother-daughter relationships, jealousy, obsession—and gaspingly surprising revenge. An irresistible story, compellingly told—and impossible to outwit. Loved this!"

HANK PHILLIPPI RYAN, *USA Today* bestselling author of *The First to Lie*

"A smart, gripping, twisted story of dark family secrets . . . will have readers feverishly turning pages until the final jaw-dropping conclusion."

ROBYN HARDING, #1 bestselling author of *The Swap*

"Begins with a gut punch of an opener: a poisoning with a fatal diagnosis, a woman with a mere six weeks to find the killer. Grief, secrets, revenge, guilt, and blame—McKenzie weaves them all together with a deft hand, turning up the heat with every chapter. A gripping page-turner that held me captive until the shocking end."

KIMBERLY BELLE, bestselling author of *Stranger in the Lake* and *Dear Wife*

"Every time I open the cover on a Catherine McKenzie novel, I know I'm in for a ride. *Six Weeks to Live* proves my theory right yet again. With its impeccable plotting and ticking clock, it is the best kind of domestic suspense—a story both heartbreaking and visceral, surprising yet inevitable. Jennifer and her triplets will shock you from start to finish."

J.T. ELLISON, *New York Times* bestselling author of *Her Dark Lies* and *Good Girls Lie*

"McKenzie readily demonstrates what a deft storyteller she is. Suspicion reigns supreme in this twisted and sinister domestic suspense, and your allegiances are guaranteed to shift faster than a ping-pong match. Cleverly plotted and expertly paced, with an ending that's sure to have you gasping out loud. Do yourself a favor and pop this on your 2021 reading list now."

HANNAH MARY McKINNON, bestselling author of *Sister Dear*

"Just when you think you know what's happening . . . there's a new twist, a new piece of information, a new direction. Unpredictable and captivating, *Six Weeks to Live* had me mesmerized right up to the shocking end."

SAMANTHA DOWNING, bestselling author of *My Lovely Wife* and *He Started It*

"Begins with a devastating premise, then takes the reader on the most unexpected ride as a mother seeks to uncover the truth about the illness that is about to take her life. With skillful plotting and flawless narration, McKenzie weaves together past and present in this twisty, page-turning, and ultimately heartbreaking novel. Thoroughly enjoyable!"

WENDY WALKER, bestselling author of *Don't Look for Me*

"A twisty tale of secrets and lies that reverberate across generations of a dysfunctional family. Gripping and unputdownable."

MICHELE CAMPBELL, internationally bestselling author of *The Wife Who Knew Too Much*

"Smart, engrossing, and richly emotional, *Six Weeks to Live* is a deep dive into the secrets and lies between a dying mother and her three daughters. Part whodunit, part family drama, this textured and utterly spellbinding story unravels in surprising ways you won't see coming. A heart-wrenching, complex story of death, regret, and the impact our pasts have on our future."

CHRISTINA McDONALD, *USA Today* bestselling author

"A subtle and unsettling novel about a family with secrets and a mother running out of time. A suspenseful story that will keep you reading past your bedtime."

KAIRA ROUDA, *USA Today* bestselling author of *Best Day Ever*

"McKenzie is at her very best in *Six Weeks to Live*; it's twisty as hell and impossible to put down. I was hooked from the first page to the spectacular ending. This was exactly the book I needed to read right now."

AMBER COWIE, author of *Loss Lake*

"In *Six Weeks to Live*, her eleventh novel, McKenzie masterfully spins an exceptional story that is darkly funny, poignant, and grippingly suspenseful. A fresh take on the whodunit, this addictive novel will both tug at your heartstrings and make you frantically flip the pages to unlock the key to the mystery. A mesmerizing read!"

SAMANTHA M. BAILEY, #1 bestselling author of *Woman on the Edge*

"McKenzie works her magic again, combining harrowing domestic suspense with a razor-sharp crime thriller that had me riveted from page one. Hands down my favorite book this year."

EMILY CARPENTER, bestselling author of *Burying the Honeysuckle Girls* and *The Weight of Lies*

Praise for *You Can't Catch Me*

"McKenzie is at the top of her game when a former cult member finds herself mixed up in a dangerous high-stakes case of identity theft.... McKenzie's best book yet!"
Mary Kubica, *New York Times* and *USA Today* bestselling author of
The Good Girl and *Pretty Baby*

"*You Can't Catch Me* has a saucy female narrator and an intriguing plot. If that's not enough to lure you in, there's also intelligent action and great characters.... One of Montreal lawyer Catherine McKenzie's best novels."
The Globe and Mail

"An action thriller that just grabs you by the throat and won't let you go."
Montreal Times

Praise for *I'll Never Tell*

"McKenzie does a brilliant job of gradually reconstructing the last day of Amanda's life, mapping each sibling's whereabouts on the campgrounds while also revealing their own potential culpability in the crime."
Chatelaine

"Should be at the top of your list."
PopSugar

"McKenzie's characters leap from the page in this compulsive, riveting tale filled with twisty family secrets, suspect loyalties, and deadly encounters."
Heather Gudenkauf, *New York Times* bestselling author of
The Weight of Silence and *Not a Sound*

Praise for *The Good Liar*

"[McKenzie] specializes in mining people's inner darkness, particularly the inner darkness of women living superficially happy lives."
The Globe and Mail

"A riveting thriller."
Entertainment Weekly

"Thought-provoking, suspenseful, and mysterious, *The Good Liar* is a true page-turner."
Megan Miranda, *New York Times* bestselling author of
All the Missing Girls and *The Perfect Stranger*

ALSO BY CATHERINE McKENZIE

You Can't Catch Me

I'll Never Tell

The Good Liar

Fractured

Smoke

Spun

Hidden

Forgotten

Arranged

Spin

SIX WEEKS TO LIVE

A Novel

Catherine McKenzie

PUBLISHED BY SIMON & SCHUSTER

New York   London   Toronto   Sydney   New Delhi

SIMON &
SCHUSTER
CANADA

Simon & Schuster Canada
A Division of Simon & Schuster, Inc.
166 King Street East, Suite 300
Toronto, Ontario M5A 1J3

This Simon & Schuster Canada edition April 2021

SIMON & SCHUSTER CANADA and colophon are
trademarks of Simon & Schuster, Inc.

For information about special discounts for bulk purchases, please contact Simon & Schuster Special Sales at 1-800-268-3216 or CustomerService@simonandschuster.ca.

The Simon & Schuster Speakers Bureau can bring authors to your live event. For more information or to book an event, contact the Simon & Schuster Speakers Bureau at 1-866-248-3049 or visit our website at www.simonspeakers.com.

Interior design by Lexy Alemao

Manufactured in the United States of America

1   3   5   7   9   10   8   6   4   2

Library and Archives Canada Cataloguing in Publication
Title: Six weeks to live / Catherine McKenzie.
Names: McKenzie, Catherine, author.
Description: Simon & Schuster Canada edition.
Identifiers: Canadiana (print) 20200314408 | Canadiana (ebook) 20200314424
| ISBN 9781982137557 (softcover) | ISBN 9781982137564 (ebook)
Classification: LCC PS8625.K4395 S59 2021 | DDC C813/.6—dc23

ISBN 978-1-9821-3755-7
ISBN 978-1-9821-3756-4 (ebook)

For Wilma,
who always saw the best in everyone

Six Weeks to Live . . .

Chapter 1

INSANE IN THE MEMBRANE

Jennifer

"I'm sorry to have to tell you this, Jennifer, but you have a primary glioblastoma in your brain. That's—"

"Brain cancer," I whisper, the words a rasp in my throat.

"Yes," the doctor says. I've been told his name, but I can't remember it for the life of me. He isn't my regular doctor, just someone in his practice I was referred to when I first came in a couple of weeks ago. The physician I'd seen for years, Dr. Turner, retired last year at the age of seventy-eight, right after my last physical. This new guy looks young enough to date my twenty-five-year-old daughters.

"I have a grade 4 cancer." The knowledge comes to me, unbidden.

He nods.

"I'm dying."

"Yes," he says gravely. "You have six weeks before . . ." He shakes his head as if he's disappointing himself for ending my life.

The world tilts and I grip the arms of the chair I'm sitting in. They're rounded at the end and slightly worn, as if they've been clung to in this way before, and more than once.

A bad-news chair.

The doctor watches me. He has watery blue eyes and a rash of acne scars near his dark hairline. "I'm sorry, Jennifer."

I squeeze the chair arms harder and focus on a spot above his head. There's a large tank built into the taupe wall behind him, with a small school of fish in it, flashing silver and red. This is what my taxes are for—fish tanks and doctors who look like the prodigies on medical television shows.

"So all of this . . ." I say, motioning to the body that's betrayed me. "It's going to get worse."

He clears his throat and looks back to his notes. I might be the first person he's ever had to deliver this type of news to.

"Yes. The tumor is in your temporal lobe, which regulates speech, memory, behavior, vision, hearing, and emotions. What this means, then, is that you can expect an increase in the headaches you've been having, but also potentially issues with your speech, mood, and . . ."

Half of me listens to him cycle through the symptoms I'm already experiencing—memory issues, achy joints, all the reasons I went to the doctor in the first place—and the symptoms yet to come— behavior and personality changes, seizures, swelling, and then . . .

The other half of me is focused on the fish and the patterns they're making in the glowing water. I've always thought I'd like to have fish, but somehow in the chaos of raising the triplets I never got around to it. Now I envy them, the fish. They're oblivious in there, circling the tank, looking for the last remnants of lunch. Do fish hear like humans do? Or is their whole life like when you sink your head under the ocean? That echoey muffled sound of . . . sound?

The doctor's stopped talking, waiting for my reaction to a question he might have asked or simply to the information he's been cataloging methodically. My hands are cramping on the chair, so I let go. The room is still spinning, though. I'm tumbling through space, a satellite off its axis.

I try to think of something to ask. Is there anything more I need to know? And then it hits me: in the litany of signs and symptoms, I didn't hear anything about treatment.

"And there's nothing we can do?"

He shakes his head like a sad dog. "There are some good palliative options for when things get worse."

"Not surgery? Chemo? Radiation?"

"Maybe if we'd caught it earlier."

"But we didn't," I say, and he agrees.

I don't know how much longer it is until I leave the doctor's inner office clutching a fistful of papers. Time slips sideways when someone tells you you're dying.

"Can I help you, Ms. Barnes?" a nurse asks as I stumble into the waiting room.

I search my brain tape and this time her name is available. Who knows for how long?

"Tiana?"

Her dark brown eyes fill with concern. "Did you need something, honey?"

"I . . . I don't know."

"Did the doctor give you those?"

I look down at the unfamiliar papers in my hand. "Yes. Should I give them to you?"

"Those are for you to take home. Here, let me show you."

The stares of the other people in the waiting room press into my back. Dead woman walking. Is that what it says on my sweater now, for everyone to see? Or is it the expression on my face that gives it away? Part of me cares, but the other part simply feels lost. How did I get here? I plan everything, and I don't have to check my calendar to know that dying at forty-eight is not on the schedule.

I hand the sheets to Tiana and try to concentrate on what she tells me as she sorts them into two piles.

"These are your prescriptions," she says, pointing to the shorter stack. Her nurse's uniform is crisp and white, like something from the fifties. "You'll need to go to the pharmacy and fill these. There's one downstairs if you need it."

I look at the top page and feel foolish. They're prescriptions. I even recognize the medications—a steroid to help manage cerebral edema and my other symptoms. Tramadol, an opioid for when the pain gets to be too much for extra-strength Tylenol. Clonazepam to help me sleep. Drugs I'd never take normally, but I guess I don't have to worry about addiction or the weight I'll gain.

I see a quick flash of light. I reach up and touch my head. It disappears as quickly as it came, as if the tap to my forehead was an off switch. I doubt it will work much longer.

"Are you all right?"

"Yes, I—I felt a . . . pain, I guess, but it's gone."

"You'll want to fill these," Tiana says again, pointing to the prescriptions.

She knows my diagnosis, I realize. *Glioblastoma multiforme.* Knows that I'm dying. She must've known before I did. Was that why she was so nice to me when I checked in?

"I will."

"Today."

"Yes," I agree, though what does it matter? Corticosteroids, benzos, and opioids are not going to cure me, or even necessarily reduce my suffering. They're the window dressing being put on my tragedy so the doctor can feel as if he did something.

She motions to the larger pile of documents. "These other papers explain about your diagnosis. What you might expect in the coming weeks. In case you didn't take it all in when Dr. Parent was explaining it to you."

Dr. Parent? Did he say that was his name? He's not old enough to be a father. No, that's not right. It's the French name, *Pa-rent.* Only she's put a twang to it, and—I'm losing it. I am going to lose it in front of these strangers and this smiling, kind nurse and—

No. I can handle this. I can breathe. Yes, I'm going to breathe. That breathing exercise my therapist taught me years ago. I need to breathe in through my nose for four beats and out through my mouth for *1—2—3—4—*.

1—2—3—4—.

I do this ten times, ticking off the repetitions with my thumb against my fingers, trying hard not to think about how weird I must look. Did I always care this much about other people's opinions? A side effect of the malignant cells that have invaded my brain and will march onward until they've shut it down entirely?

I breathe in and out again. Somatic therapy, that's what the exercise is called. It engages the somatic nervous system, which regulates anxiety and acts like a natural benzodiazepine. See, brain, you haven't lost me yet.

When I am done, I feel calmer, though Tiana looks more concerned than she did when I started counting.

"Better?" Tiana asks.

"Yes, thank you."

"Good. You've also got all your test results in here, in case you want a second opinion. And there are two more documents that are important, ones you'll want to review with your family."

She pulls two sheets out. *Palliative options*, the first one says across the top. There's a list of facilities below it, and one other line at the bottom written in by hand that I recognize from a series of controversial stories in the paper. *Alternative end-of-life options*, it reads, with a phone number. Assisted suicide, this means, now legal in Canada for cases that are bad enough.

The other document is decidedly legal—a medical power of attorney form. If—when—things get grim, someone has to be able to turn off the lights if I can't make that decision anymore. I have to choose one person to give this power to, and the choice seems obvious and exhausting.

My eyes sting with tears, muddling my words. I need to leave this horrible room with its quiet classical music and its greige paint. I shuffle the pages together as if I'm going to store them in a folder, only I don't have one. I didn't think I'd need transportation for papers. I didn't think there was anything seriously wrong with me, only fatigue and getting older and—

Fuck.

I'm dying. My life has a countdown clock.

And it starts now.

Chapter 2

PAVED PARADISE, PUT UP A PARKING LOT

Jennifer

Though the world is now listing like I'm in the middle of a hurricane, I make it to the parking lot. I can't remember where I left my car and I don't have the energy to walk up and down the long rows searching for it, so I hit the panic button on my key fob. I normally hate it when people do that, but today I think the obnoxious noise is justified. I follow it until I find my car, neatly parked between two white lines, nose out so it's easy to leave. I've always parked like that, ready to make a quick escape, and finally, now, I'm glad.

I kill the alarm and get in. I put the sheaf of papers I'm clutching on the seat next to me.

And then I lose it.

Another time slip. Better not to keep track of how long you spend sobbing alone in your car in a medical building parking lot after someone tells you you're dying. So I ride it out, my arms slumped over the front wheel, my body heaving, and wait for it to stop. Eventually it does.

I sit up and wipe my face with my sleeve. I leave a black streak of mascara on the light gray fabric. It probably won't come out. This would've driven me nuts this morning, the waste of it, the stupid decision to use one of my nicest sweaters as a tissue. But the only reaction I can muster now is *oh well.*

I look out the window. It's a pleasant day, and the lodgepole pines that ring the parking lot are swaying slightly in the breeze. An afternoon on a placid Monday at the beginning of June. The sky is mercifully blue, a day when I'd normally be out in the garden, soaking up the infrequent sunshine. My appointment was at eleven, and now it's nearly one. I should be starving, weak even, my hypoglycemia kicking in, but I don't think I can ever eat again. Perhaps I won't. I'll simply hasten this all along and starve myself to death. Maybe I'll—

No. I need to quash this now. Spiraling thoughts are not the answer. Spiraling thoughts are bad. That's not even the word I want to use, but my language is sneaking away too. That was the one symptom that stood out other than the headaches, the trouble I've been having finding words sometimes. Anomic aphasia. I mostly thought it was a natural part of aging. A perimenopausal symptom like some of my girlfriends are going through. In dark moments, usually when I couldn't sleep, I worried it was early-onset Alzheimer's. But then I'd bat that possibility away. I'm only forty-eight. There isn't any family history. My mother's sharp as a tack at seventy-five, and her mother made it to 103, living in her own home to the end.

I was right to be concerned, though. I should've listened to the alarm bells my body was emitting and pressed the panic button long before now.

My watch jolts on my arm. It's a text from one of my girls. *Thing 1*, it says, referring to Emily. A family joke left over from childhood, when the triplets were a minor media sensation and their favorite pieces of clothing were the special *Thing 1, 2,* and *3* shirts someone at Disney gave them as a promotional item.

A set of identical twins and a full sibling, that's what I'd given birth to. A polyzygotic pregnancy, it's called, when two eggs are fertilized and one splits in two but the other doesn't. A medical anomaly that's a one-in-a-million chance. One in a million—that's what I used to tell the girls they were. A statistic to be proud of.

What are the odds of developing glioblastoma? I used to know all those statistics, but my mind's a blank right now. Regardless, it can't be as rare as that.

I check Emily's text. A reminder that her twins have a talent show at their day care on Wednesday. Perfectly organized Emily's reminders arrive on time and as scheduled, forty-eight hours before any commitment.

Some people are just born old.

Jake and I were twenty-three when the girls arrived. We were outnumbered from day one, and though we had help from friends and family, it took us years to recover. More than once, when the girls were older, Jake would look across the dinner table at me and say, "We did it." We survived, he meant. We'd made it.

Jake. Shit. I'm going to have to tell Jake.

I scroll through my texts to find my last exchange with him when a text from my best friend, Suzie, appears, asking how my doctor appointment went. I'll get back to her later, after I deal with Jake.

Please, he'd texted. Please give me the divorce.

Go fuck yourself, I'd replied. If you want the divorce you know what you have to do. And then for emphasis, I'd written, $$$.

He'd never replied.

Not my finest moment, but so be it. It wasn't about the money anyway. I had plenty of my own now, but money was the only lever I had left. A large part of me wishes I never had to see him again, but he's the father of my children. If Dr. Parent's right, and I have no reason to believe otherwise, he's going to be the only parent they have left very shortly.

I need you to come to the house tonight, I write to Jake.

Why? comes the almost immediate response. Jake's never far from his smartphone, communicating with it at all times of the day and night. It's funny now, but I never use to worry about it or measure his words for the falsehoods they could easily contain.

My mistake.

I have something important to tell you, I write. The girls will be there too.

I write this without even having asked them to come, but I don't have to worry. My girls love me and will be there for me; that's the one thing I'm certain of.

Are you finally going to relent? Jake writes back. I can feel his excitement at the possibility.

It strikes me like a slap that Jake is finally going to get his way. So convenient for him, my dying.

Come to the house tonight and find out.

I can see him hesitating, that bubble of consideration floating in our thread. But he'll come. If there's any possibility that I'll let him off the hook without a nasty divorce in front of the family court judges who are looking for an opportunity to avenge their own losses, he'll jump at it.

His confirmation comes a minute later. I send a quick text to the girls asking them to come for dinner too, underlining the importance, not giving them a chance to say no. Then I throw the phone down onto the front seat without waiting for their answers. The papers I got from the doctor rustle as the phone hits them. I pick them up and flip to my test results, including those from my physical last year. CBC and blood protein testing and tumor markers—all the things you'd expect with a diagnosis like mine. I was in my third year of medical school when I got pregnant. I was supposed to take a year off and then go back to complete my degree, but when one baby turned into three, that plan got thrown out the window. I still remember the lingo, though, the terminology locked into my long-term memory.

I scan the results like clicking the beads on a rosary. There's something comforting in it, though some of the numbers are way off.

Then I get to a section in last year's tests that stops me cold. My previous physician, Dr. Turner, had done a full blood panel and it had turned up something unusual. Lead—a lot of it. The results are so far off the charts that they have to be a mistake.

That much lead in the system would make someone very sick, and might even cause—

Oh.

The world closes in like a pinhole camera.

I have just enough time to reach for the panic button before I pass out. And the last thing I hear before everything goes dark is the shrill of the alarm.

Chapter 3

DON'T ASK, DON'T GET

Aline

Aline was nursing a bad hangover, but that didn't stop her from sticking to her plan and asking Dr. Jackson for what she wanted.

"Credit?" Deandra Jackson replied dismissively. "Your name will be on the publication."

"I meant as first author."

"Pardon?"

"I want to be listed as first author."

Deandra looked startled. She rolled her chair back from the bench where she was looking at the slides Aline had prepared for her and crossed her arms over her ample chest. "That's not how it works. You know that."

Aline hid her annoyance. She knew how it worked. She wasn't an idiot. The point was, the way it had worked for the last fifty years or whatever was bullshit.

Aline ran her hand over her head, smoothing a loose hair into her signature ballet bun. "But I did the work. I wrote the paper. I'm the author."

"And I provided the resources and supervised your work and came up with the research concept in the first place."

Aline bit her lip, hit a worry spot and tasted blood. This was also bullshit, but she had to tread lightly. Deandra had made it perfectly clear since Aline had been working for her that she didn't like to be reminded about the work she'd done and, more importantly, not done on a project. Yes, Deandra brought in the money because she was a brilliant scientist, someone who'd done some amazing cutting-edge research on DNA linkages to everything from diabetes to cancer. But the reality was also that she hadn't done her own research, or even research proposals, for years. Aline doubted she even knew how to fill out a grant application anymore. Deandra wasn't alone in that; none of the senior scientists at this lab, or the one she'd worked in before, did their own applications.

"Aline?"

"Yes, Dr. Jackson?"

"Are we on the same page?"

Aline hesitated. She wanted to tell Deandra to shove it and leave, but she had ambitions. Plans. She needed a good recommendation from Deandra to get her next job. That, and a few more publications under her belt.

"Yes."

"Good. Now, is that all for today?"

Aline managed not to roll her eyes as she said that it was. Deandra stood and walked away. Aline watched her make her way to Kevin's bench across the room, her stomach in knots and her head pounding. Whether it was from the one drink that had turned into five the night before or the interaction with Deandra, she wasn't entirely sure. Aline hated it when she didn't get what she wanted, but she couldn't see how to change that now.

Aline sat down on her stool, feeling queasy. She reached into her bag and took a clonazepam out of its vial, slipping it quickly under her tongue. She closed her eyes and waited for it to kick in, trying to block out the antiseptic air and the slight buzzing sound from the bright overhead fluorescents.

Her phone vibrated in the pocket of her lab coat. It was a text from her mother asking her—no, telling her—to come to dinner with less than a few hours of warning.

No fucking way, she wanted to write, but life was more complicated than that.

Her mother had written in the family group thread, which Aline usually ignored. She flicked through it quickly—it was mostly texts between her mother and Emily, with the occasional intervention from Miranda. Aline's texts were mainly emojis, which her mother hated, which is why she did it. Like a sliver under a fingernail. That's the way Aline felt about their relationship. But was she the sliver or the nail?

Aline switched over to the group chat she had with her sisters, no mothers allowed.

You going to Mom's? she wrote.

Emily answered first. The boys have soccer tonight.

Have Chris take them.

Yes, Miranda wrote, joining the conversation. Send Sir Chris.

LOL, Aline responded.

Why is that funny?

Aline chuckled. Emily was always so sensitive about anything to do with Chris. Sir Chris was her and Miranda's nickname for Chris because he was so perfect.

Should we tell her? Aline tapped out.

She wouldn't believe us anyway, Miranda said. She never does.

Dudes. Cut it with the twin stuff.

I am not your dude, Aline wrote. Don't be so sensitive. You coming tonight or what?

I can't, Emily wrote. I told you.

So tell Mom you can't go.

She said it was important tho.

Aline sighed. Everything to their mother was a five-alarm fire. She was sick of it. Besides, she was supposed to go for drinks with Nick and some friends tonight. Though maybe she shouldn't. Eliminating a hangover with more drinking worked, but wasn't always the best idea.

So, Aline wrote. You showing, then?

Is Andrew going to be there? Emily asked.

Negatory, Miranda answered. He's at some artist colony thingy. Haven't seen him in a while.

Ugh. How can you stand being around him?

You offering to put me up?

I *did* offer, Emily wrote. You turned me down.

You live too far away.

You think the boys are too noisy.

Well . . .

You should've moved in with Aline, Emily wrote.

My apartment's too small, Aline responded, feeling guilty because she hadn't offered to let Miranda move in with her, and simultaneously pissed that Miranda hadn't asked.

Whatever, Miranda wrote. I'll be out of Mom's place in the fall.

Are you sure that's a good idea? Emily wrote. What about all the $ you owe?

It's handled.

Really?

Aline felt hot. Miranda had handled her money situation? When had that happened? How come Miranda hadn't told her? They shared everything. Well, almost everything.

Stay out of it bee-atch.

Sorry, sheesh.

Anyway, Aline wrote. Dinner yes or no?

We all know we're going, Miranda responded.

See you there!

Aline was about to put her phone away when another text popped up from Emily.

Hold on a sec.

[Jeopardy music] Aline wrote.

Nooo, Miranda wrote. That's too sad now.

Emily was back in a moment. Shit guys. That was the hospital.

The boys okay?

Not them. Mom. She's in the ER.

Why?

They wouldn't say. I need to call Chris. Go to the hospital. Will meet you there as soon as I can.

Aline's heart thudded and her hands felt slick against the phone.

Aline? Emily wrote.

Yes, coming.

Miranda?

I'll be there. But guys? What's wrong with Mom?

Chapter 4

I WANNA BE SEDATED

Emily

Even though she had the most to handle in order to free herself and get to the hospital, Emily was still there first. This didn't surprise her, though both of her sisters lived closer to the hospital than she did. They were always late. She didn't resent it, mostly—it was the way they'd been from the beginning when they'd clung to the womb for a full hour after Emily had vacated it, almost making them born on different days of the year. There had been only four minutes between their arrival, first Aline, then Miranda right on her heels, coming out one minute before midnight. If they'd only been a bit later, Emily often thought, she would've had a birthday to herself, separate from the twins.

You're triplets, her mother was always quick to correct her. Only they weren't triplets on anything other than a technical basis. They may have shared a womb, but Aline and Miranda were the ones who were truly connected, having started as one fertilized egg that split in half to create two identical people. She was the extra egg that had snuck in there, crowding them, making the whole pregnancy riskier than it already was.

It didn't help that they barely even looked like sisters. The twins had their father's coloring—thick, almost black hair, dark brown eyes, and olive skin. She was a carbon copy of their mother—light blue eyes with pale skin and strawberry blonde hair that fell in ringlets when she was young. This contrast had been part of the reason the triplets had gotten so much media attention when they were little—the triplets who weren't, three babies born together who looked as if they came from different families.

When she was in high school, people used to tease her by saying that she must be a mistake. Maybe her mother had been getting some extra on the side?

Emily had wondered about that herself over the years. It was possible. Her parents weren't married when Jennifer got pregnant; maybe she was dating someone else? Emily had even done 23andMe a few years ago, though she questioned her decision as she waited for the results. She'd read too many stories about people finding out that their father was the fertility doctor, or that they were switched at birth. No one in these stories seemed particularly happy with this newfound knowledge.

She shouldn't have worried. When the results came in, they confirmed that the girls were full sisters, whether she always wanted that to be true or not.

Going to be a while, Aline texted, Siri's slightly off pronunciation filling the car as Emily pulled into the hospital parking lot. I'm working on getting out of something.

Me too, Miranda wrote a moment later.

Emily parked her car while her hands shook on the wheel.

"Get here as soon as you can," Emily dictated as a response.

Did you hear anything? Aline asked.

"Not yet. But just come, okay? Both of you. I don't want to do this by myself."

They agreed, and Emily turned off her car. Emily had been as nice as possible to the desk nurse, but the nurse hadn't told her anything. Her mother had given Emily's name as the person to call. That was all she could say.

Maybe there wasn't anything wrong with her. Jennifer had always been a bit of a hypochondriac, though it usually stopped at the hospital door, where her own health was concerned. The triplets had been in and out of the emergency room when they were young, but Emily couldn't remember a single time when Jennifer had gone there for herself.

Emily tried to keep from leaping to any conclusions. There wasn't any use until she knew how serious this was. She climbed out of her car and locked it. It was an early June day, and the sun felt good on her exposed shoulders. This was her favorite time of year, when the world was full of life, and the sun shone for more than a few minutes at a time.

She was walking through the parking lot when her phone rang. It was Chris.

"Everything okay?" she asked.

"Yes," he said, his voice even. "Just calling to see if you knew anything yet."

"I'm on my way inside."

"I'm sure she's fine." Emily heard the sound of a small crash on Chris's side of the line. "Hold on a sec."

She smiled as she imagined the scene. The boys, her twins, were always up to something.

Because she looked so much like her mother, it seemed as if she were destined to follow Jennifer's fate, right down to getting pregnant at twenty-two, when Emily was in medical school. The only difference was that she'd had fraternal twins, two boys, now three years old, who had an insane amount of energy.

"I'm back," Chris said, slightly out of breath.

"Everything okay?"

"It was only a Duplo tower. Ethan knocked it over."

"Oh, good."

"I should take them to soccer."

"Yes. And also, maybe ten laps around the park?"

Chris laughed. "I'm thinking fifteen."

"Thank you."

"For what?"

"For being you."

"Go inside," Chris said gently. "Find out what's going on."

"Yes."

"I know it's scary."

Emily looked at the doors to the emergency bay. There was a man sitting in a wheelchair in a light blue hospital gown, hooked up to an IV. A young woman was crying into the shoulder of an older man who was patting her on the back in a way that looked uncomfortable. An ambulance blocked the view to the inside, its siren off but its lights still rotating, throwing off a flash of red, then white, then red.

She'd spent enough time in emerg to know what the inside would be like. Sick people sitting around the waiting room looking at their phones and watching the patient-response-time clock as if it were a promise. Nurses and med students rushing around trying to triage patients and order the right tests to move them along to a diagnosis. The constant tension to get it right and not send someone home prematurely. Nothing was worse than a missed diagnosis, though it happened all the time.

"She'll be okay," Chris said. "Text me when you know something."

"Will do."

Emily put her phone away and took one last look around. God only knew how long it would take her sisters to get there. She was going to have to go in alone.

She approached the sliding glass doors slowly. She couldn't help but feel that while she stayed outside, nothing was happening, but once she crossed the threshold, there wouldn't be any going back. Was she wrong to want to hold on to this moment a second longer?

The doors slid open as if in response to her question.

So she did the right thing, as she almost always did, and walked on through.

Chapter 5

DOCTOR, DOCTOR

Jennifer

"Glioblastoma?" Emily asks the resident who's been in and out of my cubicle a few times already this afternoon. Dr. Sayed is calm and focused and has the best bedside manner of anyone I've ever encountered in the medical profession. This is saying a lot for someone with rambunctious triplets who ended up in Pediatric Emergency at the Surrey Memorial Hospital on a regular basis up until the age of eight.

"Yes. In the temporal lobe. Inoperable."

Emily looks at me with panic in her eyes. "Mom, did you know this?"

"I found out this morning."

"Is that why you wanted us to come to dinner?"

"Yes."

Emily turns back to the doctor, a small pad of paper in her hands where she's started taking notes. I watch my daughter's efficient movements with pride, even though I'm embarrassed by the fact that I'm in the hospital at all. I fainted in the car, the wailing of the panic alarm summoning the help I couldn't ask for. When they asked me who to call, I said Emily because she's always the person you want in a crisis.

It wasn't the cancer that brought me here, though, Dr. Sayed is explaining. It was the lack of food and the shock of the news.

I am in shock. There's no getting around that. They've pushed fluids through my IV, and Emily gave me an energy bar from her cavernous purse. And though I don't feel faint anymore, that doesn't mean all is right with the world.

"What causes glioblastoma?" I ask Dr. Sayed when there's a pause in Emily's questioning.

She turns to me and speaks gently. Her hair and neck are covered by a beautiful teal fabric. "Mostly unknown, unfortunately. You might have inherited abnormalities in your DNA that could make you more susceptible to this form of cancer, but it's not something that's predetermined as far as we know."

"And with your history—" Emily says.

"Like the breast cancer gene?" I ask Dr. Sayed.

"Something like that, though the correlation there is much more pronounced."

I pull the thin sheet up over my hospital gown to my shoulders. It's white with blue stripes, and soft from too many washes, but it barely keeps out the cold. They've got the air-conditioning cranked up to the maximum setting, and I've been shivering since I got here. My mother believes in things like rain causes colds. If she were here, she'd tell everyone to turn the air down because it was going to kill her daughter.

Too late, Mom.

"Do you have any questions?" Emily asks me. "You must have so many."

My mind is whirring with them, but there's one that's front and center, because nothing about this feels like a natural result of my life.

"I seem to remember something about exposure to chemicals potentially being linked to certain forms of brain cancer. Could that have caused it?"

"What?" Aline asks, careening into the room like a drunk. "You have cancer?"

"Mom has cancer again?" Miranda says right behind her, then gives Emily a hard look. "How come you didn't tell us?"

"Yeah," Aline says. "How come?"

"Girls, girls. Stop it. Emily didn't know. She only just found out."

Miranda glances at Emily as if asking for permission to speak. Emily nods gently. "Are you . . . Are you . . . ?"

There's no sugarcoating this for them, though I wish with everything I have that I could. "Dying? Yes."

Miranda's hand flies to her mouth, and a second later Aline's does the same. They've always done that, their whole life, as if their motor functions are linked, tied together with invisible string.

"Oh, Mommy," Miranda says, dropping her hand and launching herself onto the bed the way she used to do when she was little. "Oh, no."

A sad hour passes while the details get conveyed to the girls and sink further into me. Doctors and nurses come and go, come and go. They take my blood, send me for another scan, and at the end of it all I've received the second opinion I never asked for. The glioblastoma has a good grip on my brain. It will continue to advance through channels and tissue until it succeeds in shutting me down entirely. A suicide mission that will take me with it, kamikaze-style, in six weeks or so. No one can say for sure.

This is tough news for all of us, but I seem to have left all the tears I have in the parking lot. It's only when Miranda breaks down when Dr. Sayed confirms the time that I have left that I crack again.

We all crack then. Dr. Sayed retreats quietly to let us grieve together, and the girls crawl up onto the bed as best they can in a way that's both a comfort and a memory. Aline on the left, Miranda on the right, and Emily at my feet. Their silken heads are bowed, their hair in its contrasting shades tossed together on my belly. I've always loved the feel of it, ever since they were babies and it started growing in. It might look different, but its touch is identical.

We stay like that until sometime around six, when Dr. Sayed says I can go home. The nurse removes my IV, and I change back into the outfit I picked out this morning when I thought I was on my way to getting the all-clear. The sweater is already trashed because of my mascara, and I doubt I'll want to wear these jeans again. Maybe I'll ask the girls to bury me in these clothes, because who cares what you get cremated in?

I wish I could stop these morbid thoughts, but they seem to be all I have left.

When I emerge from the bathroom, only Emily remains.

"The twins went to the house," she says gently. She knows this term provokes me and I think it's her way of telling me that nothing fundamental has changed. I want to smile, but I can't. "They said something about making dinner."

Despite the fluids and the energy bar, I'm finally feeling hungry. "That would be nice."

"It will probably be something healthy and vegan."

I give her a conspiratorial grin. "Maybe we should stop at Five Guys on the way home?"

"A burger with real meat? But what about the environment?"

"Sweetheart, that's not going to be my problem."

"Why did you mention that, at the hospital?" Emily asks after we've gone to Five Guys and gotten our order to go. I got a bacon cheeseburger, fries, and a chocolate shake. I haven't eaten this much in one sitting in decades, but I plow through it like a teenage boy as Emily drives us to my house in her family SUV. Despite her three-year-olds, it's almost spotless.

"You're going to have to be more specific," I say with a full mouth. Here's a side effect of terminal cancer I hope is permanent: every bite I take is the best bite of food I can remember.

"About whether exposure to chemicals could have caused your cancer?" Emily asks as she stops at a light. She puts on her turn indicator, then drums her fingers on the steering wheel.

I lower my burger, resting it on the napkins on my lap. Even though this question is front and center in my mind, it sounds silly and paranoid now that Emily's said it out loud.

"It's nothing."

"Come on, Mom. What's going on?"

I finish the last of the burger to stall for time, then wipe my hands on the napkins as Emily navigates through traffic. I feel full, too full to have a serious conversation, particularly one about what might have made me sick. Even though it can't be true, I must be wrong—the delusions the doctor warned about already starting. I should've kept my suspicions to myself, but silence has never been my strong suit.

"I was trying to understand how this could have happened."

"I can't believe it got this far without them finding it." Emily shakes her head. "You must've been feeling sick for a long time. Why didn't you say anything?"

"I haven't been feeling that bad, honestly."

"Headaches, loss of memory, confusion . . . were you experiencing those symptoms?"

"Some of them, yes."

"And you didn't go to a doctor?"

"I did go to Dr. Turner a year ago—you remember, after the boys' birthday, when I was sick? He didn't find anything."

But there was something. Something in my blood back then that shouldn't have been there.

Emily's quiet for a moment, watching the road. I've never understood how I produced her. She might look like me, but she's so much more competent and focused. The only mistake it seems she ever made was mine as well—getting pregnant in the middle of her education. I know this isn't possible, everyone makes mistakes, but that's the kind of person she is. Error-free.

If only I could say the same.

"And when the symptoms persisted?" Emily asks. "You didn't go back?"

"The symptoms went away. Mostly."

"But with your medical history—"

"I don't want to talk about it anymore." My stomach clenches around the food I ate, and I worry I might throw up. I roll down the window and breathe in some fresh air.

"Yes, but maybe if . . ."

I lean back in the seat and touch her hand. "Don't do that to yourself. Don't do that to me. Nothing can be changed now."

"You sound like me."

"We've always sounded like each other."

"True."

She turns the car onto my street and stops in front of my house. Our house. The family home we moved into sixteen years ago with help from my parents. It was supposed to be a fresh start after I got home from the hospital. An updated rambling house, with a sprawling lawn and a backyard with a firepit. There's a large oak in the front yard with an old tire hanging from it. The house had enough room for all of us, but not so much room you could get lost in it. A place I thought I'd spend my whole life in.

It turns out I was right.

The sun is setting behind it, the sky pink and purple like a bruise. This home has always made me happy, and so I held on to it despite the fractures brought on by Jake's leaving.

"Thank you, Emily," I say as she turns off the engine.

"What for?"

"For everything you've done today and for everything I know you're going to do in the next few weeks."

"A pre-thanking."

"Yes, if you like."

We smile at each other, then gather up our things and get out. Miranda's car is already in the driveway along with another one it takes me a minute to place.

"Who invited him here?" I say with rancor before I can stop myself.

Then the front door swings open and there he is, standing in the doorway as if it's his home to invite me into rather than the other way around.

If he's offended by my comment, Jake doesn't miss a beat.

"You did, dear."

Chapter 6

DADDY'S HOME

Miranda

Miranda always hated it when her parents fought, and the fact that she was twenty-five years old changed nothing.

There was something about it that made her feel so small. Not that her parents fought a lot when she was little, but when they did, they went at it. Name-calling, door-slamming, days of silence afterward. When it would start, the girls would leave their rooms one by one and gather in Emily's room, climbing into her double bed and crowding together as if they were still in the womb.

Miranda and her sisters had always made shapes, and the shape of an argument was a tetrahedron.

"I wish we had sound things," Miranda remembered saying once when she was eight, her face near Emily's feet, her breath partially muffled by the comforter. It had flowers and unicorns on it, and Emily's reading light made it glow pink.

"You mean soundproofing?" Emily said.

"Yeah, that."

"Fancy pants," Aline said.

"Am not," Emily said.

"You think you're better than us because you skipped."

"I don't."

"She is better than us," Miranda said. "Better at school."

They went silent then, listening to the thud of words from upstairs. It was during those fights that Miranda first learned that words could hurt you like a punch.

So many years later, that was still true. Her mother and father were fighting in the kitchen, and Miranda and her sisters had retreated to the basement to pretend they weren't listening. But the fight filtered down through the floor, and with each rising tone Miranda felt bruised.

Emily was sitting on the old leather couch that used to be in the living room but had made it downstairs by the time they were fourteen. Miranda and Aline had taken up spots on the floor, each of them leaning on either side of Emily's legs. The room was carpeted in a Berber weave that always felt soft and warm underfoot. There was a large TV on the exposed brick wall and a huge collage of photos and newspaper clippings above the built-in mahogany bar. A shrine to their childhood, mostly, back when they were the Famous Gagnon Triplets, a name that reminded her more of a circus act than anything. It had been a circus for a while, but they'd gotten older, and the Fantastic Sanders Quads were born, and so all that was left were the memories and the photographs and the accumulation of trinkets they'd been given.

"History repeats itself," Emily said, looking up at the ceiling.

"I can't believe Dad's fighting with her when she's dying," Aline said in a clipped voice.

Miranda recoiled at that word, *dying*. It was so formal. So horrible. So final. "He doesn't know that though."

Aline knocked her feet against Miranda's. "Why do you always defend him?"

They were both wearing Stan Smiths with pink stripes on the side. They'd bought them separately, but they often did that.

"I don't. It's a factual statement."

"We should go up there," Emily said. "Protect her."

"We never did that before," Aline said.

"Maybe we should have."

Miranda looked at her shoes. They were already scuffed, though she'd only bought them a week ago. She couldn't afford them, even though she'd needed new shoes. Like her dad said too often, she had no marketable skills. It was one of the reasons why she was back living with her mother, waiting to figure her future out.

"Mom wouldn't want us to interfere," Miranda said.

"Who says?" Emily asked.

"Because she's private. She likes to keep things to herself."

Aline scoffed. "Like symptoms of cancer? Is that why you missed it?"

"Aline!"

"What? It's true, right? I mean, hello irony. After all those times she rushed us to the hospital for the slightest thing when we were kids."

Emily leaned forward so her head was level with theirs. "She said she had some symptoms a year ago and went to the doctor, but he didn't find anything."

Miranda shivered. It was always cool in the basement, which was nice in the summer, but not comforting enough for this moment. "How can that be?"

"Sometimes cancer happens without a warning."

"Yes, thank you, Dr. Gagnon," Aline said. "We know that."

Emily leaned back quickly. She didn't like it when people called her *doctor*. Even though she was back in school, finishing her course work, she couldn't get her hospital hours in while the twins were still so young. Being an actual doctor was a long way off.

Miranda felt bad for Emily. She used to be in such a hurry to get everywhere—skipping first grade, finishing her undergraduate degree in three years, the youngest person in her med school class. When she got pregnant, she was stopped in her tracks.

Miranda often wondered how it had happened. Not the mechanics, obviously, but the accidental pregnancy. Emily was always so careful and organized. Miranda couldn't imagine Emily relying on only one kind of birth control.

"I just meant that there might not be an explanation for why this is happening," Emily said. "There isn't always one."

Miranda turned around to face her. "I know, Memily. No one's asking you to explain it."

That's what Miranda used to call her when she was little because she couldn't say Emily properly. Emily's name for her was Dadanda. Only Aline's name escaped intact.

"What do you think Dad wants, anyway?" Aline asked.

"At least we know the answer to that question," Miranda said. "A divorce."

Chapter 7

CHAIN OF FOOLS

Jennifer

There have been times in my life when it has struck me that I've made some bad choices, but never more than those moments in the kitchen with Jake going over the old scrapes and bruises of the last two years, ever since the lazy Saturday when he told me he was leaving me.

I've spent a lot of time working to move past it with my therapist. I've made tremendous strides, he's said, and most days I believe him. But sitting there at the kitchen table—the one we'd eaten sixteen years of family breakfasts at, while Jake railed on about how I was being unfair to him and why did I care so much about the money anyway, was I trying to *torture him*?—I couldn't help but be faced with the reality that I'd made a terrible choice in my life partner, a fundamental one, like the neighbors who live next to a serial killer and think that he's *such a nice, quiet man.*

It does something to you, making a mistake like that. Misjudging someone so fully. It makes it impossible to trust any other decision, from the smallest to the biggest. I might think I should eat a tuna sandwich for lunch, but would I come to regret it? Did the tuna seem off, or was I being paranoid? Paranoid, probably. But even paranoiacs are right sometimes.

Only time would tell.

"Stop it, Jake."

He doesn't hear me. Maybe I didn't say it out loud. I meant to. But Jake is still talking about his right to be happy, so I must not have.

"Jake."

"What?"

"Go and divorce me, then. Just do it."

He looks at me. He's still attractive, the man who used to be my Jake. Six feet tall, with dark French-Canadian coloring, a man who takes care of himself and would probably still fit into the same clothes he was wearing when I met him. Not that he'd ever wear the acid-washed jeans and plaid shirt he sported back then. Now he's into expensive suits and pressed shirts during the week, and dark-wash jeans with casual cashmere on the weekends. He wears a watch that costs as much as my car, and I'm pretty sure he's started coloring his hair, because it used to have gray flecks in it, but now it's an even inky black.

"I can't," he says, his voice low and menacing. "You know that."

"You can. You just don't want to be judged. But everyone already knows what you did."

"Only because you couldn't keep your stupid mouth shut."

I spit out my words. "You expected me to keep your secrets for you? You thought I'd what—absolve you?"

Jake looks at me with hatred, and I'm sure my face mirrors his. Because it is what he expected, but even he sees how terrible that sounds. It was a mistake to say it, though. Confronting Jake with his horribleness is something I try to avoid since all it usually leads to is me being punished.

I'm sure the retribution will come, but for now, he tries a different tactic, softening his features and his tone. "You don't have to keep holding on like this, Jenn. You should let go. You should move on."

"I have moved on."

"What, with that Andrew guy?" His mouth turns into a sneer. He's had his teeth whitened, and they're too bright for the age he wants to forget he is.

"Yes."

"He's a freeloader."

"You've never even met him. And he's an artist."

"Right. Freeloader, like I said."

"Jealous?"

"What? No. I just thought you had higher standards is all."

Jake turns and reaches into the fridge. He comes out with a beer. One of Andrew's, actually, but there's no point in telling him that.

"What's that supposed to mean?" I ask.

"You were the one who wanted all of this," he says, waving at the kitchen. We'd renovated it a few years before he left. *All white and expensive*, is what he said at the time, but also *whatever makes you happy*. But he means more than the kitchen.

"I thought you wanted this life too."

He twists the cap off the beer. "Yeah, well, I didn't."

I feel so angry and sad as I watch him take a calm swallow of his beer. This man has made me want to commit a homicide. After he left, I used to fantasize about it on a regular basis. Some days, the idea that he might drop dead was the only thing that got me through.

And now, I'm the one who's dying.

"I remember when you used to want to be an artist," I say. "Was that a lie too?"

Jake makes a dismissive noise in his throat. "That was a stupid dream from college. I always knew it wasn't reality. People with responsibilities can't be artists."

He takes a long swig of beer, then tosses the bottle cap in the direction of the garbage, or where we used to keep the garbage when he lived here, only I moved it after he left. The cap plinks on the floor. He makes no move to pick it up. Why should he? He knows it will bug me. Knows it's already bugging me, and that I'll retrieve it sooner rather than later.

Jake never stopped treating this house as if it were his, even though it had always been in my name, a gift from my parents when we needed it. Even after he moved out, he'd show up unexpectedly, looking for this "lost" item or that. I'd come home and find something not quite in the place I'd left it. Items rearranged in the fridge. The mail riffled through. I'd even found him rooting around in the basement last year, looking for the box that held his college essays. He'd come up empty because I'd burned that shit in the backyard firepit soon after he left.

But he didn't need to know that.

I should've changed the combination to the fancy electronic locks on our doors immediately. Instead, I left the door open for his return—metaphorically and physically. Now I'm wondering what else he was up to all those times he came over. And as crazy as it sounds, even to me, I can't help wondering if the reason he's so angry is that I'm still here, not just in the legal sense, but here at all.

I can't say that out loud, though. He'll deny it, and it will only be more fodder for his Jennifer-is-crazy file. He doesn't need anything more to put in there. That file is full.

"So you're not going to give me the divorce?" Jake says when half the beer is gone, and we've been staring at each other in silence for a full minute.

"No."

"Bitch."

"Dad!"

Jake's face falls. Part of his good-guy act involves keeping his contempt toward me in check around the girls. That way, if I say anything about him, I'm the one acting inappropriately because *he's never said a bad word about me.*

But now the girls are standing in the doorway. They've never looked more alike, with their mouths shaped into identical Os of surprise.

He shrugs sheepishly. "I'm sorry, girls. You know how your mother can be provoking."

Aline frowns. "No, actually, I don't know that, Dad. And anyway, that is a completely shitty thing to say to her, but especially today."

"What's so special about today?"

Emily looks at me. "You didn't tell him?"

"Not yet."

Jake puts his beer on the counter and slaps on his charming smile. It's not working, though, not now that the girls heard what he said. "What am I missing here? Girls?"

They look at one another, waiting for me to say it. I don't want to give Jake the satisfaction.

"Mom's dying, Dad," Emily says. "She got the news today."

A series of emotions cross Jake's face. Surprise, shock, what might even be the hint of a smile.

"Is that what you wanted me to come here to discuss?"

"Yes," I say, not taking my eyes off him.

Because the emotion his face has settled on is joy.

And I hope I'm not the only one who can see it.

Chapter 8

TIDE ONE OVER

Aline

"So, what are we drinking?" Aline asked as she stared into the wine fridge. There was an amazing array of wines in there, including a whole row of prosecco, which seemed liked the wrong choice for the evening. When had her mother become such a big drinker? Was this Jake's fault too? Or was it a change brought about by Andrew, the man Jennifer had been dating for the last year? None of the girls particularly liked him, though he was good to their mother. "What do you want, Mom?"

"Open the bubbles," Jennifer called from the living room, where she, Emily, and Miranda had retreated after Jake left.

"You sure?"

"Yes."

Aline pulled out a blue bottle with silver trim and went in search of the champagne flutes. She found them where they'd always been, above the fridge. They were dusty; it had been a while since her mother had had something to celebrate, she guessed. Or maybe she was drinking from the bottle these days? Aline didn't know. She lived on the other side of Surrey, near White Rock Beach. When she saw her mother, it was usually for lunch near the lab, which her mother would "happen" by every couple of weeks. Aline never called out the pretense. To acknowledge it would be to confess that if her mother had simply asked to have lunch, Aline would have invented an excuse.

"What's taking so long?" Miranda called. "We're thirsty in here."

"Hold your horses! The glasses are dirty."

Aline took the glasses to the sink and washed them quickly. She removed the foil and wire cage from the bottle and turned the cork in her hand until it popped.

"That's a fun sound," Miranda said, coming into the kitchen.

"Should we be having fun, though?"

Miranda shrugged. "Mom wants to. Plus, like, what the fuck, you know? Is she supposed to sit around all gloomy for the next—"

"Six weeks? I don't know. But it feels weird."

"Well, yeah."

Aline handed Miranda the bottle and glasses and followed her into the dining room with the vegan lasagna Miranda had pulled out of the freezer and stuck in the oven earlier. There was supposed to be salad and garlic bread, too, but her parents' fight had derailed that. Despite how she felt about her mother, Aline was glad when Emily had kicked Dad out of the house. Had he always been like that and she simply hadn't noticed?

"Dinner!" Aline called as she walked into the dining room, holding the hot pan with oven-mitted hands. The lasagna bubbled and smelled amazing. Aline's stomach growled in anticipation. She hadn't eaten anything since breakfast.

"Not hungry," Emily said as she walked into the dining room.

"Well, shit."

"Sorry, Mom wanted to stop at Five Guys."

Aline put the lasagna down on the mid-century modern oak table and took a seat.

Jennifer walked into the room. "Guilty."

"It's fine."

"I know you don't approve of eating meat."

Aline had been a vegan since she was eighteen, and Miranda had followed along soon after. Emily hadn't, even though she was usually easygoing, blaming her "hypoglycemia," the term both she and Jennifer used to describe their need to eat on a regular basis. Neither of them had been diagnosed with anything other than cranky pants as far as Aline knew.

"I think you can eat whatever you want, Mom. Today and every day."

Jennifer smiled at her. "I will. And please go ahead. It smells delicious."

Jennifer, Emily, and Miranda sat at their usual places, with only Jake's seat empty. The walls were a soft blue, the carpet an intricate swirling pattern. This was where they'd come every night of the week as a family, for chicken on Mondays, pork on Tuesdays, a casserole on Wednesdays, spaghetti on Thursdays, and fish on Fridays, until they'd grown up and the obligation dwindled down to Sundays. Mandatory family time that her mother insisted on even after they'd moved out of the house.

Aline had hated those dinners, and she'd been grateful when they stopped after they'd moved out for university.

"There was supposed to be garlic bread," Miranda said.

"Who needs garlic bread?" Jennifer asked.

"Me," Aline said. "I always need garlic bread."

Jennifer laughed. "I think I need a drink."

"Coming right up."

Aline poured the prosecco evenly into the four glasses, filling them to the rim. She thought about Nick as she took her first sip. He was probably at their favorite bar, with Steve and Nancy and the rest of them. They'd started dating last year, but she hadn't introduced him to anyone yet. Miranda in particular was going to kill her for that, but she wanted to keep him to herself. Mostly, she didn't want the inevitable questions from her mother about what he meant to her and *were they serious?* She was only twenty-five, for God's sake. Though her mother and Emily had been ready to settle down young, that was never something Aline wanted. Hell, maybe she wouldn't even get married. She was never having kids, that was for sure.

"What shall we toast to?" Miranda asked, raising her glass.

"To kicking Dad out," Aline said. "Good riddance."

Miranda looked confused, but Jennifer raised her glass high. "Oh, girls, I've been waiting to toast that very thing with you for years."

They clinked glasses. There was a deep silence in the room, then Emily started to laugh.

"What's so funny?"

"I'm sorry," Emily said, trying to compose herself. "This is all so fucked up."

"I agree," Jennifer said. "But what are we going to do about it?"

"Drink?" Aline said.

"That's a suggestion I can get behind."

Chapter 9

CLOSING TIME

Jennifer

We end up finishing three bottles of prosecco. My daughters and I. My daughters and me. We five. I mean, four. Man, I am drunk. Drunkety-drunk. Which is fine. FINE.

It's been a while since I was this drunk. Frequently after Jake left, and then as the pain receded, I returned to my normal consumption levels, a few glasses on a Friday night with Andrew once we started dating, a few more on a weeknight with Suzie. I stopped drinking alone and . . . Oh dear. I never answered Suzie's text. I'm going to have to tell her, along with my mother and—

"Where's Andrew?" Emily asks as we're cleaning up in the kitchen. Or Emily's cleaning up and I'm supervising. She only had two glasses because she needs to drive home. She's been in constant contact with Chris, and we even FaceTimed briefly with her boys. They sat still for about twenty seconds, and solid Chris looked like he was trying to hold back tears. Emily had ended the call and opened the second bottle.

Aline's staying over. She and Miranda are in the living room. Even though it's June, they've turned on the gas fire and are cuddled together under a blanket on the couch, their heads touching, maybe communing without words. They've always denied it, but I've often wondered if they could.

"Andrew's at an artist retreat," I say.

"Have you told him?"

"No, not yet."

"But you will soon?"

I shrug. "There's no technology where he is."

"Like a summer camp?"

"I guess. A summer camp for adults."

Emily loads the dishes into the dishwasher efficiently, rinsing each one carefully, then lining them up like soldiers. She cuts up the lasagna into individual portions and puts them into containers, then into the freezer.

"I can eat that all week," I say lightly.

"Oh, sorry. Did you want me to throw it out?"

"No, that's fine. It will be useful. One less decision to make."

Emily frowns. "Are there decisions to make?"

"They gave me a bunch of papers at the doctor's office. Oh, they're in my car . . . I left it at the doctor's office."

"I'll get it with Chris tomorrow. Then we can sit down and go through everything if you want."

My hands seem to have taken on a life of their own. They're flitting around my body, looking for a place to rest.

"Mom? Are you okay?"

"I . . ."

"We don't have to read the papers tomorrow."

"Maybe that's best."

"I'll get your car and that can be it, okay?"

"Sure."

I check the time. It's after ten. I feel exhausted. Not the low-grade tired I've felt for months, maybe years, but wrung out, so tired I'm not sure I can make it up the stairs. The alcohol was a bad idea, and I'm going to feel like shit tomorrow, but who cares. I have nowhere to be and no one to disappoint.

"I should go to bed."

"Let me help you."

I want to resist, because the time will come soon enough when I'll need someone's help to do that very thing. To do many other things too. But I feel unsteady on my feet, and the stairs to the bedroom seem like a barrier.

"Thank you."

"Of course." Emily wipes her hands on a dish towel, then takes my elbow. She's gentle, yet firm, and she will make such a wonderful doctor one day.

"You're still going back to school full-time in September, right? To start your hospital rotations?" Emily was taking a few classes a semester, working toward her medical degree.

"I don't know."

We stop at the bottom of the stairs. There's half a flight in front of us. Then the landing. Then another half flight. I've decorated the walls leading up the stairs with family pictures, the same look as in many houses. Each stair is a year in the girls' lives, and in mine. I did take down the Jake photos, but the faint outlines of where they used to be linger on the walls like the shadows of the departed.

"What do you mean?"

"I thought I might put it off a year."

"Why? Because of Chris?"

Emily starts walking up the stairs, nudging me to do the same. "No, not because of Chris. He wanted me to go back full-time last year."

I stop at the second landing. The girls are three and adorable. It's an outtake from one of the commercials they shot. They're wearing matching outfits and running around me in a ring. I look so young, only twenty-six, a year older than they are now. What would my life have been like if I'd never had them? Would I be like Dr. Sayed, calm and soothing, doling out terrible news to a flotsam of patients I'd never see again?

"What, then?"

Emily sighs. "It's my life, Mom."

We walk up the rest of the stairs in silence. Once in my bedroom, I go into the adjoining bathroom to brush my teeth. Then I pull the clothes from my body and step briefly into the shower. The warm spray feels good, rinsing away the lingering hospital smell, that antiseptic odor that I used to find attractive.

I wrap myself in the nicest thing I own, a luxurious cashmere robe I bought on a shopping trip Suzie took me on to make me feel better after Jake left. It was a time when I felt so fragile, I needed to be Bubble Wrapped in gentle fabrics. Maybe that's why I'm taking this so well. The worst has already happened to me, and in the low moments, I'd vacillate between wanting him dead, and wanting my own life to end. That's one of the things I hate Jake most for—how he robbed me of the will to live.

And now here I am dying.

Convenient, my mind reminds me. So convenient.

When I come out of the bathroom, Emily's still there. Sitting on the edge of the bed, looking at something on her phone.

She looks up. She's me twenty-two years ago. Unlined, young but not young, with a full life ahead of her. Optimistic, I hope, about the future.

"That's a nice robe," she says.

"Isn't it? A separation present to myself."

"I'm sorry Dad is such a dick."

"Me too."

I climb into bed. I bought a new mattress too, after Jake left, and all-new Egyptian-cotton sheets. This bed is amazing, and I might stay in it forever.

"We should have been here for you more, after he left."

"You were here enough."

"Yeah, but we didn't really take in what he did, you know? We didn't want to know."

"He's your father."

"You don't have to let us off the hook." Emily tucks her phone away and stands. "I'm ready, willing, and able to hate him if you need me to."

I close my eyes. "I might."

"Okay, Mom. Just give me the word."

I listen to her pad across the floor. She kisses my forehead, as if I'm the kid and she's the mom, and pulls the sheets up so that I'm tucked in properly. Then she goes into the bathroom and fills a glass of water, returning to leave it on the bedside table.

"I put two aspirin here too."

"Thank you, honey."

"I'll call you about the car in the morning."

"Okay."

"Goodnight."

She leaves and I listen to the silence as it fills up the room. Is this what dying will be like? A quiet thief, stealing through the house, who will avoid detection until it's too late?

Will I give in to it, or will I fight? There are so many things I was too tired to pursue today. They're on a carousel in my mind: the levels of lead in my blood a year ago, the texts from Jake about the divorce, how happy he looked when he heard he didn't have long to wait until he could get what he wanted.

Convenient, my mind says again. So convenient.

"I think your father tried to kill me," I say to Emily, but she's gone.

Five Weeks to Live . . .

Chapter 10

WHAT A DIFFERENCE A DAY MAKES

Jennifer

I spend most of the week after my diagnosis in mourning.

I mourn for the loss of my own life, and everything I'll be missing from now until when I should have died. Forty years from now, or longer if my grandmother's any guide. Weddings and births. The vague idea I had of doing something with my time other than watching it tick away in yoga class. Seeing if I could have a long-term relationship again, one that wasn't tainted by Jake. Repairing my relationship with Aline, which I'd let deteriorate bit by bit until I wasn't sure if either of us knew what the original injury was. Seeing Miranda find her way and settle on something, anything, that she could be passionate about for more than six months. Seeing my grandchildren grow up.

So many tiny things and big things too. I am a book that will remain unfinished, and I was very much looking forward to seeing how it would all turn out.

Then there's the way everyone is treating me. The girls—mostly Emily, but sometimes Miranda—walk quietly around the house, speak in hushed tones, bring me meals and make sure I eat them. I'm still capable of doing all these things on my own, but it's easier to let them have their way. It's a preview, though, the only window I'm truly getting to my future.

I don't let anyone else in, not even my best friend, Suzie. The news of my imminent demise has started to spread, though she's the only one I told, in a text that asked her to give me a bit of time to process and not to let anyone else know. She agreed, but then, two days after my diagnosis, the doorbell rang, and Miranda brought in a vegan casserole with a sympathy card from one of the neighbors down the street. Miranda ate it for dinner while I nibbled around the edges, and we threw the rest in the trash. The next day there was another left on the doorstep, this time from Suzie with a note asking me to please return her call. I haven't, not yet, I just burrow under the covers and try to keep the world at bay. Because the thought of visits and calls, even from those I hold dear, is exhausting. I have enough pain. I cannot be the sponge or the deflector shield for others. What this says about me, I'm not sure. I don't have to follow anyone else's guidebook to dying.

Emily comes in the afternoons. She cajoles me into showers, makes me change my pajamas. She's brought a diary to record my symptoms and meds and she writes them all down in her neat handwriting like she used to do when she was keeping track of her boys' pees and poops. Then she leaves to return to her normal life, promising she'll be back tomorrow.

These are all the visits I want or can handle right now. But there's one visit that I cannot avoid, however much I might wish to.

My mother.

•   •   •

"Darling!" my mother says as she bursts into my bedroom. No quiet entrances for Bea. She always comes into a room as if she's entering stage right in a Noël Coward play. "What is this horrendous news?"

She's been this way my entire life, and even before then. Every picture I've ever seen of her is slightly blurry because she cannot stay still. It's amazing and exhausting and I wasn't the only one who was relieved when she announced at seventy, five years after my father died from a massive heart attack, that she was moving to the desert in California and joining a retirement community.

"I don't know what to say to that, Mother."

"Oh, don't 'Mother' me. Not today." She whirls toward the bed. Bea's tiny and thin, her hummingbird energy beating away any calories she consumes. Her hair is white and chin length, her slacks perfectly pressed, her blouse without wrinkles. When I travel, I feel as if I come off the airplane looking like I've been through a hurricane. I used to blame the girls, but the truth is I've never figured out how to be wrinkle-free.

"Sorry, Mom."

My mother's deep blue eyes flit to mine. "Why can't you just call me Bea? The girls do."

"Do they?"

"Oh, you know they do. Ever since they were little. Grandma Bea."

"That's different. Emily's boys call me Grandma Jennifer, but not just Jennifer."

"I still can't believe I'm a great-grandmother."

My mother moves around the bed, straightening the sheets and fluffing the pillows. There's evidence of my illness everywhere. The laundry basket is full of pajamas, the only thing I wear these days. The garbage is occupied by several boxes of Kleenex soaked with tears. The air smells stale and I do too. My mother opens the curtains wide and props open the windows for some "fresh air," she says. The loamy smell of our backyard, surrounded by tall pines, the grass scattered with their needles, filters in.

I wish she'd sit down, sit still. Her need to constantly be in motion has always driven me nuts. Truthfully, the girls were probably the only ones who were sad to see her go. Jake and I, on the other hand? We may have opened a bottle of champagne and toasted over a candlelit dinner.

She means well, but she's a lot.

"Leave all that, Mom. Okay?"

"I don't mind, it's such a mess in here."

"Thanks."

"Oh, darling!" My mother flings herself at the bed, blocking me into the pillows. "I'm beside myself."

And there it is. The moment I knew was coming. I'm going to have to comfort her for losing me. It's always been like this. Bea relying on me for emotional support, when it should be the other way around. When I was little, I used to wish my father gave more of a shit, but I realized as I grew older that his distance was a defense mechanism. The only way to stay away from the chaos was to stay above it.

"I'm glad you're here," I say, and it might be the truth. I pat her on the back. I can feel the knobs of her spine. A hug from my mother has never been a comfort.

She squeezes me harder. My shoulder feels wet through the thin fabric of my T-shirt.

My mother's crying. She's crying. Of course she's crying. She's difficult, yes. But not a monster. Her child is going to die before her. That's a loss I'm never going to have to suffer. I should be grateful for that. But I'm not.

Mostly, I'm angry.

"Thank you for saying that," she says, and sits back. Her waterproof mascara hasn't moved an inch, and her hair's still salon perfect. Close-up, though, she looks every one of her seventy-five years. Her skin is dried out, papery, as if the desert has turned her into a husk.

"Sure."

She holds my shoulders, pulling back from me. "You look all right."

"Yes."

"A bit puffy, perhaps."

I haven't seen a change yet, but then again, my mother's always cataloged my flaws. "I have to take steroids."

"Why?"

"To control the swelling"—I tap my head—"up here. So it hurts less."

"Oh, darling. Does it hurt much?"

"Sometimes. I have pain meds too."

She crinkles her face. "Nasty things."

I have a pure sense of déjà vu. I'm ten and my mother is looking at the bottle of pills prescribed by her psychiatrist. "Nasty things," she says, then pours them down the sink. Who wants effective medication when you can be on a bipolar roller coaster instead?

"For once, I agree with you."

She stands and begins to walk around the room. "You were always into that."

"Into what?"

"Medical things. You were the only child I knew who loved going to the doctor."

"You say that as if it was a bad thing."

She smiles briefly and starts to pick up yesterday's pajamas off the floor, even though I asked her not to. There's no point in asking again. I don't have the energy to fight, and trying to get my mother to be anything other than exactly what she wants to be only ends up in one place.

"You should've finished medical school," she says as she folds my shirt, then puts it in the laundry hamper.

"I was occupied."

"We would have helped with that. We offered."

"I know."

"You didn't want our help."

"I did let you help. A lot. But I wanted to raise my kids myself, not with a bunch of nannies."

"It would have been better," my mother says, turning away from me. "If you had finished school."

I lean back and close my eyes. What's the point in arguing? My mother was both hyper-focused on me and an absentee landlord when something needed to be fixed. Both parts of her were extremely disappointed when I got pregnant. I'll never forget her shocked response to the news. "You're not keeping it, are you?"

She didn't mean adoption.

I kept the girls, and she and my father eventually paid for this house. But I always knew I disappointed her. As much as she loves the girls, she couldn't help imagining my life without them.

Wishing for it, even.

"Too late for that now," I say gently.

"Hmm."

I open my eyes. She's standing over my desk, riffling through the papers that have gathered there since Tuesday.

"What is all this?"

"Research."

"Into your cancer?"

"That's right."

"Why?"

I look away from her penetrating gaze. The truth is that I've spent much of my time for the last week trying to solve the mystery of what's happening to me. I've searched the house, late at night, while Miranda's been sleeping, looking for a possible source for the lead in my blood. I've been through all my journals, the health logs on my phone, my emails and texts, trying to reconstruct when this all started. I've read multiple articles on lead poisoning and its symptoms and causes, pouring endlessly over the same facts as if I were cramming for an exam. Because on Diagnosis Day +1, I woke up with a hangover and a clear certainty. This wasn't just life, me dying. This was something that was planned, deliberate, wanted. I was healthy and fine until last spring. Then, a sudden turn.

It had been a year since Jake left, and I was finally doing okay. I'd been on a few dates with Andrew. I no longer called Suzie with panicked crying on a regular basis. I hung out with her and our friends. I'd lost weight, but in a good way. Jake was starting to recede in the rearview. Emily's boys, Ethan and Noah, turned two, and I went to their birthday party, a loud visit to a trampoline center where we all jumped and laughed. There was pizza and a *Trolls* cake, which was rich and delicious.

I ate too much, drank too much, and in the morning I suffered for it. I felt sluggish and weak. That was no surprise. But it continued the next day, less, but lingering. After that, it came and went. Some days I'd feel tired, then others, fine. Eventually I called my doctor, went for a checkup, had blood drawn. The tests had come back negative, and I'd started to feel better. It was probably just getting older, I'd thought then, life catching up with me. Until the violent headaches started a couple of months ago, I mostly felt fine. I kept my eyes front rather than lingering on the past.

That was my mistake.

One I won't make again.

Chapter 11

I HAVE WALKED A MILLION MILES
Miranda

Miranda hit her five hundredth tennis ball with the same energy as she'd hit her first. More, even. So long as she kept hitting the ball crosscourt, landing it past the service line, she could keep everything else at bay. The hopper on the ball machine was getting low, though, and she could feel the couple who'd booked the court after her hovering in the background. She didn't have much time left, in more ways than one.

So many things in her life were going to run out at the end of this summer. Her membership at the tennis club was one of them. Her father had been paying for it until now. But he'd told her she had this last summer to find her own way to pay, or that was it. There was also her part-time job teaching kids tennis, which she'd promised herself a year ago was a one-year thing to get herself situated, and then she was going to have to find something else to do, something worth her time, or at least something that would pay her bills. Something that would allow her to move out of her mother's house, which she'd also put a clock on a year ago when she'd moved back in.

Which brought her to her mother. She was going to be over this summer too, give or take a week. Which was a horrible thing to think, even if it was true. It had been like that since Miranda had heard about the diagnosis. Awful thoughts seeping out, sometimes to herself, but often to Aline and even Emily. She'd managed not to say anything too terrible in front of her mother, but it was only a matter of time before it happened.

That's why she was hitting tennis balls.

Hitting them so hard she was developing blisters on top of her usual callouses.

"Excuse me? I think we have the court?"

Miranda hit the last ball with extra venom. It landed perfectly crosscourt and leapt to the left. A winner.

If only she had this much focus in a game, but that had never been her strong suit. All the talent and none of the focus, her coach used to tell her. That was a good summation of her life so far.

"It's all yours," she said to the hovering couple as she grabbed a towel off the sideline chair and wiped her face. They looked to be about sixty, wearing matching tennis whites required by the club. Miranda had started a petition a couple of years ago to get them to allow colors, but breaking the mold was not what this place was about. She'd even been spoken to about her "use of colorful language" around the kids she was teaching. As if they weren't swearing a blue streak when their parents weren't around.

"Aren't you going to pick up your balls?" the man asked. He was speaking to her in the same tone her father had used when they'd come up with this arrangement. *What's the plan, Miranda-Panda? What's the plan?*

How the hell was she supposed to know? She'd never been in this situation before.

"It's a club rule," the woman said. Her skin had a weird orange tinge to it, almost like jaundice, but probably spray tan.

Miranda thought about turning on her heel and leaving without picking anything up, because who cared about following the rules if she was going to get kicked out either way? But that wasn't what she was like. That was more of an Aline thing to do. A thing Aline had done. Despite what everyone thought, they were different. People always wanted to concentrate on their similarities, but she always felt more like Emily than Aline where rule following was concerned. She didn't have Emily's thousand-year-old soul, though. Miranda liked being young, and she planned on enjoying it as long as she could. Not like Emily, who'd jumped over all the good parts of youth and gone right to the bad parts of being old.

"No need to stress," Miranda said. "I'm doing it."

She picked up two of the long translucent plastic tubes that lay on the side of the court and made quick work of collecting her balls while the couple went through a useless series of stretches. When she put them in the ball machine and lugged it to the side, they took up spots on either side of the net at the service line and started warming up. Miranda could already tell that the woman was the better player but that the man had way too much ego to admit it. He was totally the kind of guy who'd claim that his wife had footfaulted on a good serve when he was behind in the point.

There were a lot of guys like that at this club.

"Have a nice game," Miranda said sweetly as she pulled the ball machine off the court and shut the gate behind her with a *clang*. She put the machine in the side hut, then walked slowly toward the clubhouse. It was hot, insects buzzing in the tall pines that provided partial shade, and she'd worked up a sweat. It felt good, though. Like she'd pulled some of the toxins from her body even though she knew that was probably garbage.

She filled a paper cup with water in the clubhouse, then went and stood on the porch. She could see all ten courts from there, lined up like soldiers. She wasn't quite sure why she loved this place so much, but the thought of having to leave it made her feel like crying.

"You're getting too close to the ball," Devon said, coming up next to her and leaning against the railing.

"You were watching me?"

"I might've been."

She finished her water and threw the cup in the trash. Devon had grown up at the club too. He was in law school, and she'd heard that he hadn't gotten the clerkship he wanted, so he was living back at home, like her, and hanging out at the club every day, also like her.

"Do I owe you a hundred bucks for that advice?"

"My hourly rate's way higher."

"That's gross. And how can you have an hourly rate when you're not even working in a firm yet?"

Devon pumped his fist into his chest. "You know how to hurt a guy. Man."

She smiled at him. The last time they'd hung out, he'd still had the skater-boy haircut he'd had through most of high school, his almost-white-blond hair shaved close to his head with a longer shingle above. That had grown out, and his hair had darkened, and now he'd cut it in a way that Miranda could only think of as conservative.

"Come on, Dev. You're tougher than that."

"Not so much, recently."

She patted him on the shoulder. "You'll bounce back."

He laughed. He was taller than her, and she could see the roof of his mouth as he flung his head back. Miranda felt a bit put off by the view, and the laughter, which seemed overdone and forced, because her joke was corny. The little kids were rubbing off on her.

"It's not that funny."

"You need to relax." He tilted his head down to her and leaned in. "I have some good edibles. You want?"

Miranda thought briefly of what she was supposed to be doing that day—going for an interview at a coffee shop she'd worked at a few years ago. It was the last place she wanted to go, with its impatient customers and the loud whine of the milk frother. Trouble was, there wasn't anywhere she did want to go. That had always been her problem. She was prone to tumbling along in the wake of whomever she was with. That was how she'd ended up in the Peace Corps last year, only to discover she didn't want to build houses in Namibia. She'd followed a forgettable girl there, and her disappointed father had wired her the money for her return ticket when that had fallen apart.

What's the plan Miranda-Panda? he'd asked when he picked her up at the airport. *You need to do something solid.*

But she wasn't solid, no. She was fluid, and not just in her choice of partners. Sometimes it was fun, and sometimes it was trouble. There wasn't any way to tell until you jumped in.

And the one thing she did have was the courage to jump.

"My mother's dying," Miranda told Devon two hours later. They were tangled up in the sheets on the bed in his parents' guesthouse, their joined limbs forming a rectangle. The guesthouse was nestled in a stand of Western white pines, half hidden from the house. The property sat at the crest of a hill, and you could glimpse the ocean through the window. If this place were hers, she'd sit out on the stone patio and watch the surf even in winter, when it grew dark and angry.

Miranda's brain was foggy, but at least she knew how she'd gotten there. If she were being honest, she knew this was probably what was going to happen when she'd agreed to come to his place. She didn't regret it—Devon knew what he was doing in bed, and there wasn't any risk he thought this was something serious between them. That wasn't Devon's style. The only thing that was weird was that Devon and Aline had had a thing in high school. Did it matter to him who she was, or were identical twins interchangeable?

"What?" Devon said. His shirt was off, the sheet around his waist. His chest was hairless, possibly because of manscaping. She'd never paid much attention to what he looked like with his shirt off before, but she was pretty sure there had been hair there the last time she'd looked. "What did you say?"

"She's dying. She has cancer."

"Like, actual cancer?"

Miranda sat up. The air-conditioning was on high, and she pulled up the sheet to cover herself. "Yes, Devon. What the hell?"

"Sorry, man. I had this girlfriend a few years back who'd say shit like that, but it wasn't true."

"That's messed up."

"It was."

"Well, I don't do things like that."

Miranda climbed out of bed. Her sweaty tennis clothes were on the floor, still damp. She didn't feel like climbing back into them. "Do you have something I could wear?"

"What?"

Miranda suddenly remembered why she didn't do edibles. People were mostly idiots when they were stoned. "Devon, focus. Do you have any clothes that I could wear?"

"Maybe some sweatpants?"

"How about you go ask your sister? I think we're about the same size."

"Valerie?"

Miranda sighed. This felt like more than edible-induced stupidity. He probably deserved to miss out on the clerkship. If his dad wasn't super rich, there was no way he'd have gotten into law school.

"Yes, Valerie. Go ask her if I can borrow some clothes."

"Then she'll know you're here."

"So?"

Devon looked sheepish. "Um, well . . ."

Now Miranda felt like an idiot. "You have a girlfriend?"

"Yes."

"Dammit, Devon. You didn't tell me that."

He shrugged, and she felt a wave of disgust, mostly at herself. She hadn't done anything wrong, but she hadn't asked any questions, either. She wanted a way to distract herself, and this is where she'd landed.

"Forget it." Miranda picked up her clothes and walked toward the bathroom. "Do me a favor, okay?"

"What?"

"Don't be here when I get out."

"This is my house."

"So?"

She didn't wait for his answer, just closed the door firmly. She dumped her clothes on the floor, took a quick shower to rinse Devon off, then called Aline.

"What?" Aline said.

"That's not a normal way to answer the phone."

"I knew it was you, dummy."

Miranda closed the toilet lid and sat down. She tucked the thick towel around her tightly. At least Devon's towels were clean and luxurious. This experience wasn't a total loss.

"I need a favor."

"What have you done this time?"

"What the fork, Aline?"

"I speak from experience. And you know I find that expression annoying, right?"

"I'm trying to swear less."

"Why?"

"Because of the tennis kids. Can you pick me up?"

"I have things I need to do."

"Fine. Forget it, okay?" Miranda looked down at her feet. There was a tan line around her ankle from where her tennis socks stopped. She held the phone to her ear, listening to Aline's breathing.

"Are you crying?" Aline asked.

"No."

"I can hear you."

"Why are you being such a cow?"

"Baby, I was born this way."

Miranda brushed her tears away with one hand. "I did something stupid."

"I gather."

"Will you just come get me?"

"I'm at work."

"Say it's an emergency. You can even—"

"Blame Mom?" Aline finished. "How is she doing, anyway?"

"You haven't talked to her?"

"Not in a couple days."

"That's not very nice."

Aline's laugh was bitter on the other end of the line. "What's your point?"

"She's dying, Aline. So maybe you could, I don't know, bury the hatchet or whatever?"

"Where are you?" Aline asked.

Miranda felt ashamed. "At Devon's."

"Devon Harper?"

"Yep."

"Well, shit. Doesn't he have a girlfriend?"

"So he just told me."

Aline sighed, but it was a sound of surrender. "Okay, I'll be there as soon as I can."

"And then you'll come with me to Mom's?" Miranda pressed.

"If you insist."

"I do."

"Fine. I'll do it. But I don't have to make up with her just because she's dying."

Chapter 12

I SPY

Jennifer

One of the last things the girls did in their famous phase as children was my favorite. Theirs too, I think. A guest spot on *Sesame Street*. They were six, and the show was looking for people to do language spots for them—those little clips between the scenes where two people would toss a ball back and forth while counting to ten in French, those sorts of things. The producers had them jumping rope, counting their steps, wearing cute pedal pushers in a trio of colors. Emily was off to the side, waiting to jump in while Miranda and Aline twirled the ropes. Then another kid came up and asked Emily, "Are those your friends?"

"No," Emily said, almost yelling because she wasn't a natural actor. "They're my sisters. We're triplets!"

The other little girl looked confused, and then one of the regulars, Maria, I think it was, stepped in and explained what a wonder they were. How special. I remember grinning from the sidelines, the whole day a smile. Once it aired, other kids would rush up to the girls and say, *"Sesame Street!"* in enthusiastic voices and ask them about it. Had they met Big Bird? Was Oscar that much of a grouch? Was there actually a street? The girls could've been embarrassed by it, but they weren't. Not then. And I was the best for arranging it.

"You're the best, Mom," one of them would say multiple times a day, and that would be my cue to start singing the theme song. The girls had a whole choreographed dance to it, one that always made us crack up.

You're the best, Mom.

Even then, I never believed it.

"How are you feeling, Jennifer?" Dr. Parent asks me at my first follow-up appointment. He's behind his desk, and I'm sitting in the same Bad-News Chair. The only difference is the presence of Emily, who insisted on coming along. Because *someone has to, Mom.* She was right, but it feels like an invasion having someone else in the room with me. Like the cancer that's raiding my body. Neither of them is supposed to be here.

"About the same, I guess."

"Headaches?"

"Yes."

"Any new symptoms?"

"No, I don't think so."

"Are you taking your medications?"

"Yes," I say. The opioids he prescribed dull the thick pain in my head, but also my thoughts, my reason, my judgment.

That's the excuse I'm using anyway, because last night I broke into Jake's email, looking for clues to determine whether he tried to poison me a year ago.

I used to know his password, but at some point he changed it. But I was pretty sure he forgot to change my email address as his recovery email. So in the deep of night when I could be reasonably sure he was asleep, I reset his password and spent an hour going through a year's worth of messages and junk mail that made me feel crazy and dirty and crazy all over again.

What did I expect to find? Articles he'd emailed himself about how to get rid of a pesky wife? I didn't have access to his browser history, and he wasn't that stupid. No. There wasn't anything in there for me, but after my search of the house turned up nothing concrete, I felt as if I had nowhere else to go. I paid for it in the messages that were there—private communications that could only hurt me. I tried not to look at them, and then I changed his password again to something that was nonsense and prayed that he didn't take the time to explore why he suddenly couldn't get into his emails. It was a stupid thing to do, a mistake I can't repeat, so I tucked the pills away this morning for when I truly need them.

For now, I can live with a headache.

"It's important for you to stick to the regimen," Dr. Parent says.

"I know."

"Anything else?" Dr. Parent asks.

"I'm tired."

"That's to be expected. Are you sleeping?"

"Sometimes."

He frowns. He doesn't look any older than he did last week, but I can see where the lines are going to form in the coming years. The creases that will be in his forehead. The streaks radiating out from his eyes. "The clonazepam should help you sleep."

I look away from him and watch the fish. They're so tranquil in there, so happy. Their life could end at any minute, but they wouldn't see it coming. Like me.

"It's fine."

"You don't have to suffer."

"Don't I?"

Dr. Parent blushes slightly, a pink rash along his jawbone. "I'm sorry, Jennifer."

"Yes. You said."

"I know this isn't easy."

"You know?"

Emily reaches out and squeezes my hand. *Enough*, she's saying. *You don't have to punish Dr. Parent.* But I do. Because a year ago, this could've been stopped, and this medical practice had let me slip through the cracks.

Dr. Parent clears his throat. "I meant . . . Do you have someone you can talk to?"

Someone professional, he means. Someone who can help me cope with the emotions storming through me like a summer squall.

"I do," I say, though I skipped my monthly appointment with my therapist last week. But I should go see him, if only to say goodbye. I've been his patient for more than fifteen years, off and on, and he's as much a fixture in my life as some of the other people I've been avoiding.

"Can I suggest . . ."

"That I go to therapy?"

"Yes."

"Work on my rage issues?"

"Anger is a natural part of grieving," Dr. Parent says.

Emily makes a noise in her throat. I turn toward her. She looks tired but pulled together. Her strawberry blonde hair is in a sleek ponytail, and she's wearing a pretty flowered sundress with a white cardigan.

Me, on the other hand. Well, I came in my pajamas. At least I put on clean ones.

"Is it?" I ask, though I know it is. I don't know why I'm being so combative, but it feels good to let it out. "Am I grieving?"

"That would be natural," Dr. Parent answers.

"Well, there isn't anything natural about this."

Emily pulls her hand away. "Mom . . ."

"What?"

"Nothing. Only, maybe you should . . . I don't know. Not get into this."

I'd told Emily on the way here that my diagnosis didn't make sense to me, and that I needed some explanations. She'd bitten the corner of her lip, a move all the girls shared when they were troubled. She hadn't pressed me on what I meant, and I could tell she wanted me to leave it alone.

That would be simpler. To let it go. To accept what's happening to me and go quietly. Consent to the natural order of things. But what I said before is right. There's nothing normal or natural about what's happening to me.

"I can't though," I say, partially to Emily but also to Dr. Parent. "This shouldn't be happening." From my purse I pull out the blood tests he gave me last week and hold them out to him. "Look at this. Look at the lead in my blood last year."

"What?" Emily asks, turning toward me, her body rigid. "I didn't see that."

"You only looked at this year's results," I say as Dr. Parent takes the sheets I've memorized by now. "The ones that doctor showed you at the hospital."

He reads through the results quickly. His eyebrows raise when he gets to the result I was referring to. "This must be a mistake."

"I don't think so."

"Why not?"

"Because it matches the symptoms I was having back then.

Aching joints, headaches, digestive issues. Look at my chart. That's why I came to see Dr. Turner."

"You told me that was a normal part of aging," Emily says. "Last week in the car."

"I was talking about my more recent symptoms. And I hadn't seen these results," I add, though that's not true. I'm not entirely sure why I'm not being up front with her or the doctor. They don't have anything to do with this.

"This is . . . concerning," Dr. Parent says. "But, as I said, it might also be a mistake. Your blood work doesn't show anything like this now."

"I know, but it would dissipate, wouldn't it? If the exposure stopped." I knew this already and I've spent a lot of time online confirming it. It's easy information to access even if you don't have a medical background. The Google autofill on things like *lead poisoning* includes *sign*, *symptoms*, and *murder*. Had someone I know done these very same searches? I couldn't help but wonder about that and many other things in the terrible darkness of my bedroom at two a.m.

Was it Jake? Hence the email break-in, which had turned up nothing.

"Is it in my charts?" I ask. "The symptoms I mentioned?"

Dr. Parent flips through the notes. I can see the page from my last visit. His handwriting is typical doctor—scrawled and illegible. But the pages below it are careful and clear. Dr. Turner was meticulous in everything he did.

Or so I always thought.

"Yes, Dr. Turner took note of that. It must've been why he ordered the heavy-metal panel along with your other blood tests."

"And?"

Dr. Parent looks wary, hesitating about what to tell me. He's worried about liability. That I'm going to sue his practice for missing it.

"Did someone review the results?" Emily asks. She's got her notebook out and she's written: *heavy-metal panel, one year ago, lead.*

"There is a note here that he reviewed them. And an annotation to the nurse to make a follow-up appointment with you to do further testing to confirm the results."

"That didn't happen."

He stands. "Will you excuse me for a minute?"

Emily nods and he leaves. She stands and walks to his desk.

"What are you doing?"

"I want to see those results."

"And what it says in my chart?"

She gives me a brief smile. My heart accelerates as I glance toward the door Dr. Parent walked out of. Is it illegal to look through your own medical file?

Emily takes out her phone and snaps pictures of the first several pages, then puts the chart back the way Dr. Parent left it. Then she flattens out the test results and does the same. She moves swiftly, with assurance, and it's done in a matter of seconds.

She sits down next to me and smooths her dress. A moment later, Dr. Parent returns. He's holding a printout that he hands to me.

"As you'll see here, there's an annotation that two calls were made to your house last year."

I take the paper from him. There the calls are: two calls last June a few days apart. *Message left*, the note next to the second one says. *Patient spoken to. Seeking second opinion with another practice.*

"I never said that," I say.

"Said what?" Emily asks.

"What it says here." I hand her the paper. "That I was going to another doctor. And I don't remember getting a message telling me to come in, either . . ." I search my memory. It's not like me to forget things—not historically, anyway—and if a doctor tells me to come in for more tests, I do it. I have no recollection at all of what it says on this paper. But there's something tugging at my brain. A faint something. "I think . . . I'm almost sure I remember a call telling me everything was okay?"

"Going for a second opinion sounds like you, though," Emily says. "Are you sure you didn't say that?"

"Yes, of course I'm sure. If I was supposed to go for follow-up tests, I would have gone for them."

"Have you been experiencing memory loss?" Dr. Parent says gently. "It's a common symptom of glioblastoma."

"Yes, but nothing like that. It's more like how no one can remember trivia anymore because of the internet. Like I'd be watching a show with an actor I know, and it would take me a while to get to his name. Longer than normal. Or it would take me a moment to find the right word. I wouldn't forget to make a follow-up medical appointment." I look at Dr. Parent. "Aren't you concerned about these results?"

"If they're accurate."

"You don't think they are?" Emily says.

"These levels are very high."

"Everyone has a different tolerance, though."

"That's true. Which is why follow-up testing was requested."

"Excuse me," I say, raising my hand. "Can you please not talk like I'm not here?"

Dr. Parent looks at me. "I apologize."

"Isn't there a way to resolve this?"

"How so?"

I shift uncomfortably in my seat. "Lead can stay in hair follicles and fingernails much longer than in the blood, right?"

"Yes, that's right."

"So let's test those, then."

"Mom," Emily says gently. "What's the point?"

I feel a shot of anger. "Because I'm entitled to know. I want to know."

"Okay, okay. Don't get upset."

I look away from her. "Can we just do the test?"

Dr. Parent nods. "Yes, of course we can."

"How long will it take to get the results?"

"Several weeks."

I might not have that long. "Can we expedite it?"

"There will be an extra fee."

"That's fine."

Dr. Parent takes a form out of his desk and checks several boxes. He hands it to me. "Give this to the nurse and they'll take the samples now. Please call if anything else comes up."

"I will."

We rise to leave. Emily hands me back the paper Dr. Parent gave me earlier, the one with the messages left at my house. The one that says someone from this office spoke to me and I told them I was getting a second opinion.

There are things in my life I don't remember. Others I wish I could forget.

But I know with a solid certainty that the person the nurse spoke to was not me.

Chapter 13

LIFE AS A HOUSE

Aline

Aline and Miranda pulled up to the house moments after Emily and their mother came back from Jennifer's doctor's appointment.

Dutiful Emily, Aline thought, brushing aside any attempt at guilt. Some of her girlfriends growing up were friends with their mothers, but Aline never felt that way about Jennifer. She was the enforcer, the rule maker, the boss. She made the house go, made sure there was milk in the fridge, that their clothes were clean, that school fees got paid. But she wasn't their friend, not Aline's anyway. Not her confidante. Aline had her sisters for that. Perhaps they hadn't left their mother any room, but they'd only been kids. It wasn't Aline's responsibility to set the tone.

She knew all this rationally, and yet there was a nagging voice inside her, probably Miranda's, that was telling her she should put her slights away. That she should make the first move toward healing what was broken before it was too late.

But why should I? Aline thought uncharitably as she watched her mother walk across the lawn, holding on to Emily for support. She felt an overwhelming urge to tell Miranda to get out of the car, and then drive away.

This urge to flee wasn't entirely her mother's fault. Aline was already in a mood before they'd reached the house. It didn't help that she'd had to pick up Miranda from her daytime walk of shame. Not that she gave a shit if Miranda slept with Devon. They had a fling in high school, but it wasn't serious. She hadn't thought about him in years. She just didn't understand what was going on with Miranda. Quitting the Peace Corps so suddenly. Teaching tennis to bratty kids. Middle-of-the-day hookups weren't her style, or drugs either, but Miranda was still clearly high, her pupils dilated, and her speech slowed down in a way that maybe no one else would recognize but Aline.

Something was wrong with Miranda, and Aline didn't know what. When she'd asked, Miranda had told her to mind her own business, that she was sick of Aline's judgment and that she didn't have to be so perfect all the time. Miranda's hostility hurt, but whatever it was masking concerned Aline more.

"Are we just going to sit here?" Miranda asked.

"I was thinking about it."

"You're in such a pissy mood today."

"Yep."

Miranda put her hand on the door latch. "Well, I'm going in. I need to get out of these clothes."

"You might want to use some bleach."

"Ugh, gross, Aline."

"Devon's been around is all I'm saying."

Miranda rolled her eyes and stepped out of the car. Aline fought the urge to back up and leave. Instead, she turned off the car and got out. But her mood followed her like a cloud as she walked toward the house. The front lawn needed mowing. Didn't her mother have a service?

Even the grass was making her angry today.

"Oh, girls!" their grandmother said, tripping out of the house and waving enthusiastically from the front porch.

"When did Grandma Bea arrive?"

"Yesterday, I think."

"How could you not be a hundred percent sure?"

"Chill, Aline. Honestly, you're so uptight today."

"Fork off," Aline said, then opened her arms wide. "Hi, Grandma!"

If there was one person Aline didn't have complicated feelings about, it was Grandma Bea.

Even when they'd gone to live with her when Jennifer had cancer the first time, and they'd had to leave all their friends behind and their house and toys, Aline didn't mind. She knew that Emily and Miranda found her a bit much, but Aline loved her pure spontaneity. You never knew what might come out of her mouth, and after the rules and regulations of their parents' house, this was a welcome change. Who wouldn't want to be woken up at one in the morning to make lasagna? So what if Bea forgot that the oven was on and it set the fire alarms off? Sure, it woke Grandpa Norman up, but he was used to it. He'd pad into the kitchen in his dressing gown and clean it all up in a flash.

It was manic depression, Aline knew now, though Bea never seemed to have the depression part. She was a bit envious sometimes, truth be told. That manic energy could be useful when she had to stay up all night in the lab because a reagent had to be added at a weird time, or she was burning through a grant proposal. Aline used crushed-up Adderall to get through those things when she had to, but it would be much easier if she could tap into a natural resource.

"How long are you staying, Grandma?" she asked. They were in the kitchen, putting lunch together. Veggie pâté sandwiches for her and Miranda, roast beef ones for the rest of them. Aline wrinkled her nose at the beef, trying not to think of where it came from as she laid the thick slices on the fresh country bread her grandmother had picked up at the store. *No frozen casseroles for her*, she'd said as she filled the fridge with grocery items from the plastic bags that Aline thought had been banned. Grandma Bea had probably been hoarding them for years.

"I'm not quite sure yet."

"Because we don't know when the end is coming?"

For once in her life, Bea looked shocked. "Aline, we shouldn't say such things."

Aline buried her head in the fridge, looking for a drink. She looked longingly at the half-full bottle of wine, but wine with lunch was frowned upon in her family. She pulled out several Diet Cokes instead. She usually avoided it because of the chemicals, but that seemed beside the point now.

"Sorry, Grandma."

"It's all right. I . . ." She pulled a tissue from the box on the counter. "I'm finding this all quite hard to bear, my dear."

Aline had never seen her grandmother flustered or crying before. "Oh . . . I . . ."

Bea gave her a thin smile. "You're surprised, I see. Yes, I was surprised too. I don't think I cried when Norm passed, and I did love that man."

"But this is different."

"Yes, dear, I'm finding that it is."

Aline's stomach was in knots. Never-down Bea was upset, and yet here Aline was, not feeling much of anything other than the lingering annoyance at the day in general. What was wrong with her?

She knew she didn't care about most things as much as other people, but this, this . . . It should be getting through to her. It should be registering.

"I'm sorry, Grandma."

"It's all right, dear. It's not your fault."

"I—"

Bea blew her nose loudly. "Enough of that. Now tell me, what are you scientificking about these days?"

"I'm still working with Dr. Jackson."

"The famous Dr. Jackson! You're so fortunate that you got to switch to her lab. She is such an amazing talent. I was reading a while back about some of her first experiments."

"You were?"

Bea picked up the sandwich Aline had finished making and took a bite. "Oh, too much mustard."

"I can make another."

"Oh, no, that would be a waste." Bea put it back on the plate and brushed the crumbs off her fingers. "Did I see wine in that fridge?"

"You did."

"Excellent." Bea opened the fridge door and pulled out the bottle. "Now, where are the wineglasses?"

"To the left of the sink."

"Yes, perfect. How convenient." Bea walked to the cabinet and opened it, then pulled down two glasses. "Anyhoo, as I was saying, I was reading about some of Dr. Jackson's experiments and they're fascinating."

"She's done some great work."

"And you?" Bea poured herself a generous glass of white wine. "Are you doing great work?"

Aline thought of the research project she'd finished a few weeks ago, the one she'd asked Deandra to let her take credit for. She'd nearly killed herself writing that article, burning the candle at both ends. She had to make up for lost time and past mistakes, but her grandmother wouldn't understand.

"The focus of our research right now is on neural processes."

"Ooh, that's interesting."

Bea took a large gulp of wine. Aline eyed Bea's wineglass with longing.

"Did you want a drink, dear?"

Aline gave herself an internal shake. It was hot out and the wine looked so refreshing, but Aline knew she'd have trouble stopping at one glass. "No, better not. I have to go back to work after lunch."

Bea picked up her sandwich and took a small bite. Bea's diet had always been 50 percent alcohol, which was probably why she weighed ninety-five pounds. Alcohol dulled the buzz in her brain, Bea had said, so it was *medicinal*. Bea always said this with a laugh, and there was no science behind it, but Aline believed it. The brief times Grandma Bea had been sober had not gone well.

"What's the theory of your research? The thesis?"

"We're trying to determine if a high-fat diet changes brain chemistry or has an effect on things like dementia and Alzheimer's."

"How do you do that?"

"You won't like it."

"Try me."

"Well, first we feed the mice a high-fat diet. Like super high in fat."

"Oh dear."

Aline didn't like it either—she was a vegan, after all—but it was a necessary evil of her job. At least she didn't participate in the killing of animals just for sustenance.

"That's not the worst part," Aline continued. "After a while we kill them—well, euthanize them, actually—and then we slice their brains open."

"How gruesome."

Aline finished making her own sandwich and picked it up. She was hungry. She hadn't wanted anything for breakfast that morning, though she knew that something with a lot of fat would smooth her out from the night before. She and Nick had closed the bar down again, even though it was a Sunday. She knew it was a bad idea, but wasn't she entitled to a bit of fun? A distraction from the fact that her mother was dying?

"It is rather."

"But you love it."

Aline took a bite of her sandwich. Did she love it? The thrill of discovery, yes, very much so. The recognition that she was fighting with Deandra to get? That too. But the daily grind of the lab? She wasn't so sure about that. Hopefully she wasn't going to be tied to the bench for too much longer. Not if everything worked out according to plan.

"Most days."

Bea smiled, then drained her glass. "That's a good answer."

"What are you two up to in here?" Jennifer asked, shuffling into the room. Aline stifled her shock at her mother's appearance. Had she even brushed her hair today? Wasn't Emily supposed to be taking care of that kind of thing?

"Aline's telling me about her research on the brain."

Jennifer's eyes lit up. "Now that's something I'd be very much into hearing."

Jennifer made eye contact with Aline in a way that made her uneasy. It was hard to place what the look was, exactly, but the only word Aline could come up with was *accusatory*.

Chapter 14

HOLD ON

Emily

By the time Emily got home from her mother's house, she was exhausted.

She'd only meant to drop Jennifer off after the doctor's appointment, but she hadn't seen her grandmother yet, and then her sisters arrived, and the next thing she knew it was midafternoon. When she'd realized the time, she'd given her grandmother a kiss and promised to return the next day.

She and Chris lived on the other side of Surrey, forty-five minutes away in midday traffic. It was a choice they'd made consciously: far enough to keep her parents from dropping in unexpectedly, but reasonable enough to make babysitting easy. Not that her dad ever offered to babysit. He'd shown minor interest in the boys when they were born, which had dwindled to twice-a-year visits on their birthday and sometime near Christmas when Emily had what she considered an obligatory second Christmas lunch with her dad and her sisters.

It was almost four when Emily pulled into her driveway. When she turned off the engine she sat slumped in the driver's seat, her hands dangling over the steering wheel, and thought back to what her mother had said that afternoon when she'd asked Aline to investigate her "poisoning," as she called it. She hadn't told Aline, Miranda, or Bea about the phone calls from the doctor, or how Jennifer thought it was deliberate. Instead, Jennifer had left the impression she was contemplating a lawsuit, and that she needed to gather evidence to show that the doctor was negligent.

Emily had listened without contradicting her but had pressed Jennifer about it when they were alone for a few minutes before she left. Her mother was convinced someone had poisoned her. She wouldn't say who, but Emily knew she meant Jake.

Emily sighed and looked at her own lawn, freshly mown with organized flower beds that Chris tended with care. She hadn't noticed it until now, but the house they'd chosen bore an uncanny resemblance to the house she'd just left. Part of it was the local style—houses from the 1950s that had been updated with Pacific Coast influences in the form of large cedar beams and porticos—but part of it was surely an unconscious wish to replace something that felt lost or misplaced. The normal upbringing that the house promised, an illusion she couldn't quite dispel.

It was what she'd always told everyone—Chris, her friends, the mothers she met in playgroup. She'd had a happy childhood, normal, nothing to complain about. But that wasn't true. A completely normal house didn't produce a mother who was convinced that someone tried to poison her, even if her brain wasn't working right.

"What?" Chris asked when she'd filled him in after pulling herself into the house. It had been hot in the car, and the air-conditioning inside felt like a cold kiss. "She what?"

They were in their kitchen, which was different from the vast expanse of white at her mother's house. The people they'd bought the house from had renovated it to sell. In fact, they'd been on one of those home-renovations shows, the ones where professional designers spruced up your house so you got top dollar for it. Emily had recognized their style the minute she walked in. She'd spent too many hours watching HGTV all night after the boys were born.

She'd even watched the episode this house had been in, she'd realized after a minute during the open house. They'd installed these amazing French doors in the family room off the kitchen that folded up and out of the way, giving them an "indoor-and-outdoor feel," and gray cabinets with white stone counters. The backyard was enclosed with a heavy cedar fence and was big enough to put a pool in eventually if they wanted, though Emily wasn't sure that the limited sunshine that came in summer was worth it.

"She thinks someone tried to poison her."

"Who?" Chris asked.

"One guess."

Chris sat down on one of the barstools and rested his chin on his hands. As often happened, Emily felt a thump of love for him. He was so kind and adorable, and she didn't know what she'd done to deserve him. They'd met when they were nineteen years old, and both in pre-med. She fell for his dark good looks immediately and had pursued him in a way that had surprised her. She'd dated in high school but never seriously, simply accepting the boys who asked her out and moving on to the next if things didn't work out.

"That's . . ."

"Insane?"

Chris frowned. "I don't like to use that word."

"I know, but . . ."

Chris hadn't gone to medical school. Instead, he'd veered into teaching. He taught physics at a high school twenty minutes away, which gave him summers off and a reasonable schedule. Perfect for the boys once they arrived, and perfect for Emily if she ever completed her MD.

"Why does she think that?" Chris asked.

Emily explained about the blood tests, all that lead that had been in Jennifer's blood a year ago, and the telephone calls Jennifer swore she'd never received and never returned.

"But it doesn't make any sense," Chris said. "There's lots of ways you can get heavy-metal poisoning, aren't there? What about Andrew? Whatever he uses to make those pieces of art he showed us? Or what about the water in her house? I was reading some article a few months ago that more towns have water problems like Flint than we know."

"Yeah, she's asked Aline to look into that."

"Aline?"

"You know she's a scientist, right?"

Chris made a face. "Sure, but she studies the brain, the last time I checked, not heavy-metal poisoning. Which, as a total aside, would be an awesome name for a band."

Emily was amazed that Chris knew what her sister was researching. He could surprise you like that, Chris. You'd think he wasn't paying attention to something, and then he'd be able to tell you all the details you didn't notice yourself.

"I agree," Emily said. "About the band name."

"Aline actually agreed to look into this?" Chris and Aline didn't like one another, and neither of them kept it secret.

"She did."

"I'm shocked."

"She's not that bad, you know."

"When you get the chance to know her?"

"Ha, ha."

Chris blew her a kiss. "Babe, you know I love you, but Aline and I are never going to get along."

"I know."

Emily walked into the great room and sank into the couch. Was this what twenty-five was supposed to feel like? She knew everyone thought she was old for her age, but this was ridiculous. She could almost understand why her mother had ignored her symptoms for as long as she did. She, too, had a low-grade headache most days, and the other day, when she'd bent down to pick up one of the boys' socks, she'd felt something pop in her back. She'd had to take a bath for thirty minutes and do a yoga DVD before she could stand fully upright. She hadn't been able to lift the boys for a week.

Emily's thoughts skidded to a halt. "Wait. Where are the boys?"

Chris laughed and came to join her on the couch. "I wondered when you'd notice."

"Oh my God. I'm a terrible mother."

"You're a wonderful mother with a lot on her plate."

She rested her head against his shoulder. He was wearing a teal polo, and it smelled freshly laundered, but there was also a hint of salt clinging to his skin.

"Did you go for a run?"

"I did."

"And did you lose our children on this run?"

"I did not."

"So, they are . . ."

"I enrolled them in summer camp. Well, summer day care. My parents offered to pay for it, and I took them up on it."

Emily looked around the room at the mess that never got cleaned up that was created by Ethan and Noah on a daily basis. Duplos and trucks and stuffed animals whose names she couldn't remember. Emily was constantly stepping on one thing or another, cursing under her breath so the boys couldn't hear her, because good mothers didn't swear in front of their children.

Was she a good mother? Sometimes she wasn't sure. Before the boys could talk, she'd lived in constant fear that she'd put them down somewhere and walk away without them. Or leave them buckled in their car seats and forget them in the car on a hot day. People always got so outraged when someone did that, and it was horrible to think of a child dying that way, but Emily had sympathy for the parents. Sometimes when she thought of all the time it would take to unstrap the kids and get them into their stroller, and the fuss they'd make in the store . . . well, she understood the temptation to leave them behind.

"How come you didn't tell me?" she asked, rubbing Chris's arm. She liked the way his hair stood up when she did that, evidence that he was still attracted to her.

"Are you mad about my parents paying?"

"No."

Chris put his hand over hers and squeezed. "I thought it would help us out. Give us a break so we could be more available for your mother while all this is happening."

"Investigating her attempted murder?"

A lump formed in Emily's throat when she said the word *murder*. It sounded ridiculous there on 22nd Avenue, sitting on a couch her father bought them as a housewarming gift, and under a roof that was mortgaged to the hilt. It wasn't a word her mother had used, but Emily could tell that had been an effort she'd made to keep things polite.

"I didn't know about that part, obviously, when I enrolled them,"

Chris said. "But come on, she can't be serious. Did she actually say that?"

"Not in those words, but that's clearly what she's thinking."

"That's truly nuts."

Emily looked at the family portrait they had done last Christmas that hung on the wall across from them, everyone in matching outfits against a washed-out background. In that picture, her family looked perfect, though if you got up close, you could see Ethan's eyes glistening from the tears that had stopped only moments before.

"Is it, though?"

"Your dad? Come on!"

"You didn't see how my dad was talking to her the other night. How he's probably been talking to her for years."

She could feel Chris scowl against her head. "But why would he try to kill her?"

"She thinks it's because she won't divorce him."

"That's not a reason to do something like that."

"Don't be naïve. People kill their spouses for that reason all the time. Don't you ever watch Investigation Discovery?"

Christ twined his hands through hers. "You know I don't like all that true-crime stuff."

"Well, they do. Men kill their wives. Breaking news alert. Plus, don't you remember what my dad told me at the boys' birthday last year?" Emily shuddered at the memory.

"But your mom doesn't know about that, right?" Chris asked.

"No way I'd tell her."

"Good. Your dad could just divorce her, though. He doesn't need her permission."

"Yeah, but he doesn't want it to end up in court. He's pissed off a lot of judges over the years representing their exes in their divorces, and he's certain they'll screw him. Plus, then they'd be able to see his financial records. He doesn't want to go there if he doesn't have to."

"Isn't that supposed to be confidential?"

"Sure. But if the great Jake Gagnon has a messy divorce? That'd be like catnip to them."

Emily had spent many summers working in her father's law office and had picked up more than a passing knowledge of his profession. Jake had hoped she'd follow in his footsteps and join him in his practice, but she'd had other plans.

"But he's not a murderer. Come on."

Emily turned around to face Chris. They both might feel old sometimes, but dressed down like this, he still looked like the teenager she'd fallen in love with. More than once people had assumed that they were babysitting the boys, and when she was alone with them, she was often mistaken for a nanny. "I agree with you, okay? I don't think he'd do something like that. But I didn't think he'd do lots of things he's done. So what do we know? What do we know about anyone?"

Chapter 15

THINGS THAT GO BUMP IN THE NIGHT

Jennifer

It's weird how a house that you thought you knew everything about can still give up secrets.

I remember reading years ago about a couple who found an old body in the walls while they were renovating their property. It had been there since the thirties, a young child who'd died. She'd been wrapped in newspapers, which was how they dated the approximate year of death. She'd died of natural causes, the investigation finally concluded, and it wasn't illegal then to privately dispose of a body.

But oh, knowing that it had been there the whole time? I would've moved out immediately. I wouldn't have been able to sleep there another night. Jake thought I was foolish. *Did I believe in ghosts?* No, I didn't, but I would've felt haunted just the same.

And that's what I am now. After Jake left, the house felt unnaturally quiet. Even though I was used to going to sleep without him because he often worked late—more and more, it seemed, in the last years of our marriage—suddenly it became hard. Jake had become that dead body in the wall—the thing I never knew was right there the whole time. Now that I knew who he truly was, it haunted me. He haunted me.

Every creak and groan in the night made me bolt awake. I'd become convinced there was someone in the house, and I'd lie in bed, clutching my phone, waiting, waiting, waiting. Was this how I was going to die? By home invasion? Or was something worse about to happen?

I stopped watching true-crime shows before going to sleep, got some strategies for dealing with it from my therapist, and eventually the fears receded. The house returned to the house it had always been. It wasn't my enemy—it was my friend. My comfort. The thing I knew best outside of myself; it would never betray me.

That was a lot to put on a house, but I needed something to sustain me.

I met Andrew and he started staying over sometimes, and I got used to having someone around. Particularly when Miranda moved back in. Now the noises had an origin, a purpose. They weren't sinister, they were the evidence that there were other people in my life that I could count on. I slept better. The dreams were less ferocious. My brain no longer felt like it was attacking me.

Then Andrew left to go to his retreat, and then the diagnosis. Ever since, I haven't had a good night's sleep. The creaks and pops are back. Doors slam for no reason. When I ask Miranda about it, she looks at me, puzzled, and tells me she didn't hear anything.

I can tell she thinks it's the cancer affecting my brain. She doesn't have to say it out loud.

So when I hear something in the night, I don't call to her. Instead, I lie there clutching my phone, wondering if the end is coming sooner than I thought.

Which means that tonight, when my phone rings in my hand, it's like an electric shock. It tumbles away from me on the bed, but when I read who it is, I answer it.

"Suzie?"

"Yes, it's me. Hi. I'm so sorry I haven't called before now, but when Miranda told me you didn't want me to come in . . . I shouldn't have listened to her. I'm a terrible best friend."

I prop myself up on my pillows and glance at the clock. It's only nine thirty. When did I fall asleep? When did I even go to bed? I must've taken a pill and forgotten about it. I need to check Emily's notes, though she left hours ago.

"That's okay."

"No, it isn't. It's shitty. I am a shitty person."

"Okay, you are."

Suzie laughs nervously. This conversation already feels weird, even though Suzie is the one who got me through the worst of the separation with Jake. She was there for me whenever I needed her, and she knows more about my marriage than my therapist. And yet, I didn't reach for her when I found out I was dying. I told her, but I told her to stay away. What does that say about me? Or her? Our friendship?

"Does everyone know?" I ask. "About me?"

"Well . . . Barbara told me the other day in the grocery store. You know how she is—sidling up to you all casual-like and then . . . *boom.*"

"How did she find out?"

"How does she find out anything?"

Barbara is the queen of the neighborhood gossips. But she also goes to the same gym as Jake. Fucking Jake. Could he not help crowing about my impending death? Of course, he'd say it in a tone that would make it seem as if he were sad and concerned. But I know better. It's no different than his phone calls. He keeps calling and leaving messages because I don't pick up. He's *worried about me*, he says. He *doesn't like the way we left things*. He wants me to call him back.

I know what he wants. To apologize, and for me to forgive him so he can go on with his life without guilt, and there is zero chance of that happening. I'm at peace with that. Forgiveness is for suckers.

"It was probably Jake," I say.

"He knows?"

"Yes. I had to tell him because—"

"Of the girls. Of course. How did that go?"

"About as well as you'd expect."

Suzie makes a low growl in her throat. I can imagine her expression. She goes for long runs every day, and she always has a tan and a healthy glow about her. She's one of the friendliest people I know, but don't get her started about Jake. "We hate him."

"We do," I say. "We hate him so much."

There's a pause, and I can hear Suzie take a sip of something. I think of all the times we spent at her kitchen island with a bottle of white and oversized glasses. So many nights like that while she tried to put me back together. Wine isn't a permanent adhesive, though. It only works in the moment.

"Can I do something?" she asks. "Can I help in any way?"

"I don't think so."

"I feel helpless."

"Yeah, me too."

"Do you want me to come over?"

"No . . . I . . . I'm sorry, Suzie, but I don't think I can handle it."

"I'm supposed to leave tomorrow."

"Oh, your trip!"

Suzie and her husband had been planning an anniversary cruise

to the Mediterranean for a year. They were going for three weeks—
the first time they'd ever done anything like that. I'd helped her research it, looking longingly at the hotels and beaches and promising
myself I'd do the same someday.

"I think maybe I shouldn't go?"

"No, no. You have to go! Please. Do not stay here for me."

Suzie clears her throat, and when she speaks her words are thick.
"I don't want this to be our last conversation, okay?"

"They have phones in Europe, don't they?"

"Of course."

"So we'll talk, we'll text. And I'll see you when you get back."

I say this with more certainty than I have. Three weeks might be
cutting it close. Who knows what shape I'll be in then? But there's no
way I'm taking this away from her.

"I love you," she says.

"I love you too. And thank you, thank you for everything."

"You don't have to thank me."

"But I do. You . . . you saved my life. When Jake left . . . I would
have given up without you."

Suzie lets out a sound that is half sob, half laugh. "Oh God, no, I
didn't. You saved yourself. But if I could save you, if I could save you
right now, my friend, I would."

"Thank you."

"You would do the same for me. You're sure there's nothing I
can do?"

"Well, there is one thing, maybe . . ."

"Yes. Anything."

My eyes travel around the room and fall on the pile of papers on
my desk. The papers that prove nothing now but might someday. "I
might need to leave you some instructions . . ."

"For, um, a funeral?"

This stops me. I haven't given any thought to that at all. Do I care what happens to me after I die? Maybe an autopsy would be in order, but I'm going to need evidence to make that happen. More evidence than I have, for sure.

"Not exactly. I can't say right now, but I'm going to write it all down and leave it in our place, okay? Go look there after I'm gone. If there's anything to do, it will be there."

Our place. She knows what I mean. The firepit in the backyard has a loose rock in it with a space below meant to hold a bottle of wine. Suzie stashes her cigarettes in there, and sometimes a bit of pot. The girls would be scandalized if they knew, I'm sure.

"What's going on, Jenn?" Suzie's voice has a different level of concern in it.

"It's too hard to explain. But I'll write it all out, okay? Just promise me you'll look into it. If there's something there."

"Look into what?"

"You'll understand if the time comes. Will you just promise?"

I can hear her hesitating, but the one thing about Suzie that I've learned over the years is that she'll do what she can to help if she's asked. She has trouble saying no to anyone in distress. I might've taken advantage of that once or twice. Add that to the pile of regrets I'll leave behind.

"Yes," she says, as I knew she would.

"Thank you."

"We'll speak again in a few days?"

"Sure."

"You're not alone, Jenn."

"I know," I say, but of course I am.

When I get off the phone with Suzie, I try to organize my thoughts. I need a checklist of the things to follow up on so I can leave enough evidence for someone else to follow. Come on, Jenn. Think, think, think.

The first thing is to check my phone records to see if I can identify the calls Dr. Parent said his clinic made. I have the paper with the dates and approximate times, so it should be easy enough to narrow down. I grab my phone to check the logs. Dammit. They only go back a month. I'm not sure if that's a factory setting or some box I checked when I purchased it two years ago, but I feel like crying until I remember that the number the doctor called isn't my cell, it's my landline.

I go downstairs to the kitchen where the base for the cordless phone is and check through it. Those logs go back further, but not far enough—only six months this time. Shit. There must be another way. Phone records. Phone records, that's what I need. The electronic bills I receive every month have the details on them, right?

I creep into the study because Miranda and my mother are sleeping upstairs and open my laptop. I go to my phone company's website and find my monthly statements. There are no call details, but there must be a way to get them. I search through a long line of submenus without success. Finally, I hit the chat window and a perky service person who might be a robot tells me that I can order my phone records going back two years but that it might take a few weeks for me to get them. I ask the robot to send a copy from June of last year. Then I close my laptop and try to think of what I should do next.

I do my somatic breathing and try to focus. It's after eleven and I should be exhausted, but my nap earlier seems to have killed the impulse to sleep. I could binge some show on Netflix, but something else is beckoning.

The basement.

I've been meaning to check it all week, but I haven't made it down there yet. The house has been too full of people—my mom, the girls.

And the expression on Emily's face when I told her some of what I was thinking has prevented me too. It's the reason I didn't tell Suzie what was going on. That *what the fuck* expression that I'm all too familiar with and the questions that follow. It makes me question myself.

Is my brain malfunctioning? Has my hatred of Jake pushed me over the edge?

There's only one way to find out.

I wrap my robe tightly around me, then grab my phone so I can use the flashlight on it. The stairs creak with each step I take, so I stop, certain I'll wake everyone in the house. But my mother sleeps like the dead, and Miranda doesn't hear things that go bump in the night.

I get to the basement and turn on the main lights. The family room lights up, the montage of the girls' life of fame prominent. They'd protested when I'd put up those photos and clippings. *It's so embarrassing, Mom!* I didn't listen to them, sure that when they were older, when they had their own kids, they'd appreciate the archive I kept of their lives. Maybe I was wrong. I'll never know.

I walk toward the back of the basement. There's a room there that I've only been in once or twice. It was Jake's domain. Where all his tools and half-used cans of paint ended up. Jake's dad was a plumber, and Jake took great pride in doing most of the repairs in the house himself. I used to love that he could change a leaking pipe or swap out a sink. Now I'm only annoyed that the detritus of his ego is still in the house. I've been meaning to call a junk company to come and empty it out, but it's been easier to simply forget the room exists.

But it's the room Jake was coming out of the last time I found him down here, so . . .

It was a month or two before the twins' second birthday, though it's hard to pinpoint the exact day or even the time. March or early April. Little Ethan had an accident at the park when I was watching the boys and I'd taken him to emergency, a frantic Emily meeting me there. I'd texted Jake to let him know, because some small part of me still wished he was the man who would've cared to know if his grandson was in emergency. He hadn't showed, but when I got home, his car was in the driveway. I walked through the house, calling his name, and finally heard a muffled sound from the basement.

When I got down here, he was coming out of the back room, a bag in his hand.

What was in the bag?

I'd never thought to ask. Instead I'd berated him for being in the house at all, for not caring about Ethan, for not caring about any of us.

He'd looked gaunt and tired under the bare basement lightbulb. He hissed angry words at me, but I can't remember them now as I creep across the floor, conscious of every single sound my feet are making.

What did Jake have in the bag?

Was it something he could use to poison my food or water? That would be smart, using something that couldn't be traced back to him and leaving it in my house. Was he that smart? I used to think he was the smartest guy I knew. But with everything that happened between us, I've seen his flaws. I've seen his weaknesses. I don't think he's so smart anymore.

I reach the door. The air in this part of the basement smells damp and rotten and feels humid. There's probably a leak down here somewhere, a slow one that escapes notice until it's too late and it's rotted away a beam, or a floor, or filled your house with mold.

I turn the handle and push. The door resists me for a moment, then gives way. I try the light, but it's burned out, so I use the flashlight on my phone to look around. There's a set of metal shelves against the far wall that contain rows and rows of old paint. Paint—oh. I pick up one of the cans. It's latex. Not lead based. Can you even buy lead paint anymore? I don't know, but some of these cans look very old, predating our occupancy. I go through each one. None of them is lead based. Not one.

The other containers are paint thinner and other solvents. Nothing you'd want to ingest, but not anything that could explain my blood tests.

Dammit. I was so sure. Though . . . maybe Jake took out whatever it was that he used. He had that bag. Was it big enough to hold several cans of paint? Was that why he was so angry with me that day? Because I'd caught him in the act?

Come on, brain. What was he carrying?

I slam my hand down in frustration, dropping my phone in the process. It lands with the flashlight pointed up, illuminating the pipes above my head.

The pipes.

The old lead pipes that we never replaced because they only fed the basement bathroom, which we hadn't renovated. Since no one drank from that tap, there wasn't any risk that it would contaminate the water supply.

I pick up my phone and examine them. They're covered in grime and rust and look as though they've been untouched for generations. Because lead is used in fewer products these days, old lead pipes and fittings are one of the main ways that people get lead poisoning. I follow the pipes along the ceiling, and when I get to the corner of the room, my heart stops.

There's a length of pipe that leads from a joint to the elbow in the corner and isn't covered in dust or grime. It's new and made of some different alloy than the pieces it's joined to, copper by the looks of it. Is the piece that's missing big enough to leach out sufficient lead to account for the levels in my blood?

My heart is hammering as I reach up to touch it.

I knew it. I—

"What are you doing down here, sweetheart?" my mother says in the darkness. "I thought there was an intruder in the house."

Chapter 16

ONE, TWO, THREE

Miranda

One of the things that always struck Miranda was how three people who'd grown up in the same house, two of whom were, as far as DNA was concerned, the same person, could have completely different memories of the things they'd done together. Why did memory work that way? What was it about the brain that chose to save some things in Technicolor and let others fade like newsprint?

Take the time for instance when their mother was sick when they were kids and they'd gone to live with their grandparents. Miranda could've sworn that their mother was the one who drove them to their grandparents' house and made sure that they had all their toys and things. She had a clear memory of a tearful goodbye, them clinging to Jennifer, uncertain why they couldn't go with her to treatment or visit her at least.

Aline, on the other hand, would tell you that they'd gone to

Grandma Bea's with Jake. That he'd been the one to throw their things together and leave them hastily at the "crazy fun house" as Aline called it, because what else could you call a place that was both crazy and fun?

Emily, who should've been the bridge between them, couldn't, or wouldn't, corroborate either memory. She'd simply shrug and say, *Who cares how we got there?* and *Why are we even talking about this?* Emily's main beef from that time was with their dad, who in her memory barely came to visit them, while Miranda remembered weekend outings and dinner with him at least once a week.

They could do this with anything. None of them was a reliable witness. The only thing they could agree on was the six-month absence—their mother gone, their inability to visit her, and how, one day, they were taken home as if the whole thing had merely been an extended vacation, and there Jennifer was, standing in the kitchen of their new house, eager to show them around.

Things felt different after that. Every house has alliances, affinities, and by the time they moved into the new house, the family had reshaped itself. Where before their family had been a pentagon, each point as important as the others, now they'd separated into two clusters that couldn't maintain a consistent form: Miranda, Jake, and Aline on one side, and Emily and Jennifer on the other. Miranda wasn't even sure how these particular alliances had formed—why had she chosen Jake? Why had Emily sided with Jennifer? Was it as simple as classifying likes with likes? Miranda, Jake, and Aline looked like one family, Jennifer and Emily another. Or did it run deeper than that? No one ever talked about it, but it lingered over everything.

That's how it felt to Miranda, anyway, though she was certain her sisters would see it differently if they ever discussed it.

But they didn't. They just lived it. And so, despite her connection to Aline and Emily, Miranda knew intimately the feeling of being a shape outside of the hole it was supposed to fit in.

Now more than ever.

Back at the tennis club a few days later, Miranda was hitting balls and trying to avoid Devon. What a stupid mistake that had been. Miranda was embarrassed at her behavior. She'd seen him briefly, in the distance, earlier that day, and her stomach had churned with guilt. She didn't know his girlfriend, at least she hoped not, and she didn't owe her anything, but still. Miranda didn't want to be someone's side piece or involved in that kind of drama. And apparently everyone knew he had a girlfriend, even Aline, who didn't come to the club anymore. How had she missed that? Everyone had seen them flirting together. Were people talking about her now? Thinking she was a slut? Because that was totally the type of language people who still insisted on tennis whites used for girls like Miranda.

She dodged a ball she'd taken her eye off of and stepped aside. She needed to chill. Most of the other club members were her mother's age or older, or their much younger kids. Both groups had their own gossip and concerns. No one gave a fork about her.

But it had happened, she couldn't erase that.

So she hit balls until her arms were shaking, and when she came off the court, Emily was waiting for her.

"What are you doing here?" Miranda asked, wiping a towel across her face to keep the sweat out of her eyes. They were having a hot summer, days of sunshine. When it rained, it was overnight. Miranda could get used to this, but she knew that the usual misty, cold gray skies would return sooner or later.

"I'm here to see you, dummy," Emily said, smiling at her. Sometimes when they were little, one of them would pick a card from a deck and hide it from the other two. Emily would always scrunch up her face and try to guess what it was with all her might, but she never got it right. Neither did Aline or Miranda, mostly, but every once in a while, probably through dumb luck, they would. Emily resented this, Miranda knew. It made her feel left out and emphasized their weird biology. But Miranda had always envied Emily. She could move through the world as a single person. No one ever came up to Emily and assumed they knew her when they didn't. Miranda could've cut her hair differently, or dyed it, she supposed, but the hairstyle she and Aline both wore, a long bob that ended at their shoulders, suited them. Besides, her dark coloring didn't fit well with anything other than her natural hair color. Was she supposed to make herself deliberately ugly just to distinguish herself from her sister?

"Mom told me you'd be here."

"Ah." Miranda hadn't told her mother that, but she wasn't hiding the fact that she spent her day in tennis clothes, either.

"You training for something?" Emily asked.

"Not really."

"Why so intense, then?"

Emily was wearing a flowered summer dress, which she seemed to have an endless supply of, and her hair was in loose waves. The dresses made Emily look like what she was—a mom, which wasn't a bad thing, only it was sad to think that Emily didn't have any room in her life to make the kind of mistakes most twenty-five-year-olds did. She couldn't have sex with random men on a lazy afternoon and get stoned. Or, she could, but that would be highly irresponsible, and that wasn't Emily.

"Just working out some stuff I guess," Miranda said.

"Mom?"

"Sure."

Emily frowned. "That's what I came to discuss, actually."

"Couldn't we talk at the house? You're there practically every day."

"This is an out-of-the-house conversation, I'm afraid."

"Drink at the bar, then?"

Miranda was kind of joking, because it was only noon, but Emily agreed. They walked past the courts to the clubhouse. Devon was playing on Court 1 against one of the pros. He was red in the face and lunging from one side of the court to the other. The pro had a grin on his face, clearly enjoying putting Devon through his paces.

"Is that Devon?" Emily asked.

"Yep."

"Didn't he and Aline have a thing once?"

"Yep." Miranda shrugged. "Everyone had a crush on Aline."

"True enough." Emily chuckled. "It's funny, isn't it? How girls like bad boys and boys like bitchy girls? What is that?"

"She's not a bitch."

"I said bitchy. Come on, you know what I mean."

Miranda felt pissed, the same way she felt whenever anyone said something bad about Aline, even when it was true. They didn't talk again until they reached the clubhouse bar. It hadn't been renovated since they were kids, and it was all dark wood and red leather club chairs. Sometimes Miranda felt as if she could still smell the cigarette smoke leaching from the thick carpet even though no one had been allowed to smoke in there for twenty years.

"What do you want to drink?" Miranda asked as Emily sat down at one of the tables. "Dad's buying."

"White wine?"

"Sure."

She ordered two glasses from the bartender and brought them back. She handed Emily hers and sat down. Her clothes felt sticky and she needed a shower, but that could wait.

"What did you mean just now?" Emily asked. "Dad's buying?"

"He still pays for my membership, which includes the bar tab, though I'm not sure he knows that. But only for this summer."

"He's cutting you off?"

"Yep. Time for me to grow up."

Emily made a face. "He's an asshole."

Her dad was kind of an asshole, but Miranda didn't have the luxury of telling him that. She took a sip of the wine. It was a bit too sour for her taste. She put it down.

"He is. But I shouldn't be living off Mom and Dad, you know? I should grow up."

"Chris's parents have helped us a bunch. That's what parents are for, right?"

"Yeah, I guess, but . . . I don't know. I should get my act together."

"You don't have to make decisions now. You can make them after . . ." Emily shivered.

"After Mom dies?"

"I mean, there's probably going to be some money."

"There is?"

Emily tasted her wine, then took a large gulp. "Come on, Miranda, don't be naïve. You know she inherited a pile after Grandpa died."

"I didn't, actually. She never talks to me about that kind of stuff." Miranda tried not to sound resentful, because she wasn't, but it came out that way.

"Trust me, you'd rather not be her confidante."

"Why?"

Emily took another large sip from her glass and put it down. "That's what I wanted to talk to you about. What do you think of Mom's obsession with finding out what caused her cancer?"

"I wouldn't call it an obsession."

"Okay, maybe that's not the right word, but she was asking about it in the hospital, and it keeps coming up."

"I didn't hear her ask that."

Emily waved her hand. "It was before you got there. When I was talking to the doctor. She was asking about lead poisoning and cancer. I guess she'd seen the results of her blood tests from last year, though she told me later when I asked her that she hadn't."

"That's weird."

"Right? And now she's getting Aline to check the water in the house."

Miranda leaned back and put her feet on the edge of the chair to the left of her. Her thighs made a sound as they unstuck from the leather. "She's probably trying to distract herself. Like who wants to sit around and think about their impending death or whatever?"

"That's what I thought at first."

"But not now?"

"No."

"Why?"

Emily looked away. Miranda loved her sister, but she wasn't always the best about getting to the point.

"What is it, Emily?"

"She thinks someone poisoned her."

"She doesn't mean it literally."

"No, she does."

"Then why is she having Aline look into the water thing?"

"I think she's trying to make sure. Eliminate all the suspects."

"Suspects?"

"She wants to make sure before she accuses anyone formally that there isn't some innocent explanation."

Miranda felt a chill. "Accuses someone formally? What? Like files charges?"

"I don't know. We didn't get into that."

"Who does she think did it?"

"Dad."

"Dad?" Miranda let her feet drop to the floor. Then she picked up her wine glass and drained it. Who cared if it was sour? In fact, she probably needed something stronger. "Is this a joke?"

"No."

A wave of nervousness spread through Miranda. "This has to be related to the cancer, then, right? Like doesn't it affect your brain function? Make you see things that aren't there?"

"You've been researching."

"Well, yeah. I want to understand what's going to happen to her."

Emily reached her hand out. "It's fine, Miranda. I wasn't accusing you of anything."

Miranda pulled her hand away. "Dad didn't try to kill her."

"I know that."

"So what are we going to do about it?"

"I have no idea. That's why I came to you."

"Me?" Miranda asked. "Why not Aline? She's the brilliant one."

"Aline's good at science, sure, but she's not that good with people. And she and Mom don't get along."

Miranda thought back to Emily's comment earlier about men liking bitchy women. As much as she hated to admit it, it was true. Aline could be a bitch, it was kind of her persona, but that wasn't why she and Jennifer didn't get along. That went deeper and was never something Miranda truly understood. "Okay, but what am I supposed to do?"

"You could help me figure out a way to convince her to leave this alone."

Miranda looked around the room. Her hands were shaking slightly. That was probably from hitting all the tennis balls, but it could also have been from the dread that was creeping up from her stomach as the realization of what Emily was saying sunk in.

"This is scary, Emily. Mom thinking stuff like that, telling people . . . this isn't right."

"I know. We'll figure out what to do," Emily said, using her assured voice, the one that always got them through any situation, from haunted houses to home sickness at camp to navigating their complicated family.

Only this time, Miranda wondered if she was faking that assurance. Because Emily had come to her for help, and that could only be a sign of desperation.

Chapter 17

UNDER THE MICROSCOPE

Aline

"You coming to the bar?" Nick asked when she picked up his call. Nick was funny about texting. He had this weird paranoia that someone might be hacking into his phone. She never quite understood where it came from, but it made him stand out from the rest of their generation, that was for sure. He seemed less concerned about voice calls for some reason, which didn't make any sense, though she never challenged him about it. She preferred to have some way to reach him.

"I need to do something here first."

Nick's voice contained a laugh. "Deandra makes you work too hard."

"She doesn't make me do anything. I told you. I'm choosing this. For me."

"Well, right now you should choose to come to the bar."

"I'll be there in about an hour."

She hung up and returned to what she was doing with some annoyance. It's not like Nick didn't understand the nature of her job. He'd worked in a lab too and was ambitious. It's how they'd met, at a conference in Seattle last year, when they'd ended up in the same group of colleagues at the hotel bar after the day's lectures. They'd quickly connected, since they'd both done post-docs at Simon Fraser University and knew some people in common. When they realized they lived within a short drive of one another, Aline knew where things were heading.

So Nick should get it when she said that she had work to do, though it wasn't work for Deandra. It was for her mother. Ha! She was in the lab working at night on an unauthorized project for someone she didn't even get along with.

She'd done that before—unauthorized research—and it hadn't always worked out amazingly for her. On the other hand, you didn't get anywhere if you didn't take risks.

Aline put the water she'd taken from her mother's house into the testing kit she'd bought at the store. She laughed to herself as she did it. Why go to all the trouble of replicating something that was so easily available? But she didn't need to tell her mother that. While she waited for the results, she put a bit of water on a slide and placed it under the microscope to check for bacteria. This wasn't a view that most people wanted of their drinking water. All the microbes swimming around, the whole other level of life that was going on around us. Aline still found it fascinating.

"What are you doing?" Deandra asked behind her, a deep voice in the muted lighting of the after-hours lab.

Aline jumped and hit her head on the microscope. "Ow."

"Are you all right?"

"Yes, I think so." Aline rubbed her head. She felt a bump forming, but it was small and covered by her hair. She turned her chair around slowly, her heart thudding, wondering how this was going to go. She didn't expect Deandra to be here. She was never at the lab after six, though she expected her minions to work till all hours of the night. It was after eight—high time for her to have gone home. Except here Deandra was, wearing her lab coat and ID badge like she did every day, peering quizzically at Aline.

"Is that the assay from the Bjorn study?"

Deandra was obsessed with security and getting scooped by other labs, so she gave each of their projects a code word that Aline could never figure out the origin of.

Aline thought about lying, but it would be too obvious if Deandra checked. "Um, no."

Deandra frowned. "What, then?"

"Just a personal project."

"Oh?"

"I was checking a water sample for bacteria . . . But I was thinking of investigating whether local drinking water has elevated levels of neurotoxins."

"Interesting. What gave you the idea to do that?"

"My mother, actually."

"Oh?"

"Yes, well, I didn't want to make a big deal about this because I know you want us focused on our work and not personal things . . ."

Deandra gave her the charming smile she used on regulators. "Come on, now. I'm not as bad as all that, am I? We take pride here in our work/life balance."

Aline suppressed a laugh. That was a joke. Work/life balance to Deandra meant coming back to work way before your year of maternity leave was up and tolerating having to work from home if your kid was sick.

"Of course; I'm just a private person."

"What's going on with your mother, Aline?"

"She, um, well, she was diagnosed with glioblastoma."

"And the prognosis?"

"Not good."

Deandra reached out her hand and placed it gently on Aline's shoulder. "I am so sorry."

"Thank you."

"You should be with your mother right now, not here putting in extra hours."

"She's sleeping," Aline lied. She had no idea what her mother was up to, or what the schedule was. Emily was updating them in their group thread, which Aline was monitoring as loosely as she always had.

"All right. But why the research?"

"She thinks it might have been caused by contaminated water."

"Heavy metals?"

"Yes."

Deandra cocked her head to the side. "There are a few papers on this that have been published recently, you realize?"

Aline gritted her teeth. Of course she knew that. But Deandra was trying to be nice, and Aline should use that to her advantage. Who knew that the way to Deandra's heart lay in personal tragedy rather than in hard work?

"Yes, I was reading the research last night."

"Is there any indication that the water in her house is contaminated?"

"That's what I'm trying to determine."

Deandra put a hand on her arm for a moment, then retreated. "Well, I'll leave you to it, then. But do tell me if you find anything. There's an unassigned envelope of funding that we could use to pursue this if it looks promising."

"Thank you."

"What's your mother's name?"

"Jennifer."

Deandra smiled again. "The Jennifer Project, then."

"The Jennifer Project," Aline agreed, though the words felt strange in her mouth.

Like betrayal.

Two hours later, Aline crept into the bar like a cheating husband trying not to get caught. She needed a drink more than ever tonight. It wasn't a feeling she was accustomed to, but Aline felt a bit . . . well, *dirty* was the word, having used her mother's tragedy like that with Deandra. Aline needed to wash that feeling away with something strong and antiseptic.

She ordered a vodka soda from the bartender who knew her by name and went to their usual table. Nick was there alone, nursing a beer.

"Where are the others?"

"Early day tomorrow, apparently."

"Losers."

"Right?"

She sat down next to Nick, who leaned over and gave her a sloppy kiss. He was a year older than her and had worked in Deandra's lab until two months ago, when he'd started a sessional teaching position in the neuroscience department at Simon Fraser University as a tryout for a faculty position that was opening. He'd gotten her the job at the lab, after they'd started dating. But they'd hidden that from Deandra because she disapproved of relationships among her employees. Aline tried not to show it, but she was pissed when Nick got the teaching job. She'd applied too, but Deandra's recommendation had gone to Nick and not her. She always favored the men. Aline had that on good authority from the other women she worked with, who met once a week on Thursday nights for a drink to bitch, mostly about Deandra. Project D, they called that one. Not the best cover.

"What were you working on?" Nick asked.

She thought about keeping it to herself, but Nick knew about her mother's diagnosis, so she filled him in as she downed her vodka and then ordered another. She savored the slow liquid feel that was coursing through her. It was fleeting, she knew from experience, and hard to maintain, but for right at this moment it felt perfect.

"Interesting reaction from Deandra," Nick said. "She doesn't usually offer up funding that easily."

"I guess."

Nick squeezed her arm. "This could be good for you. Get you that paper you're missing on your resume."

"I'd have the paper if Deandra wasn't such a publicity hog."

"It's the way it is."

"It's bullshit. You know that. The system favors the patriarchy."

Nick laughed. "Is Deandra the patriarchy now?"

"You know she is. The one girl inside the tent, pissing out. She should be making it easier for those of us who come after her, not harder."

"Slow your roll there, sister."

"Easy for you to say." Aline threw back her second drink and rattled the ice in the glass. The pop song playing over the sound system was loud and grating. She couldn't remember why they'd started coming to this bar, a no-name place that was close to the lab. Its only virtue was its proximity. "Anyway, it doesn't matter. I'm not going to find anything."

"Why do you think that?"

"Because my mother is crazy."

"She's going through a trauma."

"Sure, now. But, historically, loco." Aline spun a finger near her ear.

"Everyone thinks that about their parents."

Aline looked at her hands. Her nails were ragged, but she didn't care. Who had time to care about nails?

"Sure, but . . . I don't know. You know how medical students imagine they have everything they're learning about?"

"I've heard that."

"She was in med school when she got pregnant with us, and, well, it was like that pattern never went away for her. Only it was focused on us. I can't even tell you how many times I went to the emergency room when I was little."

"A lot of mothers are like that."

"I guess. I'm not explaining it right."

"You're tired. And probably sad."

Was she sad? Aline didn't think so. Not sad like when she didn't get the university job. More like guilty because she wasn't feeling the emotions she was supposed to be feeling.

"Well, whatever it is," Aline said, "I didn't find anything."

"In the water?"

"Nope. It's clean. Clean for a city, anyway."

Nick made a face. "It's a good topic regardless. You could turn it into something."

"I guess."

"Hey, come on, what's going on?"

"What's the point?"

Nick sat back in his chair. "Look, your mom is dying. You didn't get the job you wanted, and you're a bit further behind on your life plan than you thought you would be—"

"Are you saying I'm having a midlife crisis?"

"No, just that you should take it a bit easier on yourself. You don't need to perform or anything. You can take your foot off the gas while this is happening. It will all still be here when you get back."

Nick had had too much to drink and so he was mixing his metaphors, but Aline understood what he meant. She was being too intense. That was always her problem. She pushed and pushed until she broke something. In ballet, it had been a tendon in her leg. Later, it had been relationships. She pushed herself too hard, and it made others feel bad. Inadequate.

When they were young, and semi-celebrities, TV personalities always laughed at her mature responses when they had the triplets on their programs. But she wasn't that young or cute anymore. Now she was the girl who needed to slow down so she didn't cause an accident.

But the thing that no one ever understood was sometimes the proximity of an accident was the point. It was the only way you could get to what you wanted. Most people weren't ready to take the risk of getting hurt.

Aline, on the other hand? Well, to her, the possibility of pain was part of the fun.

Chapter 18

THE PENNY DROPS

Jennifer

It's Sunday night dinner. That used to be a thing around here. As the girls grew up and Jake became busier and busier in his practice. As schedules no longer permitted us to eat together as a family every night. As I saw our traditions slipping away even though I wouldn't have characterized it like that, I instituted the mandatory Sunday dinner. We all had to stop and sit around the table for a meal. Sometimes I'd cook. Sometimes Jake would. Sometimes my mother would come and turn the kitchen inside out. One hour. That was all I asked for.

It didn't seem like much.

It's been a while since the last one. They'd tapered off when the girls went to university, relegated to holidays and the summer. Jake and I used to keep up the tradition, though, mostly with the girls joining us when time permitted. Then Jake left. The girls came over more often after that, but like it is for anyone with a trauma, the support retreated before the wound had healed. They went back to their lives and I tried to move on. With life. Then with Andrew, the third guy I had met on an online dating site for those over forty-five, a little more than a year ago.

I'd been bombarded by men in their sixties and seventies when I first joined. Was that supposed to be good for my ego? It wasn't. But then the men more my own age appeared, mostly divorced, some never bothering to have married and happy to date in their age bracket so there would be no expectation of kids. Andrew and I clicked right away. He was very different from Jake. So he didn't give a shit about his career; it was a relief. He was emotionally available and actually engaged in conversation rather than with his phone. He liked making long, elaborate meals. I let the girls off the hook. I had my own life now, my own plans.

But those plans have been canceled, so I've asked the girls to reinstate the dinners. There won't be many more, maybe only this one and the next, but we don't discuss that. And we don't discuss that we're eating takeout, when the meal was always something we cooked at home before. I'm tired, and none of the girls volunteered, and I couldn't face the disaster my mother would create if she were left alone in the kitchen. The result—we're sitting in the dining room eating Indian food, and I've brought out the good china and the silverware, which needs polishing. Someone lit candles and found leftover napkins from Christmas, red and green, and it almost feels festive.

"Can you bring the twins by at some point this week?" I ask Emily as she pours me a glass of champagne. My mom found the bottles in what used to be the wine cellar after she caught me in the basement the other night. She started poking around the other rooms and opened the door to the wine cellar, a wine closet really, that I'd also been avoiding. Jake had emptied it when he moved his things, something I'd discovered when I came back to the house after leaving it to him for the day. He never liked champagne, though, so he'd left a crate behind.

Did he think I'd need it to celebrate?

I'd told my mother I'd heard a clanging noise in the pipes and had hurried her out of the room, feeling full of triumph. There's a piece of lead pipe missing from my home and I had lead poisoning. This cannot be a coincidence. Jake could have easily leached the lead from that section of pipe using a corroding agent.

"Yes, of course," Emily says, her chin quivering slightly.

My throat closes. The thought of saying goodbye to those two precious creatures . . . but it's the right thing to do. I don't even know if they'll remember me as time goes by, but I have to hope Emily will make sure that they do.

It's trite to say, but grandchildren are a blessing. They are the gift of doing things over again with an accumulation of experience and the fresh love of innocence. I hadn't done anything to cause any strife between us, and that felt good to me. I'm even a tiny bit happy that I'll die before I've had the chance to screw things up.

"Are we toasting?" Aline asks. She's already greedily sucked down a glass of champagne and is on her second. Does she always drink this way? I've never noticed before. There are so many things around this table that I'm not going to know the answers to.

"How about to memories?" I say, feeling silly.

Everyone raises their glasses and mumbles the word, and we drink for a moment in silence. Then Emily begins doling out papadums and curry and rice. The spices smell wonderful, and I feel hungry in a way I haven't in days. Should I do a tour of the cuisine of all my favorite countries? The Last Meals Tour.

"Did you find anything in the water, Aline?" I ask.

Aline finishes her glass and eyes the bottle. We'll have to open another soon. "I ran the tests. Your water is fine."

I feel strangely happy at this news. Jake won't have a ready-made excuse for my test results. "Are you sure?"

Aline nods. "There are the usual traces of things you'd rather not hear about in your water, but it's all within acceptable limits."

"Thank you for checking." I scoop up a small bit of lamb rogan josh with a corner of naan. It's terribly spicy, but I swallow it down anyway. I want to feel these last meals, sear them into my fading consciousness.

"Sure."

"Can we leave it alone now, Mom?" Emily says.

"Leave what alone?" Bea says. She's sitting at Jake's place at the other end of the table and she's also through her second glass of champagne. She opens a new bottle without asking. She hasn't said how long she's staying, and I haven't the heart to ask. My mother made a lot of mistakes with me growing up, but I've had a lifetime to punish her for that. I don't need to reject her now. Besides, I know she'll leave before it gets messy. She's restless and she doesn't deal well with the hard stuff unless it's alcohol.

"About what caused her cancer," Emily says.

"Not this again," Miranda says.

"What's that supposed to mean?" I ask.

"Nothing, Mom, I . . ." Miranda glances at Emily.

"You've talked about this without me?" I say to Emily. She's shredding a piece of garlic naan into tiny pieces as if she's about to feed them to one of her kids. Perhaps it's out of habit. Or does she eat like this regularly, almost nothing?

"Yes."

"What's going on?" Aline asks.

"Yes, I'd like to know as well," my mother says.

I make eye contact with Emily. My left eye has been bothering me for the last two days, new floaters clouding my vision. I've stopped wearing my contacts and switched to glasses, and it helps a bit but not enough. I should ask Dr. Parent about it at my appointment tomorrow, but it's one of the things that can happen as the cancer feasts on my brain.

"Go ahead, Emily."

"This is your thing, Mom."

"Fine, well, I think someone did this to me."

"What?" Aline asks. "Gave you cancer?"

"Yes."

"You can't give someone cancer."

"You don't know that. No one knows that."

Aline looks down. I've spoken more sharply than I meant to, but I can't seem to help myself with her. I never could. Or she never could. Does it matter who started the fight? It was my job to end it and I didn't.

"Be that as it may, I was poisoned."

"There's no evidence of that," Emily says.

"There's the blood test." I look at Aline and Bea. "A year ago, I had very high levels of lead in my blood."

Emily shakes her head impatiently. "That was probably a mistake. Particularly now that we know your water is clean."

"There are other ways that you can get lead poisoning."

"That's true," Aline says.

I smile at her. I have to admit, I like it when Aline agrees with me. It's so rare. Her whole life she was always the one who said no first, who ran away and had to be forced into her clothing, bed, everything.

"And lead can cause cancer," I add.

"Yes, but you could never be sure of that result," Aline says. "It's not *a* plus *b* equals *c*."

"Well, I don't think that was the intended result. It's just . . . extra." This much I've figured out. The poisoning had gone wrong. It made me sick, but it didn't kill me. Not right away.

"This is nuts, Mom," Miranda says. "I'm sorry, but it's true."

"The tests don't lie."

Emily shakes her head. "Well, sometimes they do. Lab test results are wrong all the time."

"Why do you keep saying that?"

"Because what's the alternative? That someone, and by someone we all know who you mean, wanted you dead?"

I look down at my plate. "It's not so far-fetched, is it?"

"Come on. Are you listening to yourself? Dad has been . . . disappointing, okay, we all get that. But that doesn't mean he tried to kill you."

Bea gasps at that word as if it's a blow. And it is. It's the reason I've been walking around for two weeks trying to catch my breath.

I look up. Tears are clouding my vision now, but I don't care who sees it. "None of us know what he would do. We don't."

"So how is he supposed to have done this, then?" Aline asks.

I turn to her. Her glass is half-full again, but I've lost count of how much she's had to drink. My own glass is empty, I realize. When did that happen?

"Work with me here, Aline. You can contaminate water with lead on purpose, right?"

"Yes. You can leach lead into water or another solvent."

"Would that taste of something? If it was put on food, say, or in a drink?"

"I don't know."

"And would one dose be enough to produce the results I had?"

"I haven't seen your results, and I'm only at the beginning of my research . . ."

"What?" Miranda says. "Your what?"

Aline looks uncharacteristically embarrassed. "I'm thinking of a new research project."

"On?"

"The path between neurotoxins and glioblastoma."

"I can't believe you're encouraging this." Emily's fork hits her plate. "Or that you're turning what's happening to Mom into research."

Aline lifts her chin. "You have a problem with that, Mom?"

"It's fine," I say. "Do what you want."

Aline picks up the bottle and refills her glass. "Why is everyone being so judgy? Mom asked me to look into this and I have. If it sparked a research idea, so what? Why is that any different from you going to medical school to help sick people because of when Mom had cancer before?"

"What's that?" Bea says.

"When we came to live with you, Grandma," Miranda says. "Don't you remember?"

"Of course I do, dear. Don't pay any attention to the old bat."

I close my eyes, and no one notices. I listen to the sound of forks scraping on plates. There are lots of things I didn't pay attention to in my own life.

I didn't notice the missing piece of pipe.

I never went looking.

That was my mistake. One I'll pay for with my life.

Chapter 19

BROKEN

Jennifer

The girls have left, leaving me and Mom and Miranda behind. I admit, it's nice having my family around me again, fussing over me, concerned. I can hear the two of them from my bedroom as they rattle around cleaning up, talking in whispers the way you do when someone is sleeping during the day because they're sick. Only it's night, inky black, and they don't have to whisper; this is not when I sleep anymore. Nighttime is full of thoughts and terrors and memories. It's only when the sun comes up, in the hours between six and noon, that I can drift away. Even then I'm only skimming along the surface.

And tonight, like two weeks ago, I am drunk. Drunk on champagne—the stuff Jake left behind, like me. Drunk on suspicions. Drunk on the painkiller I took an hour ago because the headache felt like my head was going to split in two. I snuck away from the table and went to my room, my medicine cabinet, and I stared at the bottle of pills. It would be so easy to take them, to leave this all behind a few weeks early. But no, I'm not ready for that. I haven't said goodbye to my grandchildren, and despite everything that the girls think, that they said, I know I'm not wrong.

There's still time for me to prove it.

So I took one pill and climbed into bed with my thoughts.

Despite the drugs and the booze, or maybe because of it, everything is clearer tonight than it has been in the past two weeks. I can imagine Jake doing it. Like now, he'd been calling and calling, spring of last year. I mostly avoided his calls, but they'd echo through the house at night, over and over. I'd turn the ringer off on the phone, and then the texts would start. Threatening in a way I'd understand because I knew everything about Jake, or so I thought, and Jake knew everything about me.

I should've given in to him. I'm not sure why I didn't, only that it didn't feel like justice. Giving him what he wanted in the circumstances. It was something I could control. In refusing the divorce, I was taking my power back in the only way I could.

It's not that his words didn't affect me. Part of me was scared. I'd worked so hard to put my life back together and I'd succeeded. Until Jake left, I'd had everything handled. If Jake really knew, if he actually told, well, then he'd be implicating himself too.

No, Jake wasn't going to tell. So I mostly ignored him. When I answered, I told him no. I told him to leave me alone and stop calling me. He seemed to listen eventually. The calls subsided, the text thread went silent.

Then the birthday party. The boys' second birthday. The party was at one of those trampoline places. Twenty kids from Emily and Chris's neighborhood, and all their moms and dads. A large table full of chips and homemade nut-free brownies and nonalcoholic punch.

I'd watched Jake as he'd moved through the crowd, being charming, shaking hands. He'd bought Ethan and Noah matching miniature golf sets. He was going to give them lessons, he promised Emily, be more involved. I watched as Emily smiled at him, but I could tell that she felt uncertain. She moved her face away from his kiss at the last moment, and he kissed the air. Jake's face fell for a second, the mask slipped, and then he papered it with a smile.

He walked over to me a few minutes later, a red Solo cup in each hand. I'd willed him to stay away, but I didn't want to make a scene, not at my grandchildren's birthday party. I tried to keep my face calm, and I breathed in and out like my therapist had taught me, praying for calm.

"Hi, Jenn."

"Jake."

"You look nice."

It was something he always said, but he probably meant it. I'd taken extra care with my appearance. I'd lost weight since he'd left, and I'd bought some new clothes, had my hair cut and blown out. I was looking my best, everyone said so. Part of me wanted to look like the disaster I was inside, so he could see what he'd done, but that wasn't the part that won.

"Thank you."

Jake looked fine, but not like my Jake. Like the new Jake, the Jake who cared about what polo shirt he wore, what slacks. I hated to admit it, but I missed the old Jake. The Jake who didn't care if his pants were rumpled, or if I was rumpled too.

"You want one?" he'd said, holding out the cup.

"No thanks."

"I put something extra in there."

I couldn't help but smile. "The flask?"

"The flask."

I'd given it to him. A silver engraved flask that we used to bring to children's parties, because how were you supposed to get through those things without alcohol?

He pushed the cup toward me again. "Come on, Jenn. Peace offering."

"All right."

I took it and we clinked cups and drank. I could feel the girls watching us. They'd gathered at the food table as if drawn together by a magnet. They were waiting. But for what?

"What's in here?" I asked.

"Vodka."

"Tastes funny."

"It might be flavored."

I made a face. "Mint?"

"I think I grabbed the wrong bottle." He took a large swallow and grimaced. "Oh well. Needs must."

"True."

He turned and stood next to me to watch the tableau of our children, Ethan and Noah running around among their friends. They'd inherited Emily's strawberry curls, but their skin was darker and their eyes brown like Chris's. Like Jake's. They were the mix I thought we'd make, instead of the genetic anomaly of Emily, my twin, and Miranda and Aline, his.

So typical that he'd get two and I'd get one, I thought, though I'd never thought that before.

"I wanted to say I was sorry," Jake said.

I felt nervous. "Oh?"

"I was calling too much."

"You were."

"I shouldn't have . . ."

"No, you shouldn't."

"We should work this out."

"Not today though, okay, Jake?"

"Right. Not today."

He took another sip and I joined him. Maybe I took more than a few. I must have, because in a few minutes my cup was empty. Jake left briefly to retrieve more punch and came back with a fresh drink for me. I wasn't sure why I took it, only that I needed the buffer the alcohol gave between him and me. Between everyone who was watching us, or trying not to, giving us the side-eye, wondering when the show would start.

"Emily seems to be doing well," he said eventually.

"Yes—" I stopped myself from saying he'd know that if he were around more. If he hadn't disconnected not just from me but from the girls as well.

"It's hard, having multiples."

"It's hard having children," I said. "But that's not . . . It was post-partum."

"Oh, I didn't think . . ."

Emily hadn't thought that's what she had either. None of us had. Emily, who always had it all together. Emily, who never missed a beat. She'd hidden her sadness away, chalked it up to not enough sleep, mourning for her lost career, external factors. It was Chris who encouraged her to seek help, Chris who saw more than anyone that she wasn't herself. The rest of us had missed it, even me. When she called and asked for my therapist's number for a referral, I assumed at first that there was something going on with her and Chris.

"There's a family history, you know," I said.

"I do, but—"

"Don't worry. She's much better now. And it wasn't like . . . Not like Bea or anything."

He looked relieved. "That's good."

"She's had a lot to handle in the last couple of years."

He turned toward me, searching my tone for accusations.

"You all have," he said eventually, leaving himself out of the equation for once. I see it now for the act it was, but then, I was so happy to see the Jake I'd known my entire adult life show up that I fell for it. The alcohol helped. He'd spiked the drink hard, but he hadn't made me drink it.

I did that on my own.

"We have."

"I miss you guys."

"Jake."

"It's true."

"What is this?" I asked. "Why are you saying this?"

"I don't want anything. I just wanted you to know."

"The girls haven't gone anywhere." As much as I'd wanted to tell them, beg them, order them to never talk to him again, I hadn't. They were adults. They could choose what they wanted. We had a "don't ask, don't tell" policy. I assumed they saw him, but I didn't want to hear about it.

"I miss Sundays," he said.

"They still happen every week."

"You know what I mean."

"I can't help you if you miss the family," I said gently.

"I wasn't asking you too."

"Weren't you?"

We looked at one another. What did he see? A woman he loved once? A woman he wouldn't have been with but for a mistake, compounded by three? I didn't want to know which was which, I realized for the first time. I'd wanted explanations, details, closure. But in that moment, I knew that it didn't matter what he said. It wouldn't change anything. It wouldn't make me feel better. There was no explanation that would erase the scars he'd caused.

"Let's just leave it at that, okay?" I said. I finished the rest of my drink and handed him the cup. "Thanks for the peace offering."

"No problem."

I walked away and spent the rest of the party on the other side of the room. My mind was whirling from the drinks, too many drinks, and after the cake, I made my excuses and took a cab home.

But I was wrong to think I didn't need answers. I'm full of need now. I need to know. I need to talk to Jake, not on the phone or through texts, but face-to-face. Only then will I know if he's lying. Only then can I be sure.

I slip out of bed. I pull on some jeans, a sweatshirt. I walk down the stairs as quietly as I can. I go through the garage, putting on an old pair of tennis shoes I discarded there long ago. I've had too much to drink to drive, but Jake is not far. That fucker went and bought a house less than a mile away. That was deliberate, I always thought, though he swore it was a coincidence, that the right house had just come along.

The night is warm, the streetlights bright. I'm weaving a bit, but not too badly. I take in some deep breaths to clear my head, but it's cloudy. I am cloudy. A dark cloud, storming down the street to Jake's, as I should have done long ago.

I'm there in twenty minutes. I've been feeling weak, but tonight I have my strength.

I stand in front of his house, marveling at the size of it. More bedrooms than people. A half-acre lot. So new I can still smell the freshly sawn wood. Jake had torn down the old house that had sat there since the fifties and built this.

Look at me, look at me. Look how well I'm doing now that I'm free.

I don't want to ring the bell. The element of surprise, that's what I need. Jake loves gadgets, and he's installed the same key panels on this new house as he'd installed on ours years ago. Mine. And the code. He wouldn't use the same one, but he'd use something easy enough to remember. I try his birthday, and nothing happens. Then I try the girls' birthday and the lock clicks and beeps green. I did it. I guessed right. I still know Jake well enough to break into his house. That's something, isn't it?

I open the door and enter. The foyer is dark, and I stand there, breathing in. The house smells both familiar and foreign. Now that I'm in here, I don't know what to do. Go upstairs? Call for Jake to come down? I'm not sure how to manage this confrontation, how to bring it about.

I didn't think this through. I should go. Come back in the morning. Come back when I'm sober and I have a recording device on me. I should—

A light snaps on.

"What the fuck are you doing in my house?" a voice asks, furious.

But it's not Jake.

It's her.

Kim.

Four Weeks to Live . . .

Chapter 20

CAUGHT

Jennifer

I've never been interrogated by a police officer before, and it wasn't on my list of things to do before I die. Now that I'm in the middle of it, sitting in the small study on the main floor of Jake's house, I'm wishing that I'd done the conventional thing when I was given my diagnosis. Put my affairs in order, said goodbye to my loved ones, and then gone to a beach somewhere so I could drink in peace and slip quietly away while I watched the waves crash onto shore.

But no. Instead I had to go and do something stupid, the second stupidest thing I've ever done in my entire life—breaking into Jake's house to accuse him of trying to kill me and get him to what? Confess? Explain to me why he'd done it? Give me the evidence I needed to convict him? It all sounds insane now.

Stupid, so stupid. Stupid people get caught. Stupid people get punished. I guess it makes sense that I'm here, under threat of arrest for breaking and entering into Jake and Kim's house.

Kim. Kimberly Carpenter. Kimberly Anne Carpenter. Her. The woman Jake left me for. Thirty pounds lighter than me and more than twenty years younger. Born in the 1990s. Her parents and close friends call her Kimmie—at least according to her Facebook page and the Instagram account where she posts photos of herself in bikinis and in exotic locations #livingmybestlife. I know that and so much more about her from spending all the hours I couldn't sleep after Jake left going through years and years of posts about her ready-for-social-media life.

But I knew her before that too because Jake, stupid fucking Jake, had an affair with the senior partner's daughter when she was interning at his firm after her second year of law school.

Yep, that's what happened. Jake had an affair with someone half his age and joined the club of clichéd men everywhere. It feels so fucking predictable, except when it's happening to you.

All those late nights and being glued to his phone when I thought he was working and responding to demanding clients? Turns out he was stealing out of the office to fuck her in her apartment while her roommate was at work. That's what he told me before he left, sitting in his favorite chair in the living room, his voice so calm I thought one of us was having an aneurysm. But it was happening, it wasn't a product of my imagination or some sort of psychosis. He was in love with someone else and he was leaving. That's why he wanted the divorce: so he could marry her, the woman he loved more than anything.

As if he hadn't said that to me when he'd pursued me relentlessly in college. Like he hadn't promised me everything when we'd found out I was pregnant and we were trying to decide together whether to go ahead with the pregnancy. As if he hadn't told me how much he loved me on a regular basis for the twenty years we were together. Not that we had a perfect marriage, who does? But we'd found a way through all the tough times and still figured out how to be with one another in laughter, intimacy, and friendship—all the best parts of long-term love.

But that was all wrong, you see? Jake had said. That wasn't what had actually happened, even though I was right there the whole time. He'd rewritten our history, and the true story, apparently, was this— he'd married me because it was the honorable thing to do. He stayed with me because he loved the girls and couldn't imagine not being there for every moment of their growing up. Even once they were grown, he'd accepted his situation. Divorce would be a disruption. We were great friends. It was enough.

Then, like a miracle, true love walked in. *True love, Jenn!* He talked about it as if he'd seen a unicorn, a mythical thing that no one rational believed in unless you saw it with your own eyes. Only it wasn't a miracle that he'd slept with someone almost half his age. That was typical, not exceptional.

True love. That's why he'd cheated on me and left the family, didn't I see? That's why he'd violated every promise he'd made, in- cluding his promise to the world that he was the kind of guy *who would never.* Jake was the *last guy who would do that*, everyone al- ways said about him, unprompted, if cheating came up, as if to reas- sure me when I wasn't supposed to need reassurance. But now that he had done that, Jake had to have an explanation. So it was the love that made him do it, he'd said again and again, as if repetition would convince me. Why couldn't I understand that and accept that we'd all be happier now?

The narcissism of the man knew no bounds.

The only satisfaction I got from the situation was thinking about Kim and how she must worry whenever he is out of the house. I never did, because I had no reason to worry—*he would never*. Kim knows he would, though. That he could. And though I'm not usually a vindictive person, I can't help but wish that she ends up where I did—betrayed, abandoned, alone.

Of course, that wish looks silly now that I'm sitting across from a police officer with a hysterical Kim outside in the hall. I should've just run away when she found me, but she was holding a knife and she knows where I live, and I was suddenly so tired I couldn't make my legs work properly. So as she called the cops, I walked into this study and waited for them to arrive, trying desperately to come up with an explanation of why I was where I shouldn't be.

As I waited, I got angrier. At myself, but, as always, at Jake. Jake is the one who should be in trouble, not me. Jake should be the one waiting to speak to a police officer. Jake and Kim, who must've poisoned me together to get me out of the way. I can even imagine him broaching the subject one night in that smooth, reasonable voice that makes you question your sanity for disagreeing with him.

His litigator's voice.

"Ma'am?"

I look up. A police officer is looking at me with a quizzical expression, and I'm worried for a moment that I've been talking out loud.

"Yes?"

"Are you ready to talk now?"

"About?"

"What you're doing in your ex-husband's house?"

"He's still my husband, actually."

The officer frowns. His last name is Frances, and he's about forty, with short black hair and a moustache that doesn't suit him. This is one fashion trend that I wish had stayed in the seventies where it belonged.

"Is that relevant to the discussion?" he asks, his voice a drawl.

"Well, doesn't it mean that it's my house too? Community property and all."

Officer Frances takes a seat across from me. This study is eerily like Jake's study in our house. Same shelves on the wall, same dark leather chairs, same desk. It's disorienting. "Well, I don't know about that."

"It's true," I say, pulling up information I'd heard from Jake during all the years we were together. Jake loved talking about his cases, the divorces, the custody battles. He specialized in high–net worth individuals because they were the ones who could pay his exorbitant fees. "Until we're formally divorced, what's mine is his and vice versa."

"I don't think that means you can go into his house in the middle of the night, ma'am, uninvited."

"But I didn't. Jake wanted to talk to me. He kept calling and asking me to meet up. If I had my phone, I could show you."

"Well, now—"

"And I didn't break in. I had the code."

I look down at my bare feet while Officer Frances doodles on the pad that he's pulled from his shirt pocket to take down my statement—a series of stars, and a box that he's made 3D. I'd kicked off my tennis shoes while I was waiting to be questioned, rubbing my feet into the thick carpet in a bid to orient myself in something solid. "Did Mr. Gagnon know you were coming over?"

"Well, not the exact time, but he was working late, wasn't he? He always works late."

"Yes, that's true, he wasn't home yet . . ."

I lean forward. I'd watched Jake talk and talk his way out of things for so many years; I could do it too. "See? I was going to wait for him to have the conversation he wanted to have."

"Why didn't you ring the bell?"

"Jake comes into my house all the time without ringing the bell. I didn't think he'd mind."

"And Ms. Carpenter? What about her?"

I make a face I cannot help when I hear her name. *Do not call her the whore*, I repeat to myself silently. *Do not call her the whore.*

"What about her?"

"She was asleep. You scared her."

I try not to smile. Good. She should be scared. "I didn't know she'd be asleep. She's young. It's not that late. She's much younger than Jake," I can't help adding.

"Ms. Carpenter said that your husband left you for her, correct?"

"So?"

He sighs. It's late and he's tired. "Is that your story, ma'am? That you were at your husband's house to talk to him?"

"Yes."

"What about?"

This is my chance to tell the police exactly what's been going on. What Jake tried to do to me. I can show them the papers I have from the doctor, explain the timeline, let them investigate. But not with Kim on the other side of the door. Not in my present state, in these sloppy clothes, the smell of alcohol on my breath, the painkillers still in my system. It will sound crazy, I will sound crazy, and I'm more likely to end up in the hospital on a psychiatric hold than getting them to open an investigation. Because a crazy, scorned woman is so much easier to swallow, even though the murdering husband is statistically more likely.

"We had a disagreement," I say.

"About your divorce?"

That's not right but it's the easiest answer. "Yes."

Officer Frances's eyes travel to the door. He let me wait in here for half an hour while he spoke to Kim. Getting her side of the story first, because of course it's more important than the true victim's. I couldn't hear what she was saying, but her shrill tone said it all. She calmed down when the low rumble of Jake's voice joined in. I haven't seen him yet, safe from that humiliation as long as I stay inside the study, but I'm sure it's coming.

"Was that what you wanted to talk about, ma'am? The divorce?"

"Yes."

"Why? Why after ten p.m. on a Sunday night?"

"Because that's when I wanted to talk. Maybe you've also heard, I don't have that much longer to live."

Officer Frances lowers his pencil and focuses in on me. "What's that?"

"I'm sick. Dying."

He seems genuinely surprised. "I'm sorry to hear that."

"Thank you."

He doodles for a moment, to let the awkwardness pass. He adds a few more stars, squinting as if he's concentrating hard. He finishes one and looks up at me. "I'm puzzled, though. If that's true, why did you need to talk to your husband about a divorce?"

My heart rate increases, and I start to feel like a hamster caught on a wheel. I keep running, the wheel keeps spinning, but I'm not getting anywhere.

"I don't have to explain myself to you."

"I think you do, ma'am. Given the circumstances. So why don't we start again? Why don't you tell me what you're doing here?"

The anger returns. At myself, but also at this entire situation. This isn't fair. It isn't fair, and it isn't right. "What you should be asking is why my husband wants the divorce so badly and what he'd do to get it."

Officer Frances blinks slowly. "What are you saying, ma'am?"

I sit back in my chair and cross my arms over my chest. It's cold in here, their air-conditioning up too high. "I'm dying, like I said. So Jake doesn't need his divorce now. Isn't that convenient?"

"Are you suggesting that he has something to do with that?" Officer Frances says gently, with sympathy, but also with pity.

My God. I'm so sick of everyone thinking that my reaction to Jake's behavior is over the top. Why am I the one being monitored, being questioned? He's the liar and the cheater and the person who snuck around. Yet I'm the one who's supposed to forgive him, to act nice, to be polite. I'm supposed to hide my sadness away so it doesn't make anyone feel too uncomfortable, or remind them that people do these types of things. If I don't, then I'm confirming something for them. That I must've done something to make the guy *who would never* act out of character.

"Forget it."

"Are you in trouble, ma'am? Is that what you're trying to tell me?"

"I don't know, am I?"

"If you're referring to your break-in tonight, then no. Mr. Gagnon doesn't want to press charges."

"How nice of him."

I should've guessed. Jake pressing charges would make him a bad guy. A good guy wouldn't lock up his dying wife no matter how crazy she's acting. But this story will circulate, me breaking in, him letting me go, and everyone will know that he was magnanimous, because that's part of the act too.

Jake can only rehabilitate himself in contrast to me.

"Why are you asking me questions, then? Why am I still here?"

"I wanted to make sure you weren't a danger, ma'am."

"Me?" I let out a bitter laugh. "Don't tell me that Jake's been saying he's worried I might hurt him?"

Officer Frances looks down at his doodles.

"Her? The . . . his girlfriend? Please. I'm not a violent person."

"I believe you did send her some rather, shall we say, nasty emails, though?"

My hands start to shake. So that's what she was telling them about. Fucking bitch. "That was right after I learned about his affair."

"You threatened Ms. Carpenter in these emails, I believe?"

"I was mad. I didn't mean it."

"Are you certain, ma'am?"

"That was almost two years ago. Wouldn't I have done something by now?"

Officer Frances raises his shoulders. "Your circumstances have changed, though, haven't they? Given your impending . . . demise, you might have thought it was safe to act."

I cannot believe what I'm hearing, but part of me has to admire the genius in it. Jake. Jake is not as smart as I used to think, but he's still smart. He knows how to turn a situation around so that you're the bad guy, not him.

"She's the one who had the knife," I say, grasping at the first thing that comes to mind.

"That's true."

"I haven't made any threats."

"Besides the emails, you mean."

I stare at him.

"Are you denying it, ma'am?"

"I came here because Jake wanted to talk to me. I thought he'd be home. That's it."

"Are you certain?"

"Yes, I already told you."

"You've told me several things tonight, Mrs. Gagnon."

It's Ms. Barnes, I want to say, but don't. I never took Jake's last name, but I bet Kimmie will. I hate her so much.

"Do I need a lawyer?"

Officer Frances starts, and I instantly regret saying these words. This is always the part in the show when the officer gets suspicious.

"It's your right, ma'am."

"Am I being charged with anything? You said no, right?"

"That's correct."

"Then I'd like to leave."

Officer Frances stands. "All right, ma'am. You're free to go."

I push myself up, relief shuddering through me. I just want to get out of here. I want to go home.

"A word of advice?" Officer Frances says as he opens the door. "I'd spend what time you have left on something other than Mr. Gagnon. No good can come of it."

I stare into his watery eyes and fight back the tears that are forming in mine.

"You're looking at the wrong person," I say quietly. "I'm the victim."

He shakes his head sadly and walks through the door. I consider saying something more, but what's the point?

If I've learned something these last two years, it's this—no one ever believes the woman scorned.

Chapter 21

GET OUT OF JAIL FREE CARD
Miranda

Miranda stood awkwardly in the hall of her father's new house and watched as her mom left the room where she'd been questioned.

When Jake had called Miranda to tell her where Jennifer was and that he needed her to come and pick her up, Miranda's first thought was that it was a joke. It had been a while, but Jake used to be the jokester in the family. One morning, for instance, he convinced the girls that they forgot they were supposed to be leaving for camp, and they'd rushed around their rooms packing up their things only to discover Jake bent over in laughter while Jennifer looked on with a disapproving frown. Jake's jokes were one of the reasons that he was *the best*. That's what they'd always said.

No one said that anymore, and this time it wasn't a joke, Miranda realized quickly, it was true. Jennifer had left the house when

Miranda and Grandma Bea thought she was asleep and broken into Jake and Kim's place to do God knows what.

Miranda didn't know what to think, she only knew that things were getting out of control.

"Mom," Miranda said to get her mother's attention. Jennifer looked disoriented, dressed in an old sweatshirt. She was wearing her grandmother's engagement ring on a simple chain around her neck. Her feet were bare, and she was carrying a pair of old tennis shoes. She looked lost, and in this grand home her father had built, diminished.

"Mom," Miranda said again.

The police officer touched Jennifer's shoulder briefly, and she turned around, searching for the source. She was surprised when she saw Miranda, then sad.

"Miranda. What are you doing here?"

"I'm here to get you."

Miranda made eye contact with the police officer as Jennifer walked toward her. Her hair was wild, and she had dark circles under her eyes. She looked around furtively. Looking for Jake and Kim, Miranda guessed. But they were in the kitchen. Miranda had asked them to stay there until Jennifer left. She'd had enough humiliations already tonight.

Guilt flooded through Miranda as the police officer turned away and walked toward the kitchen. How had she let it come to this? They needed to take better care of her. Miranda knew she slept soundly, but how had she missed her mother leaving the house like that? More importantly, why had she felt the need to?

"How did you know I was here?"

"Dad called me."

"Where is he?"

"In the kitchen with . . ."

Jennifer glanced over her shoulder, as if she felt someone creeping up behind her. Miranda couldn't blame her. She hated this house. It was too new, too modern, too cold.

"When did he call you?"

"Around eleven?"

Now it was after midnight. The call had been brief, his voice a reproach. She'd *let him down*, he'd said, and not for the first time. She hated when her father used that tone, treating her like she was still a child.

"Did you want to talk to him or something?"

"No. Can we go home?"

"Of course."

They walked toward the front door and Miranda opened it. The night felt sticky, especially after the overly air-conditioned experience of Jake's house.

"Um, Mom?"

"Yes?"

"Did you want to put your shoes on?"

Jennifer didn't say anything in the car, she just stared out the window and refused to answer any of Miranda's questions. Her behavior was freaking Miranda out, reviving long-buried memories of how Jennifer had acted sometimes after the girls had returned home from Grandma Bea's house once Jennifer's cancer had gone into remission. Miranda hadn't thought about that in forever, but now the memories were coming in thick.

Like how sometimes Miranda would find Jennifer sitting at their new kitchen table staring out into the backyard, so out of it that Miranda had to shake her arm to snap her back to reality. She'd guessed it was the pain meds Jennifer was on, but it felt like more than that to nine-year-old Miranda. Jennifer seemed hesitant around them, as if the six months they'd spent apart had made them strangers.

Miranda seemed to be the only one who noticed. Emily told her she was imagining things, and Aline had started her slow journey to anger every time she was around Jennifer. Miranda thought it was probably because Aline wanted to stay at Grandma Bea's house. Miranda, not so much. She didn't enjoy Grandma Bea's moods. Aline might think it fun to be woken in the middle of the night to go on an adventure, but Miranda knew it meant feeling sleepy in school the next day, if they made it there at all.

No, it was good when they were home—back with their mother and father. If they behaved, Mommy would go back to being like the Mommy they remembered. Hyper-focused on them. Fixing all their scrapes and bruises, real or imagined. Smiling and kissing away their pains. Eventually she did. Who knew now how much time it took? Childhood time is not the same as adult time. But gradually, the time at Grandma Bea's faded. Life replaced those memories. Growing up. The slights and disappointments of high school. Falling in love.

"You can talk to me if you need to," Miranda said as they approached the house.

"I know."

"Can I be honest?"

"Of course," Jennifer said as she stared out the window like someone who was seeing their neighborhood for the first time.

"Sometimes it feels like you've already left."

Jennifer's head snapped around, and Miranda instantly regretted her words. Why did she have to go poking at something? Why couldn't she leave well enough alone?

"I'm still here. Whether people want me or not."

"Mom . . ."

"Forget it, Miranda, okay? I just want to get home and go to sleep."

Miranda made the final turn onto their street. Their block was a ghost town, each house shrouded in the shadow. She cut off the engine and before she'd even retrieved the keys, her mother had her car door open. Jennifer ran up the front walk and slipped quickly into the house.

As Miranda listened to the crickets grinding in the night, Jake's words came back to her. This was *her fault*, he'd said, and she hated him for it, resented the blame being shifted. Miranda might not be the most insightful person, but it didn't take a genius to guess the reason Jennifer had been at Jake's.

And that was all of their faults.

"Mom, will you please let me help you to bed?" Miranda asked her mother in the living room. She was speaking low, but there wasn't any worry about waking Grandma Bea.

"You don't have to," Jennifer said, holding herself tight. She peeled off the sweatshirt she was wearing and slipped on the old cashmere sweater that she often wore around the house.

Miranda had a sense memory of how soft it was, and the little girl that still lived within her wanted to crawl into her mother's lap and rub her face against it.

"Mom, come on. Let me help you, okay? It's late. You need to rest."

Jennifer agreed reluctantly, and Miranda took her arm the way she'd watched Emily do in the last couple of weeks and led her up the stairs. Once in the bedroom, she helped her mother strip off her clothes, feeling shy and avoiding eye contact. When was the last time she'd seen her mother naked?

"Why don't you take a shower? Or a warm bath? That might help you sleep."

"Nothing helps me sleep."

Miranda wanted to say that her mother was being dramatic, but she bit her tongue. What did she know? Who was she to judge? She wasn't the one dying, not the one who'd had her life stolen away.

"Let's try a bath, okay?"

Jennifer agreed, and Miranda ran a bath, checking the temperature like she did when she looked after Ethan and Noah and they got all sweaty running around the park. When it was ready, she found an old bottle of bubble bath in the cupboard and poured it in. Partly for her mother's modesty, but also because it felt luxurious. That's what Jennifer always said when she offered to let them take a bubble bath when they were kids. *You're living in the lap of luxury, girls! Enjoy every second of it.* There was even a picture on the stairs of her and her sisters in a bath where the bubbles were so high it looked like they might get lost in them. It was one of her favorite pictures, though she didn't remember the incident other than through the reconstructed memory from the photograph.

Her mother stepped into the bath. She was thinner than Miranda remembered. Was this the cancer, or the product of the separation and she'd just never noticed?

"Temperature okay?" Miranda asked once Jennifer had slipped beneath the bubbles. Miranda handed her a small towel to put under her neck.

"Sure, it's fine."

"Are you okay?"

Jennifer sighed. "Obviously, no."

"Sorry, I know you're not okay long term, but I mean . . ."

"You want to know what happened tonight?"

"Yes."

Her mother sank down in the bubbles up to her shoulders. She'd pulled her hair into a topknot. She looked young and vulnerable. She looked like Emily.

"I wanted to ask him face-to-face."

"Ask him what?"

Jennifer turned away and looked at the tile.

"Mom."

"What?"

"Dad didn't do this to you."

Jennifer turned a weary face in her direction. "No? Well, some-one did. Someone isn't telling the truth."

Miranda wanted to contradict her, to tell her she was wrong. That just because something unfair was happening didn't mean there was an explanation. Life was like that sometimes. You didn't always know why it was happening. There wasn't always an answer.

But the problem was: in this case, that wasn't true.

Chapter 22

THE TWIN THING

Aline

"**W**ho was that?" Nick asked as Aline hung up the phone.

"My sister."

Aline lay back down on the pillow and pulled the sheet up over her. It was always cold in Nick's apartment, but it was closer to the bar than hers was, and by now, half her things had migrated there. They weren't living together officially, but Aline didn't care. She was never looking to put a label on things.

"Which one?" Nick asked. "The twin or the triplet?"

Nick, like many of the men who she'd been with over the course of her life, was fascinated with the "triplet thing," as they always seemed to call it. It didn't surprise her; it was a fact of life. Why else would all those TV shows and companies want to have them on their programming and in their advertisements? Why else would they have gotten all that stuff for free, the T-shirts and toys and pony rides? *Freak stuff for the freak show*, she used to say as a teenager, copying some adult she'd overheard. She never liked being the center of attention, and she was happy when they got too old and were no longer cute enough.

It didn't matter though, if there was fresh content. A lot of those commercials had followed her and her sisters all the way to high school and beyond. Even when she'd interviewed with Deandra, it had come up because Deandra had googled her, and despite all her accomplishments, the first hit was still the bit they'd done on the *Today* show.

"It was Miranda," she told Nick.

"Why was she calling so early?"

Aline looked at her phone. It was just after six. Miranda was never up this early normally, but today was already out of whack.

"Wait for it. My mother broke into my dad's house last night."

"Whoa. I was not expecting that sentence."

Nick rolled over and propped himself up on an elbow. It wasn't fair, how together he looked in the mornings. His sandy hair only tousled, his faced relaxed and tan. Aline, on the other hand, looked and felt like shit. She didn't need a mirror to tell her that her hair was all tangled and her face was puffy. She needed to dial back on the drinking. It wasn't doing anything good for her, and especially not when she was woken up two hours before her usual time by a frantic call from her sister.

Aline smoothed her hair back. "Me either."

"Why did she do that?"

"Remember what I was telling you the other night? About how she thinks he might have poisoned her?"

"How could I forget?"

"Well, I guess she went to confront him, or something."

"She was trying to get him to confess?" he asked.

"Only, he wasn't there."

"How did she get caught, then?"

"Kim was home."

"Kim?"

Aline scrunched up her face. "Kim. My dad's almost-my-age girl-friend?"

"Go, Jake!"

Aline punched Nick in the arm. Hard.

"Hey, I was joking."

"It's not funny. It's gross."

Nick rubbed his arm. "I thought you didn't care about stuff like that? Wasn't the guy you dated before me like forty or something?"

He'd been forty-three and her former chemistry professor. But that was different. He wasn't someone in her parents' life like Kim was now supposed to be in hers. And it had been right after the separation. Maybe she had been trying to conduct an experiment. What could anyone see in a guy twice her age? Turned out, not that much other than he had coin to pay for nice dinners. Was that what Kim was about? A gold digger, even though she came from money? Whatever it was, Aline didn't get it.

"Yeah, but I didn't, like, bring him to family dinners or anything."

"Did your dad do that?"

"Yep."

The first time had been for their birthday dinner last year. Emily had been so upset, she'd almost left. She was still struggling with the end of her postpartum depression. Miranda had just come back from her stupid attempt at the Peace Corps. Even without any of that drama, Jake had strongly miscalculated their reaction.

"Yeah, a couple of times."

"That sucks."

"Yep."

"Did he ask your permission first?"

Aline thought back to that meal. That's what Emily had said over and over after Kim had stormed out in tears. *You didn't even ask our permission.* Aline didn't quite understand her fixation on that. Jake hadn't asked her mother's permission to do a lot of things, including Kim, so it shouldn't have come as a surprise. Aline supposed Emily thought that was between them, her parents. That the girls were outside of the shit that had gone down in their marriage. But it wasn't true. They were right there in the thick of it.

"Nope," Aline said. "That's not his MO."

"So he lives with her?"

"He built this big house and a bunch of other stuff. I guess that's what she wanted."

"That's heavy."

"It was. It is. I think it's driven my mom crazy, to be honest."

"Didn't you say she was always crazy?"

Aline looked up at the ceiling. There was a water stain on it, yellowed, not fresh. She'd never asked Nick what had happened, if he even knew. Life was full of things like that. Stains left behind through some unforeseen event. Sometimes you knew where they came from, but often you didn't.

"Yes, but not like this. I mean, sure when he first left, she was devastated. Even I felt bad for her. We all did. But I thought it would . . . not go away exactly, but slow down? Stop being the sole focus of her existence. Maybe it's the glioblastoma?"

"It can cause personality changes, and delusions."

"Yeah. I just wish they weren't focused on my dad. She needs something else in her life, which sounds ridiculous, but . . . ugh, I don't know."

Nick tapped her on the elbow. "Am I going to be meeting any of these people anytime soon?"

Aline turned to look at him. "Why? Do you want to?"

"It's not like there's all the time in the world to meet your mom, right?"

"Yeah."

"Sorry, I didn't mean . . ."

"No, it's fine. You're right. There isn't."

"So?"

Aline thought about it. Did she want her family to meet Nick? What would it be saying about them if she refused? Why was everything so fucking complicated?

"Maybe you can come for Sunday dinner. It's this thing we do. Used to do. Doing again, I guess. For now."

"I don't want to intrude."

"I'm sure she'd like to meet you. She's always worrying that Miranda and I will end up alone together in some old folks' home."

"I could pretend we're engaged if that would make things better."

She reached over and kissed him. Her breath felt terrible, but he didn't seem to mind. "I don't think we need to go that far."

She pulled away and got out of bed.

"Where are you going?"

"Work."

"This early?"

"There's something I need to do."

The lab was a graveyard when Aline arrived at seven. She went to her bench and retrieved the samples she'd taken from the house and ran a second set of tests. She came up with the same result. There was nothing wrong with the water. Aline started taking notes on what Miranda had told her, what she'd eked out of her mother after she'd picked her up at Jake's house and brought her home, and what Aline herself had picked up over dinner, and she began crafting a timeline.

If she could get it all down in the right way, maybe she could convince her mother that what she thought had happened wasn't possible. Aline knew enough about Jennifer to know she didn't let go easily. Whatever had happened between them, however Aline felt about their life together and her mother's impending death, Jennifer deserved some peace.

Aline wanted to give her that, if nothing else.

She stared off into space, reaching for some other explanation that would satisfy her mother. Miranda had told her the other day that Emily had asked her to find a way to convince their mother that she was wrong. That stung, that Emily hadn't asked both of them. Aline loved Miranda more than she loved herself, but Aline was the competent one; she thought that was understood.

Emily probably thought Aline wouldn't help if she had asked. That was also probably why Jake had called Miranda to get their mother from Jake's house and not her. Not that Aline wanted to be called in the middle of the night to go get her mother, but still. It stung.

Aline knew things were bad between her and Jennifer. How could she not know that when everyone was always on her about it? She should try harder, she should fix it, she should make the first move, but she couldn't help also wondering why it was her move to make. It wasn't as if it was one thing that had caused the rift between them. It was more like they were oil and water and try as you might to emulsify them, they were going to separate eventually.

Anyway, what did it matter? If Aline was fine with it, why did it bother everyone else so much? Lots of people died with unresolved issues. The only issue that needed to be resolved right now was whether Jennifer could be reasoned with.

She could only think of one person to answer that question: Grandma Bea.

•   •   •

"This is so fun," Grandma Bea said the next day. "Me getting to see your lab. Us having lunch."

"I'm glad, Grandma."

Aline had taken her grandmother on a brief tour before lunch. She'd introduced her to Deandra, because why not get the points from that? Her grandmother was in town because her mother was dying. How could Deandra refuse when she said she needed to spend the afternoon with her? Aline should feel guilty at the subterfuge, but she didn't. Add it to the long list of things Aline didn't feel guilty about.

They had gone to a restaurant near White Rock Beach, one that wasn't too far away from Aline's apartment—a small one-bedroom that she'd lucked into when the previous tenant needed someone to transfer the lease to ASAP. It wasn't a place she'd normally be able to afford on her lab salary, but the owner was picky about who he rented to, and so as long as she checked in on the other apartments in the building once in a while, he cut her a deal on her rent. Which meant she got to live near the beach. As she inhaled the brine in the air, Aline couldn't understand why anyone lived anywhere else if they didn't have to. For her, that salty tang was perfection, even on a windy, cooler day like this one, even in the winter months when the ocean grew choppy and it was so dark in the morning you needed a headlamp to run along the sea path.

They were sitting on the balcony at the Crab Shack and had ordered a large serving of Dungeness crabs in a spicy sauce. Some kind of Cajun fusion thing she'd seen on a Netflix documentary that used to only be available in the Gulf of Mexico but had spread like it was contagious. It was delicious but messy, so they were wearing bibs like they used to do as children. A stack of wet wipes sat on the table between them.

"This is very good," Bea said after a few small bites. No matter how wonderful the food, Bea wasn't going to eat a full meal by Aline's standards.

"Right?"

"I thought you were a vegan, though?"

Aline felt guilty. "Yeah, well, I make an exception for this place. Don't tell Mom. Or Emily."

"Of course not, dear, if you don't want me to. Everyone's entitled to a little cheat now and then." Bea looked around. "I never come down here."

"I discovered it a couple of years ago because a friend lived nearby. I love it."

Bea smiled at her. "You're doing well for yourself."

"Not exactly where I wanted to be but I'm getting there."

"You'll get there." Bea took another bite of crab and wiped her mouth. "Maybe we could get your mother to come for a meal?"

"Maybe."

"I wish you two got along better."

"I know."

"Don't you think you should try?"

Aline sighed and put down her fork. "It's what I wanted to talk to you about, actually."

"Oh?"

"Yes. The other night at dinner . . . I noticed when Mom's first bout of cancer came up that you didn't seem to know what we were talking about. It got me thinking. I don't think I ever heard you talk about it. Not even when we were living with you. And why were we living with you in the first place? Why didn't we just stay with Dad?"

Bea wiped her mouth with a napkin even though she didn't need it. "He was busy working, and you three were a lot."

"Sure, I get that, but there's something else, isn't there? Like, I don't ever remember Mom going for follow-up appointments or cel-ebrating cancerversaries, which is totally the sort of thing she would do. I don't even know what kind of cancer she had."

Bea shifted in her seat uncomfortably. "You should leave this alone, Aline."

"I can't."

"Why?"

"The fact that you're telling me to stop asking is making me think there's something there, for one thing."

Bea took a sip of her water. "Why are you asking about this now?"

"Because everyone wants to know why I have a problem with Mom, even you. Why we've never been close. I've been thinking about why that is. The only thing I can come up with is that it always felt weird to me that she would leave us like that, just abandon us. I've had other friends whose mothers were sick, and they didn't dis-appear for six months."

Not to mention how strangely she acted when they were all re-united. Vacant, distant. Aline had told Miranda she didn't notice it, but she did. She just didn't want to talk to Miranda about it. Aline didn't know what was wrong with her mother back then, only that she could tell even then that her mother wasn't reliable anymore, if she ever had been.

"It was complicated, Aline, with three of you and—"

Aline put up her hand. "No. I don't believe that anymore, and Mom is acting crazy, you know that? And don't tell me it's because of her brain cancer. It's more than that."

"What do you mean?"

"This whole thing with Dad. Her thinking he's responsible for her cancer. Did you know that she broke into his house the other night?"

Bea looked down at her hands, bowing her head as if she was praying. "No, I didn't."

"I guess it happened when you were asleep. Anyway, she was going to confront him, apparently. But instead all she ended up doing was scaring Kim."

Bea's look was fierce. "Maybe that girl needs to be scared."

"Not the point, Grandma."

"All right."

Aline felt bad about this next part, but she went on anyway. "Okay, look, I know this is another thing we never talk about, but I know about your diagnosis. Mental illness obviously runs in the family. So I'm putting two and two together and I'm wondering if that's what's going on here? Is that what happened all those years ago? Was Mom in some institution somewhere?"

Bea's face was a mess of worry and confusion. Aline knew she should stop, that she was pushing too hard. But she had a right to know. She had a right to know if her DNA was something to be afraid of.

"Well, was she, Grandma?"

Bea made direct eye contact with her for the first time since Aline had started this conversation. Her eyes were pooled with tears, but there was truth there as well.

"Yes," she said. "Yes."

Chapter 23

HOW DO YOU FEEL ABOUT THAT?

Jennifer

When I recover from my humiliation of being caught in Jake's house, I decide to take one piece of advice from Officer Frances and one from Dr. Parent. I'm going to put my affairs in order and go to therapy.

I need Emily for the first, and so I prepare everything for her next visit, hoping we can skip past the break-in. Her sisters have surely told her about it, though I didn't ask Miranda, just thanked her for her help and the eggs she'd made for me without asking when I came down the stairs after hiding in my room for a day. Then she left for the tennis club, and I pulled out the papers I got from Dr. Parent—palliative options and the medical power of attorney—and texted Emily to come over.

"Mom?"

"In here," I call from the kitchen.

I listen to Emily tread lightly across the first floor. She enters the room with her keys dangling from her finger. Everyone has the code to the house, but you can also use a key to get through the side door into the garage in case there's a power failure. Emily has always preferred to enter that way, and her key ring—the gift I gave each of the girls on their eighteenth birthday—has a large silver *E* on it.

"How are you feeling today?" she asks, dipping quickly to give me a kiss on the cheek.

"Not too bad."

"You got some sleep?"

She definitely knows about the break-in.

"Yes, thank you."

My phone dings with a text. It's Suzie, sending me pictures from the boat she and her husband are on. Today she's in Greece. Tomorrow Italy. We've kept it light while she's been away. She checks in, asking if I'm okay. I downplay what's happening to me. I don't tell her any of the bad stuff. She sends me beautiful photos of the places I'll never make it to. It's the one part of my life that feels normal.

"What's all this?" Emily asks, eyeing the papers laid out before me.

"Don't worry, it's not more stuff about Dad."

"Good."

"I need you to sign some papers. And also to help me decide something."

Emily sits on the bench on the other side of the kitchen table and dumps her keys. She has enough to make her a prison warden. A set for me, a set for her, and a set presumably for Aline's apartment, and maybe also Jake's house. Emily is the type of person that everyone gives their keys to, which is why she's also the person I'm going to give the keys to my life to.

"What is it, Mom?"

"I am making you my medical power of attorney."

Emily shakes her head. "Oh, no. Not me."

"Yes."

"Can't it be the three of us? I don't want to have to make this decision myself."

"It will be simpler if it's just you. You three girls so rarely agree on anything. I know it's a lot to ask, but please, will you do it?"

Emily won't make eye contact with me. "What do you want me to do?"

"I don't want to suffer. And if I'm not me anymore, then I don't want to be kept alive."

"How am I supposed to determine that?"

"You'll know."

"And what if I don't?"

"I trust you."

Emily folds her hands in her lap as her cheeks flush. "What do I have to do?"

"Nothing. Someone came over from the bank this morning to witness my signature and notarize it." I push the paper across to her. Her copy; I made three. I filled out my wishes, checked a series of boxes. This is not the sort of thing you should fill out when you're already dying, though I don't suppose there's any good time to do so.

"Okay." She folds it up and puts it in her purse. "And what's the other thing? The decision."

I slide her the palliative options sheet.

"Jeez, Mom, a little warning."

"Sorry."

"No, it's fine. I shouldn't have said anything." She takes the document and starts to scan it. "I heard okay things about the Health Center from a friend of mine. Her grandmother was there I think."

"Whatever's more convenient for you."

"Do you want to visit some of these places?" Emily asks.

"Nope."

"I'll make some calls?"

"That would be good."

"What's this?" she says, pointing to the bottom.

I pull the paper back and see the note written there that I noticed in Dr. Parent's office waiting room. *Alternative end-of-life options*, and a phone number.

"I think that means euthanasia. It's legal now, right?"

Emily pulls the paper away from me. "Is that what you want?"

I raise my right shoulder. "It might be nice, leaving this world on my own terms."

"You can't be serious."

"What?"

Emily shakes her head. "You've been so upset . . . so convinced that someone tried to . . . well, you know, but now you want to do it to yourself?"

"It's not the same thing at all."

"Isn't it? How?"

Her words exhaust me, and I'm already so tired. "I don't want to argue about this."

Emily stands, folding the paper and putting it into her purse. "I've got to go. I'll call some of these places and let you know what I find out."

"Emily. Please, don't leave like this."

"I'm sorry, Mom. But I can't do this right now."

Emily maneuvers around the table, her heels clicking quickly across the floor.

"Em."

"Yeah?"

"You forgot your keys." I pick them up and turn, then on impulse lift them into the air and arc them toward her. "Catch."

My therapist's office has been in the same place since I started going to see him. So much of my life has been unspooled in this building, a white semi high-rise that is remarkable only for the ugliness of its design. It holds so many of my secrets. The reason I went there in the first place. All the things I let go when everything happened with Jake. All the moments in between, the highs and lows of life.

"I don't think I've ever been lower than this," I tell Paul.

"Are you sure about that?" he asks when I've filled him in on what's happening with me. He listened the way he always does, one leg crossed over the other, his eyes keen in his bearded face. He's one of those ageless men who could be thirty-five or sixty. In all the time I've known him, nothing about him seems to change.

It's funny because I used to feel like my life moved at a glacial place. Not in the everyday, but in the big events. Years went by and my life was exactly the same: I was the mother of triplets, married to the same man, lived in the same house, had the same routine and friends. But ever since Jake left, my life seems to be moving at warp speed. Ludicrous speed.

"Pretty sure," I say. "I broke into Jake's house to accuse him of trying to murder me, and instead of proving my point I got interrogated by the police and basically accused of trying to harm him or that terrible woman. Where is there to go from here?"

Paul uncrosses his legs. He always wears slacks, never jeans, with a rotating collection of plaid shirts, the only personal item the thick gold ring he wears on his ring finger. He knows everything about me, and I know almost nothing about him, which is the way it should be.

If I thought that little speech was going to get a rise out of him, I was wrong.

"I'm not sure that's the right way to look at it," Paul says in his even voice. "But I am curious about what led you to make those decisions that night."

"I was drunk. I took a pill. Maybe it's the cancer."

"It could be, but from what you tell me, you have had these suspicions from the beginning. Are you sure it's not more than that?"

I push back into the couch. It's leather and soft and there's a chenille throw I can wrap myself in and tissues on the table. It's a calming space, though the room is soaked in tears and has absorbed too much sadness for any one location.

"What do you mean?"

"Is this the first time you've thought that Jake was harming you?"

"Yes, of course."

"Are you sure? Your mind went there so quickly."

"Because of the test results."

Paul shakes his head. "But that's not what most people would assume if they saw those results. Most would think there was ground contamination or something in their home that caused it. You went right to poisoning."

"Without passing Go?"

He chuckles. "If you like."

"You think I have a habit of assuming the worst."

"Well, don't you?"

"But the worst is happening."

"Yes, it is. You have terminal cancer. And yet, you're trying to make it more than that."

My stomach churns. Dammit, Paul. "I'm not trying to . . ."

"Jennifer, you and I have known each other a long time."

"So you know me."

"Yes."

"And you think that this—what I think Jake is doing—is some sort of attention-seeking behavior."

"Well, is it?"

I shake my head so hard it hurts. "No, no it's not. If that's what I wanted I would have told the police before the other night. I would've gone to the media. I would've done something. Told my doctor. Something."

Paul considers what I'm saying. He's looking for patterns, I know. That's one of the things he does, what he brings to the table. Because he can see things that I can't. The bigger picture of my behavior and that of others that gets lost in the fog of my own life. But he's wrong here. This isn't something that ties to anything from before except that Jake has a motive to want me gone.

"What about the phone calls?" I say. "The ones I never received?"

"Maybe the doctor's office was mixed up."

"Twice? With a specific annotation that I was seeking a second opinion?"

He nods. "All right, that's unusual. But how is Jake supposed to have done that? What's your working theory?"

I pause. Part of the problem is it's constantly changing. I can't fix on one explanation because my thoughts can't stay still. "I never changed my password. To the voice mail that comes with the home line. I never changed it."

"You think Jake was accessing your voice mail?"

"I know he was." Another fact that had fallen out of my memory when I couldn't sleep.

"How do you know that?"

"Because after he left, sometimes messages would disappear. Messages for him."

Paul gives me a look.

"I know it sounds crazy, okay. I know it does. But he was kind of religious about checking that voice mail. His mother would still call the house when she couldn't get him at work because he took forever to tell her he moved out. And I think . . . I know this is going to sound paranoid, I know, but I think he was spying on me, trying to figure out something he could use against me to get me to give him the divorce."

"Why didn't you change your voice mail password, then?"

"I did. Eventually. When I realized what was happening."

"When?"

"About a year ago. A bit more. I'm not sure. After I found him in the house the last time. He came over again a few weeks after my grandchildren's birthday party, the one where he gave me the drink? Did I tell you about that? I can't remember.

"Anyway, he called before he came that time, didn't just show up like he had the time before. I'm not sure how much longer after, but it was after, I'm sure of it because he said something about how he was happy that we were on better footing now because we'd had a civil conversation at the birthday party. But he was wrong, things weren't any different and we had another massive argument. That's when I changed everything. I realized that he'd been in the house a bunch of times. I hadn't noticed, I was in such a haze, but things were moved around, my papers, and like I said, there were a couple of messages that got erased and I didn't erase them. And when I found him in the house, and he was so horrible to me . . . I put two and two together."

I pause for breath. I don't make any sense, even to myself. It all sounds made up, impossible, fractured.

Paul considers his words. "Assume I go along with that and he was monitoring your voice mail up until you changed the password. Why would he call your doctor?"

"Because he needed to cover his tracks. If I came in for additional testing, then he would have been discovered. I would've started asking questions. It would've been traced back to him. To the pipe he took from the house."

"How would he have done that?"

"Oh, Jake is handy, I'll give him that. It would have been easy for him to take the pipe out. And then he could leach the lead out and keep it soluble so it could be added to a drink or food. He probably didn't keep the pipe, though. He's not that stupid. But motive . . . opportunity. Those are two things that people look at, right? When a crime has been committed."

"But a woman called the doctor's office. A woman they thought was you."

"I thought about that. It was Kim. *Her.*"

Paul's face droops with sadness. "So you think that not only Jake but now he and Kim are in some conspiracy to kill you? And they chose lead poisoning to do it? Jennifer, are you listening to yourself? Can you hear how improbable that is?"

I shrink into myself, feeling sick. "I thought this was a safe space."

"It is, of course, and I'm sorry if I've made you feel otherwise. But I wouldn't be doing my job, either, if I simply indulged your thoughts when they don't make objective sense."

I put my hands on the couch to lift myself up. "I should go."

"No," Paul says. "You should stay. We should work through this."

"What's the point? I think I'm right. You think I'm crazy. But it doesn't matter, because either way I'm going to be dead soon."

"Please don't think that way, Jennifer."

"What, don't say the truth? Isn't that what you just told me I had to do?"

"I just meant . . . I'm sorry. This is not how I want to leave things."

"Me either, but I don't seem to have been given the choice."

Chapter 24

NAUTICAL KITSCH

Emily

Emily had a child hanging off each arm as she tried to get them from her car to the entrance of the summer camp Chris had signed them up for.

"Don't wanna go," Noah was saying over and over. "Don't wanna."

"Come on now, Noah. It's fun, remember?"

Noah wobbled his dark head of hair. "Noooo. No fun. NO FUN."

Emily dropped down to his level. "But you told me last night what an amazing time you were having. You said it was the best day ever."

Noah gave her a look of reproach. "Noooo. Ethan said. Not Noah."

Emily sighed. She was going to be late meeting her sisters for the family summit Miranda had called. Emily already felt anxious. Everything had turned into such a shit show, and so quickly, it was almost impossible to keep up. She couldn't believe her mother had broken into their father's house. Even the fact that Miranda of all people was calling family meetings—this was going too far.

"Ethan, is it okay if you go to camp without Noah today?"

Ethan cocked his head to the side. He liked to keep his hair longer, but Chris always insisted on getting it cut, a tug-of-war that Emily didn't involve herself in. Right now he was due for a cut, so his hair covered his eyes. "Alone? No Noah?"

"That's right. All by yourself. Like a big boy."

Ethan was always asking to do things by himself, but when it came down to it, the minute he was away from his brother, he'd start to wail.

"I don't think so."

"Wouldn't it be good, just for one day?"

"No. Twins stick together."

Oh God, where had he heard that?

"Mommy, I am going with you," Noah said. "Me and Ethan. We go with you."

Emily knew she should just shove them through the front door and let the counselors deal with it, but she didn't have the heart to. "Will you be good?"

"We are always good," Noah said with an angelic smile. "Unless we are being bad."

"What's it going to be today, kids?"

Ethan and Noah shared a look that reminded her of the thousands of times she'd seen Aline and Miranda do the same. "Good!" they said together.

"All right, then. Don't make Mommy regret this."

"Mommy will be regretting this for sure," Ethan said. "Guaranteed."

•   •   •

"So," Emily said once she'd joined her sisters at the restaurant near Aline's lab. It had a nautical theme and seemed to serve crab in everything, including the eggs. None of it appealed to Emily, but she ordered a muffin and a fruit plate to occupy the boys, something that came sans crab, thankfully. "What's going on?"

"You mean besides our mother breaking into our father's house?" Aline asked. She was wearing a white poplin shirt and work leggings that looked like dress pants. Her hair was pulled back in a low knot at the base of her neck, a small variation on the ballet bun she usually wore. She looked professional and put together, and Emily thought she should have taken more care with her own appearance. She was wearing a loose cotton dress that hid the belly fat she hadn't lost after the twins were born. She often felt as if her body had never returned to normal after that, and she certainly didn't have the energy or the time to bring it back to the taut thing it had been before she'd birthed two humans.

"Yes."

"Well . . ."

Emily held up her hand. "No bad words in front of the kids."

"Or you'll get a spanking!" Ethan said, clear as a bell.

Emily looked around. They were alone except for the waitstaff. "OMG, I don't actually . . ."

Aline ruffled Ethan's head. "A little spanking never hurt anyone."

"You don't mean that?" Miranda said. She was—as usual these days, it seemed—dressed for tennis. How many different tennis outfits did she have, anyway? "Come on."

"What? So Dad spanked us a few times when we were little. We survived."

"Spanking not okay," Noah said. "Mommy?"

"Can everyone please stop saying that word?" Emily said.

"Don't worry, Memily," Aline said. "Everyone knows you're a great mom."

Emily wasn't entirely sure why, but this whole conversation had her feeling panicked. She'd never hit the kids, not ever, but she did sometimes threaten to when she was at her wit's end. She and Chris both did, but she was the only one her kids seemed to take seriously. As if they knew that Chris didn't have the heart to do it, but she might.

She'd almost done it once, when the twins were one and a half and the thing they loved to do most in the world was bat things off tables. Their sippy cups. Plates full of food. Anything within reach. Each time Noah did it, he'd look at Emily and laugh, giving the impression that he knew exactly how much it frustrated her. And maybe he did. Kids were smart. They knew how to push your buttons, and sometimes they did it on purpose. She'd warned Noah, warned him and warned him and when he'd knocked over his bowl of cheerios and sent milk and cereal soaring all over the kitchen, Emily's hand had gone back reflexively. She'd stopped it an inch from Noah's suddenly terrified little face. Her hand was shaking, and she'd called Chris crying. He'd come home and she'd hidden in the bedroom for the rest of the day.

She'd almost hit her child. No, *slapped*. That wasn't good. That wasn't safe.

"Mommy, I'm bored," Ethan said.

Emily reached into her bag and pulled out two identical coloring books and some crayons. She'd forgotten the iPad at home, another sign that things were crumbling. "Kids, can you go sit at that table and color like good children?"

"Yes, Mommy. We can," Noah said, answering for both of them. He plopped down off his seat and carried the coloring book against his chest. "Come on, Efan."

Ethan gave a small shrug and followed his brother.

"They're adorable," Miranda said.

"You can take them anytime," Emily said. "Anyway, we'd better focus. That will only keep them occupied for twenty minutes if we're lucky. How is Mom? I haven't seen her since we talked about those horrible end-of-life papers two days ago."

"She went to therapy yesterday. Other than that, she's hiding in her room."

"That's not good. I'll go see her later."

"I think we should all go see her," Aline said. "And get some answers."

"About what?" Emily asked.

"What Grandma Bea told me."

"Which was?"

"Remember when we went to live with them when we were eight?"

Emily picked at a piece of fruit. "Of course. When Mom had cancer the first time."

Aline raised her eyebrows. "Yeah, well, here's the thing. She didn't. She didn't have cancer."

"What?" Miranda said. "Grandma Bea told you that?"

"Yep."

"What the fork?"

Aline rapped her knife against the table. "I've told you a million times that I hate that fucking expression."

"Keep your voice down," Emily said. "And watch your language in front of the kids."

"Yes, Mom."

Fuck off, Emily mouthed to Aline.

"Why did we go live with Grandma, then?" Miranda said. "Were she and Dad having problems?"

"No, she was having problems." Aline laid her arms out flat on the table. "She flew over the cuckoo's nest."

Miranda paled. "She was in an institution? For real?"

"Yes, for real."

"For what?" Emily asked.

"Depression, Grandma Bea thought."

"Manic depression?"

"No, I don't think so."

Emily considered the muffin in front of her. The kids had shredded it and picked at the crumbs, trying to get away from the raisins, which they hated. "It must have been bad if she needed residential care."

"I guess."

"Why didn't we just stay with Dad?" Miranda asked.

"He was probably fucking someone else."

"Aline!"

"I mean forking, whatever."

"I don't think so. He told me that Kim was the first time he'd ever been unfaithful."

"Gross," Emily said. "Why were you even talking about that?"

Aline made a retching sound. "Double gross. And you believed him?"

"He seemed sincere."

Even Emily had trouble believing how naïve Miranda was sometimes. "When did he tell you this?"

Miranda tugged on the end of her ponytail, her face flushed. In her tennis whites, she looked seventeen, ready to take on the nearest challenger. "I see Dad sometimes."

"You see Dad sometimes?" Aline repeated, incredulous.

"Yeah, sometimes. For lunch or whatever."

"For lunch. You see Dad for lunch."

Miranda glared at Aline. "What the hell, Aline? Why do you keep repeating what I'm saying?"

"Because I'm trying to process it."

"Why is it so hard to process? He's our father. Sometimes we have lunch. Why is that weird?"

"You know why."

"Because of what he did to Mom? You don't even like her, why do you care?"

Aline opened her mouth to object, but stopped herself.

"Mommy, my crayon is broken," Ethan called from the other table.

"Can you use another one?"

"Yes, I can do that."

"Thanks, baby."

Ethan stuck out his chin. "I am not a baby."

"Okay, little man. Keep coloring please." Emily turned back to the table. "Did Grandma say why we went to her?"

Aline shrugged. "Dad had to work. Three of us is a lot, so they thought it was easier that way."

"But why lie, though? Why tell us it was cancer?"

Emily thought back to when they'd been told that their mother was sick and they had to go live with their grandparents. They'd been devastated by the news. Someone in their class had a mother who'd died of breast cancer the year before. Cancer meant death to them.

"Now that you say that, Miranda," Emily said, "I don't remember them ever specifically saying that word. Maybe we just filled it in because of what happened to Carrie. Remember her mom?"

Aline and Miranda nodded somberly.

"I agree," Miranda said. "When I think about it, I'm not sure they actually said it was cancer. They just said that she was sick, and she'd get better, but she needed time to rest."

"Bull—" Aline said. "They totally said it was cancer."

"We could ask Dad," Miranda said.

Emily recoiled at the thought. "I wouldn't believe a word Dad said."

"He's not a monster."

Aline scoffed. "He's treated Mom so badly, she thinks he tried to kill her. So I'm pretty sure that's the definition of a monster."

"I like monsters!" Noah said. "I'm going to draw one!"

Emily wondered what the long-term impact of overhearing part of this conversation was going to be on her children. She should have left them at camp. Chris was going to be pissed.

"Aline's right," Emily said. "You shouldn't hang out with him."

Miranda squirmed in her seat. "Maybe I'm not in a position to say no."

Aline wheeled on her sister. "What's that supposed to mean?"

Emily felt exhausted by the bickering. They were also nowhere closer to a plan, which was what this meeting was supposed to be about. "Guys, can you please stop. Since when did you start fighting, anyway? We need to figure out what to do."

"About what?"

"About Mom. We need to . . . address this with her, I guess. Try to help her see that she shouldn't be spending her time on this. It's not good for her. It's not good for any of us."

"How are we going to do that, though? Didn't you already try?"

"Not hard enough, obviously. Maybe . . ." Emily stopped. Every fiber of her body was telling her this was a bad idea, but it was the only way. "Maybe we should do the opposite of what we've been doing."

"I don't follow," Aline said.

"Instead of trying to convince her she's wrong, maybe we should help her figure out if she's right."

"You want to help her pin this on Dad?" Miranda said. "I'm not going to be a party to that."

"No, I think we should help her run down every 'lead' she has so we can show her that there's nothing there. But in a positive way. Telling her no is just entrenching her in her beliefs."

"So lie to her, then?"

"We don't have to lie, we can just . . . not tell."

"Like with the cancer?" Aline said.

"Exactly. She'll fill in the blanks and hopefully we can resolve all of this before it's too late."

"Too late for what?"

Emily looked at her children, so young and innocent and happy. You only got a few years to be that way, she knew. You had to treasure them when they happened.

"Too late for her."

Chapter 25

WHITEBOARD

Jennifer

"**Y**ou sure you're up to this, Mom?" Emily asks me as I walk into the living room on Sunday evening after a quick call with Suzie. It's very early morning for her but she can't sleep. She tells me she's having an amazing time on her trip but feels like she committed a crime by going. I try to reassure her as best I can and end the call before we both get emotional. *Send more pictures*, I say. *I love you*, she answers.

We've had an abbreviated Sunday night dinner, and now we've moved on to the reason we're actually here. The trial of Jennifer Barnes.

"Yes, I think so."

"You'll tell us if not, though, right?"

"Of course."

Actually, I've had a splitting headache for the last two days and almost no appetite, so I feel weak and disoriented. I've never felt this tired, not even when I was up all night with the girls when they were babies. But they wanted to speak to me, so I pushed myself to eat something and took enough medication to dull the pain, and here I am.

I look around the room. In front of the TV, there's now a large bristol board, and Aline's standing beside it holding an array of colored pens and wearing large-framed glasses that make her look like AOC.

Emily and Miranda are on the couch; I've taken Jake's chair, perhaps out of spite. My mother left yesterday for a few days to go visit a friend. She didn't give many details, and I didn't ask. If she's found a replacement for my father, I don't want to know.

"I brought this from the office," Aline says, tapping the board with one of the pens. "We use it sometimes to map out experiments."

"Am I an experiment?"

"Of course not, Mom," Miranda says. "And I for one am against this whole thing."

"You already made that clear, Miranda." Aline opened the cap. "You can leave if you want."

"I'm staying."

I adjust my position in Jake's chair, trying to get comfortable. I had it steam cleaned along with the rest of the furniture to get his smell out of it, but it had only been partially successful. It was the most comfortable chair in the room, though, which should've been a clue to his personality right there.

"So what's the plan?" I ask.

Aline writes something and steps back. She's written *timeline* in dark blue letters across the top. "I thought we could put everything you know up here and we could see what's missing. See if it all fits together."

"To prove me wrong?"

"Just to try to figure it out, one way or the other."

I feel shy and suspicious, but I asked my girls to believe me and here they are, willing to listen, so what do I have to lose? Maybe they'll be more receptive than Paul.

"What's the first thing you think should go on here? What did you notice first?"

I think back. "After your father moved out, he kept coming back to the house. Some of the visits I knew about because I caught him a couple times, but other times I'd come home and things would be out of place. Like something would be missing from the fridge, or one of the stools wouldn't be where I left it. Stuff like that."

Emily curls her feet under her. She looks tired, and there are dark circles under her blue eyes. Even as a baby, she's always been the one to show it when she's had a fractious night. "You think Dad was coming over here and making himself a sandwich?"

"More likely he was here getting stuff he'd left behind and helped himself to something while he was at it. You know your father. He always treats everything as if it's his."

"Well, it kind of is his, isn't it?" Miranda asks. "What? It's true, right?"

"Actually, the house is in my name. Grandma and Grandpa bought it for me after I was sick."

Emily coughs. "About that—we wanted to ask. What did you have exactly?"

Her voice is too casual, and I realize that the usual answer won't cut it. If I want them to believe me, I have to come clean. Clean enough, anyway, depending on what they know.

"I didn't 'have' anything. I was . . . I was in a mental facility."

"For what?" Emily doesn't sound surprised.

"Depression, anxiety, a few other things." I shudder, thinking back to my time there. It wasn't like in the movies, not the place I'd gone, anyway, which my parents had paid for and which also contained B-list celebrities drying out. But it was awful just the same. Endless therapy, suicide watch when I'd first arrived, group. Eventually, I'd gotten better. I was better. The girls are proof of that. "Was it Grandma who told you?"

"Yes," Aline says.

I feel a wave of relief.

"Why didn't you tell us?" Miranda asks, her voice etched in hurt.

"When I left, when I had to leave, there wasn't much time to do anything other than tell you goodbye. I was in a bad place. Your father and I agreed to tell you that I was sick and needed rest and that we'd answer your questions when you had them."

"But you let us think you had cancer," Emily said.

"I didn't know you thought that. Not until I got out. You know, girls, your grandmother is not well. But she's never wanted to deal with it. She thinks medication and therapy are for the weak. So I hate to say this, and I've never asked her, but I think she probably told you I had cancer because that was something she could understand."

"We thought you were dying," Aline said. "Not cool."

My heart clenches. "I know, honey, and I'm so sorry. But when I got out, and I could show you I was okay, well, I guess it seemed easier to let you continue believing that than to explain what was going on, which would have scared you all over again."

"But your hair was short," Miranda says. "When you came home. I just remembered that. I thought it was because of the chemo."

"I cut my hair in . . . well, a bad moment."

I look around at my girls. Each of them seems lost in thought, re-evaluating their childhoods, replacing their memories, swapping out their view of me. Have I told them enough to regain their trust? Only time will tell. Only, I don't have any.

"Could we speak more about this another time? I'm very tired and I'd like to discuss your dad."

"Are you sure you want to continue?" Aline asks.

"I'm sure."

"So Dad came to the house after he moved out." Aline writes: *multiple visits to house*, then turns back to me. "When did that stop?"

"The last times I remember are around the boys' second birthday in May of last year. Right before you moved in, Miranda."

"I moved in at the beginning of June."

"Right, and the boys' birthday is May 1."

"But we celebrated on May 3," Emily says, checking her phone. "On the weekend."

Aline writes some dates on the board.

March–April: visits to the house

May 3—twins' bday party

Early June—Miranda moves in

"Are you sure that's right?" Emily asks. "I thought it was earlier. Because you were back for the boys' birthday."

"I stayed with a friend for a couple months before I moved in."

Emily rolls her eyes. I guess that Miranda means some boy. Maybe that boy Devon from the club who'd called for Miranda a week or so ago but had sounded vague when I'd said she was out. I'd told her about the call, and she'd looked embarrassed. So probably not him, then. Oh well. I never could keep up with Miranda's love life.

"But you were around," Emily presses.

"Yeah, I guess. But so was Andrew."

"Andrew?" I say to Miranda. "You don't think he had anything to do with this?"

"Well, why not? He paints or whatever, doesn't he? Why didn't you test his supplies?"

My brain skips, wondering for a moment if I've missed something so obvious. But then logic returns. "This happened last spring, right when we started dating. You think Andrew tried to poison me after a couple of dates? Am I really that bad?"

Miranda blushes. "No, of course not. Sorry, Mom."

Aline makes a noise of annoyance. "When did you get sick? The first time you remember?"

"Well, I wasn't feeling well off and on all spring of last year, I don't think, but I got super sick the day after the boys' party."

May 4—sick

"How long were you sick for?"

"A week, at least."

May 4–11—sick

"And then you went to your doctor, right? When?"

"May 23."

"And when did they call you?"

I close my eyes and think of the paper the doctor handed me. "June third the first time. Then again on June seventh."

Aline writes it all down. "So you think that Dad gave you something at the birthday party?"

"He had that flask there, and I . . . I drank quite a bit of it. Or . . . I guess he could've been contaminating the food in the house? Or the water?"

"Don't you use the water from the fridge dispenser?" Emily asks.

"Yes."

"So not that, then."

Could Jake take apart the fridge and rejig the system so that it was serving me contaminated water? Technically, probably. But that could be discovered. He wouldn't do that. He'd do something that could be explained away, that would disappear.

"No, I don't think so."

"But, Mom," Miranda asks. "Why? I mean, I know he's been mean to you, okay? I get it. He's been a total asshole. But he told you about the affair. He came clean about that. And he has his own money, right? He wasn't expecting to inherit?"

"No, I changed my will and the beneficiary of my insurance."

"When?" Emily asks.

"Probably three months after he left. I thought I told you? I'm leaving everything to you. All three of you."

"I knew," Emily says. "You told me."

"Oh, did I? I thought I told all of you. Well, your grandpa left me a lot of money and the insurance is a big policy. We got it years ago, your dad and me. Because of you girls. In case one of us died before you were adults."

"Thank you," Emily says. "But did Dad know that? Did you tell him?"

I look down at my hands. There's still a faint line where my wedding band used to be. I'd taken it off before I started dating and had been covering up the puckered skin with a ring I'd inherited from my grandmother. I took that off and started wearing it on a chain around my neck when the steroids made my hands swell.

"No, I didn't tell him, but . . ."

"What?" Aline says.

I look up. I'm not proud of this. "You know he wanted a divorce."

"Yes, we know."

"Well, I wouldn't give it to him."

"You've never really told us why."

I feel a surge of anger. "Because why should he get to win? Why does he get to behave however he wants without consequences?"

"He doesn't need your consent to a divorce, though," Emily says. "Right?"

"No, but he doesn't want it in the courts. All those judges he appears in front of, they hate him. He's represented too many of their wives when they got divorced. And judges protect their own. So he's convinced that they'll get revenge on him by giving me whatever I ask for."

"And what did you ask for?"

"A lot of money. I'm not proud of it, but it was the only way to hurt him back."

"Okay," Aline says. "Assume that's his motive; why then? Why spring of last year?"

Miranda and Emily share a glance, then look quickly away from one another.

"What is it, girls?"

"Nothing."

"No, come on, there's something. Something about last spring?"

Miranda coughed. "I asked Dad for a lot of money."

"You did?"

"Um, yes. You know the whole thing in Africa didn't work out . . . I had a lot of credit card debt, and, um, well, I asked Dad to pay it off."

"All at once?"

"Yes. I didn't want to be saddled with debt for the rest of my life, and Dad had the money. So why not?"

"Did he pay it?"

"Yeah, he did."

"How much?"

Miranda expels a deep breath. "A hundred thousand dollars."

"Jesus Christ, Miranda!" Emily said. "Did you have a meth habit we don't know about?"

Miranda hung her head. "There was that restaurant I invested in. That was a lot of it. And then the flower shop."

I'm stunned. I knew about Miranda's various misadventures, of course, but I'd never added up the costs. I assumed that she had investors in the restaurant and the flower shop, not that she'd gone into personal debt. But I'd never asked, either, which I clearly should have done.

"So," I say, feeling queasy. "He was feeling a financial pinch."

"Yes. Maybe."

Aline scoffed. "He probably paid your credit cards off to diminish his assets. And here you were thinking he was being a good guy."

"Fork off, Aline."

"Girls! Stop it. It's fine, Miranda. I understand."

But I don't. It was a selfish thing to do, getting Jake to pay off her debts, then crying poverty and asking to move in with me.

"You sure, Mom? I feel super bad about it."

"When did all this happen?" Emily asks. "When did he pay them off?"

"When I got back from Africa. April of last year."

"That's when he started really pressuring me. For the divorce. He was calling and calling."

Aline turns back to the board and writes at the top. *Motive: financial.* "There's something that doesn't make sense though. Assume he wanted to kill you, okay? I mean, he had a motive and he's a lying jerk, so yeah, I believe he could do it. But what about the rest of it? Assuming he found a way to poison you, maybe at the party, what about the calls from the doctor? And when it didn't work, why didn't he try again?"

"I think he was accessing my voice mail. And the . . . Kim could have helped him with the doctor thing, to cover his tracks."

I'm pretty sure Miranda is rolling her eyes, but I'm avoiding making eye contact with her at the moment. I can't believe she took money from Jake. That she did it and didn't tell me. That she lied to me, lied, lied, lied.

"But what about him not trying again, though?" Aline asks. "Why would he give up?"

"He didn't have access anymore. I changed all my passwords and the door and alarm codes after the last fight we had. And also,

I'd started dating Andrew more seriously, and he was around a lot. Maybe he thought if he waited it out, I'd want the divorce."

"Mom," Emily says, looking like a lightbulb has just gone off in her mind. "Where the hell is Andrew, anyway?"

"I—"

"Did someone say my name?"

Chapter 26

A LIE IS A LIE

Jennifer

"Why, Mom?" Emily asks after Andrew has appeared in the middle of our investigation. "Why did you lie to us? Again?"

"I don't have to explain it to you," I whisper angrily in the kitchen while Andrew sits in the living room holding one of his beers.

"I think you kind of do, though," Aline says. "Since you want us to believe you and everything." Her arms are crossed, and her body language screams anger and distrust.

"I don't see what the two things have to do with one another."

"No?" Aline arches her eyebrow in a way that Miranda never does. It's one of the ways I can tell them apart, ever since they were little. Aline seemed to have been born with a sarcastic streak in her. One of her first sentences was "I don't think so."

"Did Andrew break up with you, Mom?" Emily asks. "Is that it?"

"It was mutual."

"Then why keep it from us?"

I don't want to tell them about the last conversation I had with Andrew before he left. How he'd said he wouldn't be in touch for several weeks and maybe we could use that time to think. I hadn't asked him what we needed to think about: I knew he meant whether we should be together.

It was a question that hung over us wherever we went. Everyone who met us came away with a quizzical expression on their face. Because we were so different. And because he was so different than Jake. Somehow my friends expected me to settle down with some Jake carbon copy. To go on with my life as if nothing had changed, even though Kim was as different from me as possible. But apparently, all I needed was a new-and-improved Jake who wouldn't cheat on me but was basically the same man in all other respects. Maybe he'd be an accountant instead of a lawyer. Or a doctor, though they worked bad hours too. A school principal, perhaps? All of these had been suggested to me and more. It was what the dating apps thought too, their algorithms pumping out Jake carbon copies.

Even actual men named Jake.

No thank you.

"I was embarrassed, okay?" I whisper to the girls. I die a little, admitting that. A preview of what's to come. There are so many in-dignities to this process. Will they never stop?

"Why?" Emily asks.

"Another failure. Another man who didn't want to be with me. You don't know what it's like."

"You're beautiful and smart and wealthy. You can date whoever you want."

I look at Emily and wonder if she truly believes what she's saying, or if this is simply the polite lie we all tell ourselves. That we choose the person we're with. That we're not stuck with them. That if we're unhappy we can move on to someone else and it will be different but not worse. Better even, maybe.

"I'm a forty-eight-year-old divorced grandmother, Emily. That is not what most men are looking for."

"Well, maybe leave out the grandmother part on your profile?"

"That's not funny, Aline," Miranda says. "But Mom, this is not okay."

As if I need to be scolded by my own children for something they'll hopefully never understand. "I'm not going to apologize. I'm not the one who did anything wrong here."

I give Miranda a hard look. She can go and sleep at Emily's or Aline's apartment tonight, the ungrateful girl. I regret the thought as it blooms in my mind, but I can't help it. She is ungrateful, and she chose Jake over me. And then she moved into my house without a word about it. I don't know who this Miranda is. She's certainly not the sweet girl who couldn't pick something to do with her life. There's something deeper going on there. Something more sinister.

Take tonight. Miranda's the reason Andrew is here. Andrew, who she never liked. Andrew, who she made perfectly clear I shouldn't be seeing. Andrew, who she texted when he never came back from the artists' retreat. And now, as if things aren't complicated enough, my daughters are convinced I'm a liar. Which I am, yes, but not for the reasons they think.

"What?" Miranda says, but she knows. "I didn't think it was right that he didn't come back. Not with what was happening to you."

"So you told him I was dying?"

"Not in so many words."

"What did you say?"

"I said you were going through a hard time and he should come by." *Before it's too late*, she must have implied.

"You had no right to do that."

"I know. I'm sorry."

"Are you going to talk to him?" Emily asks.

I lean against the counter. I am so tired of all of this. So tired in general. I want to disappear. To wave my hand and make this day evaporate. "I don't know."

"I can get rid of him if you want, Mom," Aline says, speaking surprisingly tenderly.

"No, it's fine. I can handle it."

I run my hand over my shirt, trying to press out the wrinkles. There isn't anything I can do about the pajama bottoms. He's seen me in them already, and truly, am I going to be vain in this moment?

I walk into the living room, leaving the girls behind. Andrew's standing in front of the bristol board, reading it with a puzzled look on his face. We should have hidden it away, but no one thought to do it.

"Hi, Andrew."

He turns. His salt-and-pepper hair is a bit longer than the last time I saw it. It needs a cut. His face is also tanned. He's been in California—that part I didn't make up.

"Hi."

"Did you want to sit?"

"Sure."

I glance over my shoulder to find Aline standing there. "You can go, Aline."

"Okay. We're in the kitchen."

"You can go home. I'll be fine."

"I'm going to stay."

I sigh and turn back to Andrew.

"What's all this?" he says, motioning to the board with his beer. "You guys playing some kind of game?"

I almost laugh. Because yes, it feels like that. *Who murdered*

Jennifer Barnes? Was that a game others wanted to play? Was there a solution? Where were the instructions? I could use them right about now.

"I guess you could say that."

"What's this about? Jake?"

"It's nothing. Ignore it, okay?"

"All right."

He sits and crosses his legs. He's wearing long cargo shorts that end past his knees and a T-shirt for an obscure band he must've had for twenty years. That's one of the reasons people didn't see us together. Andrew only bought a piece of clothing when it was to replace something that had become completely unusable. He made no spontaneous purchases. He liked to keep things light and simple. Which meant his entire wardrobe could fit into a large backpack.

"Why didn't you tell me?" Andrew asks. "That you're sick."

That I'm dying.

"We said no contact."

"Come on, Jenn. I didn't mean that if something serious was going on."

"I've barely told anyone."

"I don't know what to do with that." Andrew puts his beer down on the coffee table. "What is it? What do you have?"

I tell him about the glioblastoma. The prognosis. He listens, and when he works out that half of my time is over, he does something unexpected. He starts to cry.

"I'm sorry," he says, wiping at his eyes. "I'm so sorry."

"Me too."

He stands and walks to me. I don't want him to touch me because I'm barely holding it together, but I don't react in time to stop him. Andrew wouldn't have listened anyway. He's a hugger. *Touchy-feely*, Jake would call him, and me too for that matter. It has taken some getting used to, but his arms feel good around me, and so I let him hold me. I let his wet tears fall into my hair as he grieves for me.

Then I pull away and sit down. Back in Jake's chair, the one Andrew would never sit in, as if he sensed it was Jake's without me telling him.

"I'm sorry," Andrew says again. "I didn't mean to lose it like that."

"It's okay."

"Can I do anything for you? Do you want me to stay?"

"I don't want pity."

"No, Jenn, it's not that. You know I love you."

He'd said it early, taking me by surprise. The last time I'd been in love with someone, those words had seemed like a quest, something I needed a map to find. When Jake had finally said it, after we'd gotten pregnant, it hadn't felt entirely earned. But why did I feel that? What made me think I needed to work for someone's love instead of receiving it as something that was due?

"I love you too."

"So let me be here for you. Let me help you."

It would be so easy to give in to him, but nothing has changed since we had that conversation a month ago. I've had enough of being with someone because he thinks he should, rather than because he wants to.

"Thank you. But no."

Andrew is surprised. He expected me to give in, the way I had through most of our relationship. I'd been the easy girl, the one who went along with what he wanted most of the time. I felt grateful he wanted to be with me, so if he wanted to eat Indian rather than Chinese, what did I care? He looked at me with lust rather than disgust. That was enough.

"Come on, Jenn. You deserve it."

"I know I do, Andrew. And if you hadn't left, if we'd still been to-gether when I got the diagnosis, maybe then I would've said yes. Or maybe then you would have been out the door anyway."

"I wouldn't have done that."

"You don't know what you'd do. You don't know everything that's happening. Everything I'm going through."

"Is this about what's on that board? Did Jake do something?"

Andrew has never met Jake. But he's heard all about him, all the stories, and he has hated Jake for me. It was one of the things I loved about him.

"It doesn't matter."

"Are you sure?"

"I don't know, Andrew. My head hurts and I'm tired and I've got a lot of things to work out with my family. I'm glad you came, I am, and thank you, but it's time for you to go, okay?"

"Am I going to see you again?"

I shake my head, my throat suddenly tight. When he'd left, I didn't know if it was permanent. I thought he'd probably be back. We hadn't had a big fight. We were easy together. But there was this expectation, that if we continued the way we were going, that we needed to do something. Not get married, necessarily, but some-thing official. Andrew didn't do official. He did transitory.

"Maybe? Maybe not."

He looks like he's going to break again, his shoulders shaking, but he holds himself together.

"I want to," he says. "I'll call in a few days, okay?"

"Okay."

We say goodbye and then I go to the kitchen where the girls have all been listening to every word. I shoo them out. Miranda protests, but I give her a look and she goes to get some things for the night and leaves with Aline, so now I'm truly alone. I have the whole night to listen to the wind in the trees or the creaks of the house or to take enough pills to make me sleep through till morning.

And this, I finally decide, is what I want. I don't need to be looking for more evidence, to be putting together a case file that's never going to get prosecuted. I can spend my last few weeks on earth thinking about me, not Jake.

Me, not Jake.

Me, not Jake.

It's a mantra I should've adopted long ago. But there's still time.

Three Weeks to Live . . .

Chapter 27

GUESSING GAME

Emily

When she got home after midnight, Emily tried to creep into the bedroom quietly, but it was hard to climb into bed with both Ethan and Noah splayed out with their limbs like starfishes. It took Emily a moment to realize that Chris wasn't in the bed with them. She felt a moment of panic, then realized he must've gone to the twins' room to get a night of sleep without constant kicking and toddler snoring.

This sounded like a good idea to Emily, so she padded through the house after changing into her pajamas and found him in Noah's bed. Their room was painted a deep blue and had two twin beds surrounded by toys. There was a mobile night-light in the corner, turning slowly on its axis, casting stars and spaceships onto the wall. They went with the glow-in-the-dark cutouts on the ceiling—a galaxy that Chris had pasted on laboriously last summer. Their room was the only place that still smelled like them as babies, the delicious scent of their skin that she couldn't get enough of.

She climbed into Ethan's bed and tried to find a comfortable position. It felt weird to be in a bed alone. It wasn't something she'd done in years, other than if she was sick. She probably also hadn't had a full, good night's sleep in years, not even one. She was exhausted. Emotionally, physically, every part of her wanted to succumb and emerge twelve hours later. But instead, her brain whirred and whirred like her laptop when it was frozen on a task, and try as she might, there was nothing she could do about it. It was one of the reasons that instead of going directly home after their mother had thrown them out, she'd driven around Surrey until her eyes felt heavy.

"You back?" Chris said, speaking to the wall, his voice muffled by a comforter with a train set running across it.

"Yes. Shush. Go to sleep."

"What time is it?"

"Late."

The bed Chris was in creaked and shifted as he turned toward her. "How did the whole thing go with your mom?"

Emily turned on her side so she could see Chris better. He was only a dark shape, but a familiar and comforting one.

"About how you'd expect?"

"Oh?"

"I mean, we went through everything, and it doesn't add up."

"Does Jennifer see that?"

"We didn't get a chance to ask her."

"Why not?"

"Andrew came home."

She could see Chris smile as her eyes adjusted to the dim light. "*Dun, dun, dun.* Where has he been?"

"They broke up."

Chris blew out a long breath. "Like, because of the cancer?"

"No. Before."

"And she didn't tell you?"

"Nope."

"Huh. Why not?"

"I guess she was embarrassed."

"That makes sense."

Emily drew the sheet over her shoulders. She could feel the impression of Ethan's body in the bed beneath her. She wanted to hold her babies close and never let go. "Do you think my mom is trustworthy?"

"Why do you ask that?"

"Well, between lying about Andrew and the whole thing with her not having cancer . . ."

"What did she say about that?"

"She was depressed. I guess very depressed. She checked into a mental health facility."

"Yikes."

"Yes."

"It's good that she got the help, though."

"Yes."

Chris moved again, the bed whining under his weight. These beds weren't meant for adults. "Are you . . . are you feeling like this is bringing things up for you?"

"You mean my depression?"

And there it was, like a third person in the room. Depression. Something she'd never thought she'd suffer from because she was an optimistic person, driven, someone who usually looked ahead, not back. But that wasn't how it worked, she'd learned. Postpartum depression had hit her like a truck, as if she'd stepped into oncoming traffic. Or no, that was wrong. It had started slowly, like a missed night's sleep. If it only happened once, you could shake it off and power through. But it kept on coming, a faucet's slow drip, and before she knew it, she was drowning. Chris had reached in and saved her before it was too late. She'd gotten help, she'd gotten meds, she'd come out of it with more knowledge of herself, her life, and a new purpose.

She and Chris hadn't talked about it in a while. She knew he didn't want her to feel as if he was watching her, waiting for signs. She didn't want that either. She'd made that clear. She'd promised to let him know what she was feeling, if she was feeling it, that dark cloud descending, and they left it at that. But he did watch her sometimes, she knew. Checked that she was taking her meds, which had been dialed back to a small dose. Put her vitamin D on the counter in the mornings where she couldn't help but see it.

"Are you depressed?" Chris asked.

"No."

"It would be a normal reaction to what's going on with your mother."

"I know."

"What, then? And don't tell me nothing. Something's been going on with you."

"I'm . . . I'm angry."

Emily did feel angry. Sometimes it caught her unawares, how strong it was. Other times it was like a slow, simmering boil, just beneath the surface, ready to explode at any moment.

"About your mom?" Chris asked. "The lying?"

"That's part of it."

"That's understandable."

Emily didn't know if it was. In the hours between midnight and dawn, she could never be sure of her thoughts, her intentions, who she was or what she wanted.

"Do you ever think that you live your whole life thinking one thing and then something else ends up being true?"

Chris coughed. "Like with your dad?"

"That's a good example."

"I'd never do anything like that."

"So you say."

"Hey, come on. I mean it."

"I know, Chris. And maybe my dad meant it too. I'm just saying . . . I don't expect people to be true to their word anymore. If I ever did."

"Easier not to be disappointed, I guess."

"Yes."

"We should go to sleep."

"Okay."

"That means you too, Emily."

"Yessir."

She heard Chris chuckle and turn onto his back. In a minute, his breathing deepened and then he was out. She'd always resented that about him, the easy way he lost touch with this world and went into another. She'd never been like that, not even when she was a child, not even when she was exhausted to her core with the boys. Did that say something about her? Was it the guilt-free who slept easily?

She imagined the board in her mother's house, the timeline they'd written on it, the members of her family moving around it like chess pieces. The pawns with their little steps. The knight with its L-shaped movements. The pieces that were free to move wherever they wanted, wreaking havoc.

What her mother thought had happened was wrong. That much was clear.

But all the facts weren't out yet. Emily was forgetting something, she was sure.

Was it malignant or benign?

Only time would tell.

Chapter 28

THE ENEMY OF THE ENEMY

Aline

Aline felt uncharacteristically nervous as she waited for her father to show up to the meeting she'd asked for.

She'd wanted to do it in a restaurant; he'd insisted on his law office. She was sitting in a glass-walled conference room, staring at the view of South Surrey. It was cold in the room, *office cold*, as she always thought of it, and she wished she'd brought a sweater. Her eyes traveled to the expensive art that was abstract and ugly, in her view, and the fancy-looking phone that was sitting on the credenza.

It had been a while since she and Jake had had a one-on-one meeting. Aline remembered their last one with complete clarity, though. It was a week after he'd told their mother about the affair, and he'd asked to meet with her to explain his side of the story. She didn't get how there could be two sides to that story. Maybe her mother wasn't someone he wanted to live with anymore, but that didn't give him license to cheat on her and treat her like garbage. But Aline had shown up and listened to his justifications, and as he wound on and on, it became clearer and clearer that she probably wasn't going to ever have the same relationship with him.

Until then, she'd always felt as if she was on Jake's team in their family. Her and Miranda and Jake, that's how it had been ever since she could remember. But you couldn't be on the team of someone who didn't have your back. She'd thought that then, and she knew it with certainty now.

Take today. She'd arrived on time at eleven, but Jake was late, even though the meeting was in his own office. She knew he did that sometimes, made clients wait to show them how important and in demand he was, but she wasn't a client, she was his daughter. She wished he'd hurry up. She felt like crap. She'd woken up early, having sweat through the sheets at Nick's, where she'd been staying since the disaster that had been Sunday night dinner at her mother's. Miranda was staying at Aline's apartment, no longer welcome at Jennifer's.

Aline didn't blame Jennifer for that. There they all were, calling her a liar, or crazy, or worse, and it turned out that Miranda had been staying in the house under false pretenses all along.

What had made Miranda do that? Aline had asked and asked her at the bar after they'd left their mother's, and Miranda didn't answer. She just hung her head in shame and said it *was complicated*, and she *didn't want to talk about it*, and finally, *leave it alone, Aline*. She'd stormed out then, Nick watching the whole thing play out like it was a bingeable show on Netflix. Aline couldn't blame him. Her life had turned dramatic and episodic. She wished she could watch it like a TV show too.

She hadn't spoken to Miranda since. Instead, after a few days of avoiding it, she'd texted Jake and asked him to meet her. He'd proposed a time at his office on Thursday, and so here she was.

"There's my girl," Jake said, striding into the conference room as if this were a normal corporate meeting. He was wearing a dark suit, his French-cuffed shirt starched and perfect. He leaned down and kissed her on the cheek before she could stop him. As his lips grazed her face, and she breathed in his scent, the spice of his deodorant, the mint of his toothpaste, she felt her heart constrict and tears spring to her eyes. She looked out the window quickly so he wouldn't see. Someone was running along the road, her face red with the exertion. That's what she should be doing with her mornings instead of recovering from alcohol.

Running against the morning wind.

"Hi, Dad."

Jake sat down across from her and signaled the receptionist in a way Aline felt was arrogant. Like he was in a hurry and didn't have time to wait for her to come over on her own time.

"You look well," Jake said, glancing at her.

That was the advantage of being twenty-five. It was easier to hide how you felt inside.

"Thanks."

There was a pause where Aline realized he was expecting her to say that he looked good too. Only, she couldn't get the words out. His hair was obviously dyed, and his teeth were too white. He looked like a caricature of her dad. What had happened to him?

"How are you?" she said instead.

"Good, good. Ah, here she is," Jake said as the receptionist walked into the conference room. She looked twenty-one and unsure of herself, despite the sky-high heels and the tight column dress.

"Can I bring you anything?" she asked.

"Water for me," Aline said. "Thank you."

"I'd like an Americano," Jake said.

God, her dad was a total jerk. "He means coffee."

"Black, please," Jake said.

The receptionist left.

"No more cream in your coffee?" Aline asked.

Jake flashed his white teeth. "Got to watch the waist." He patted his flat stomach. He used to have a bit of a paunch there. Aline liked it. She used to poke it teasingly sometimes, making Jake chuckle.

"Sure."

"I'm so glad you called me, Aline." He reached across the table and brushed her hands with his. His nails were manicured.

Aline hated that she was cataloging everything that was different about him. She also hated that there were things that existed to log. Who was this pod people version of her father?

"How are you dealing with all of this?"

"All of what? You mean Mom?"

"Yes, of course."

"Or did you mean what Mom thinks you did?"

Jake picked up a pen and started fiddling with it. "Not sure what you're referring to."

"Really? Miranda didn't tell you?"

The receptionist returned and gave them their drinks. Aline took a sip of the water, which was too cold for this frigid office.

"What is Miranda supposed to have told me?" Jake asked once the receptionist left.

"It doesn't matter."

"Is this about the break-in?"

"Partly."

"Your mother is very troubled."

Aline felt a flash of anger. "She was fine before you left."

"I'm sorry, but that's not true. You don't know everything . . ."

"She told us about being institutionalized."

Jake tried to keep his expression neutral and failed. "She did?"

"Yes. We know everything now."

"I highly doubt that."

Aline put up her hand to stop him. "Dad, I didn't come here to hear you trash-talk Mom."

"What, then?"

"Why did you pay off Miranda's credit cards?"

Jake picked up his coffee mug and leaned back. "She told you about that?"

Aline pushed the question away, her anger bubbling. "How could you? How could you do that when I asked you to loan me money last year and you said no?"

"So that's what this is about?"

"Yes. I want to know. Why did you pick her over me?"

Jake's eyes narrowed and Aline could feel the heat of his anger across the table. They were cut from the same cloth, Jake and her. Quick to anger, long on resentment.

"That's a simplistic way to look at it, dear."

"I don't see how that's true. When I left my last lab, I came to you and I asked you to help me out. To loan me enough money so I could take the time I needed to apply for a university position. I laid it all out for you and you said no, even though it was way less money than Miranda asked for."

"I did."

"And then, like what? Right afterward, you told Miranda yes. You paid for her to come home from that stupid African disaster and you cleared away all her problems."

"What's your point, Aline?"

"It's not fair. I'm the one who's worked hard all my life to get where I am. I'm the one who hasn't started and stopped and changed course. And yet, you're financing her."

"Life isn't fair."

"Oh, fuck off, Dad. I know that."

Jake turned red. "Don't talk to me like that."

"I can talk to you how I want." Aline slammed her palm down on the table. "This was stupid. I was stupid for even coming here."

"I'm sorry I've made you angry."

"But you're not sorry at all. You're not sorry for any of it. Maybe Mom is right."

"Right about what?"

"About you."

Jake's lip curled. "Been filling you with her poison again, has she?"

Aline stood. "No, Dad. That's what you did."

Jake reached out and tried to grab her as she left the room, but she swerved in time and avoided his grip.

"Come back here, Aline."

But she didn't. Instead, she headed for the exit without looking back.

Aline's blood was still boiling from her interaction with Jake when she returned to the lab. Ever since she was young, fairness was something that was important to her. And the thought that she never would have ended up in the situation she was in now if Jake had given her what she'd asked for was driving her mad.

She used her keycard to get in. It was lunchtime, the benches half-full. Aline went to the kitchen to make herself some toast with a thick coating of butter. She needed to fill her stomach with empty calories to overcome her lingering hangover. She spotted a plate of donuts sitting on the counter. There was a note next to them. They were apparently gluten- and nut-free, and one of her lab mates' *first experiments in donut-making!*

God, people were such suck-ups.

Aline picked one up and shoved it into her mouth. It wasn't as good as a real donut, but it was sweet and full of carbohydrates. It would do.

She took a second donut to her bench, where Deandra was waiting for her, looking pissed. Could this day get any worse?

"What is this?" Deandra said, waving a set of pages that were stapled together.

"Hi, Deandra. How are you?"

Deandra looked momentarily surprised, then collected herself. Aline used the reprieve to put her coffee down on the bench and wipe her fingers on her lab coat.

"I've been asked to review this piece," Deandra said. "Be part of the peer-review panel."

"Okay."

"It's yours." Deandra thrust the pages at her.

Oh no.

"I can explain."

"I'm waiting."

Aline took the pages from Deandra. It was research that she'd done at her previous lab. A paper her supervisor hadn't wanted her to pursue. She'd done it herself, on her own time, but using that lab's resources. When she'd been caught, she'd been let go. Quietly, and with a good reference because they didn't want to make a stink. That's why she'd gone to her father for money. That's how she'd ended up at Deandra's lab.

"Dr. Perkins didn't want to pursue it."

"But you did it anyway?"

"I should have told you, but I wanted to work here very badly, and I was worried if you knew, you wouldn't take me on."

Aline felt no guilt at the lie. She needed a certain amount of post-doc time in order to get hired at the university. She also needed a certain number of publications. If she was lead author on something this early in her career, it would make all the difference.

"Why didn't Perkins want to pursue it?"

"He didn't think it was going to pan out. But I also suspect . . ."

"Yes?"

"Well, men his age aren't always so receptive to ideas from women my age. I'm sure you understand. It must've happened to you dozens of times."

Deandra gave her a rueful look. "More than I can count."

"So you understand?"

"That you went ahead and did the project anyway and used lab resources, I assume, to conduct it?"

"Yes."

"No."

"Oh."

Deandra tapped the pages Aline was holding. "But I do think this is a good piece of research that should be published."

"You'll tell the reviewing committee that?"

"No."

Aline felt sick. "Why not?"

"I can't review your work with you working here. That would be a conflict of interest. They must not have known you were in my lab."

"I wasn't working here when I submitted this."

"That's good, because then I'd have to fire you."

"Deandra, I—"

Deandra held up her hand. "We don't have to discuss this any more. I admire your ambition, Aline. I do. But you know the rules. No outside projects. No using my lab for anything other than what I direct you to do. Yes?"

"Yes."

"Excellent. Now, what's going on with Project Jennifer?"

"Oh, I . . . I didn't find anything in the water. It was fine."

"Hmm. Did you investigate household products?"

"Yes, I thought of that, but I don't think my mother uses any products that could cause lead poisoning."

"That's curious."

"Yes."

"You should double-check. There must be some other source."

"Agreed."

Deandra put a sympathetic hand on her arm, surprising Aline. Deandra was like a weathervane, spinning this way and that at the slightest breeze. "Keep looking for something in the everyday."

"What do you mean?"

"Heavy-metal poisoning in adults is almost always the result of long-term exposure."

"Right. I read that."

"So it's probably something that's been under your nose the whole time."

Chapter 29

PEACENIK

Jennifer

It's worse this week. The symptoms, the cancer. Because I sent everyone away, I was left alone with myself. Perhaps the cancer sensed my weakness. Knew it could move in when my defenses were down. More likely, this was all going to happen anyway. The world closing in. The pain. The fractured thoughts. It won't be long now. More than half of my allotted time has passed, assuming I've been given an accurate diagnosis. That they can pinpoint the moment when I'll be gone forever.

What have I done with it? Squandered it chasing down ghosts. Trying to reconcile my past, but not in any helpful way. I'm at war with my life and I want to be at peace. I need to be at peace.

So here I am, walking—limping—back into therapy on a Friday morning because I don't know how to get there on my own.

"How are you feeling, Jennifer?" Paul asks as I sink exhausted into the couch. He's wearing brown corduroys with an orange striped shirt that doesn't match. Paul never dresses for the weather. I'm not sure he knows how to. Is he impervious to it? Another one of the million things I've never asked him over the years.

It's warm but gray outside the window behind him, and I've kept my sunglasses on because my eyes are now ultrasensitive to light. The migraine to end all migraines. But the fact that I can feel it means I'm still here, so there's that.

I tap the side of my head. "It's winning up here."

"I'm sorry."

"It's all right. Nothing to be done, apparently."

"Why the sunglasses?"

"My eyes hurt."

Also my life. My life hurts. I hurt.

"What if I put down the blind?"

"Sure."

He does it and I lower my sunglasses and remove them, letting them rest in my lap. My eyes sting, then adjust, though the room is blurry. Everything is going to be taken from me, inch by inch.

"Better?" he asks.

"A bit."

"What brings you in today?"

I fiddle with the sunglasses. "I didn't like how we left things last time."

"I'm sorry about that."

"It's all right. You were trying to give me good advice. I didn't want to listen."

"And now?"

"Now I want to know how to let go."

"Of?"

I raise my shoulders. My body's stiff from spending too much time in bed. My back aches and the painkillers are never enough. "Everything. All of it. The past, the present, the future. I'm dying and I'm not at peace with it."

"You think you should be?"

"Shouldn't I?"

"If you can, of course. One should always be at peace with their life."

Whenever Paul starts speaking theoretically, I know he has more to say.

"You don't think it's achievable, though? For me?"

"I didn't mean to imply that. You still have a lot of anger about what's happened to you, and a lot of relationships that are broken in one way or another. I doubt that healing those is the work of a—"

"Few weeks."

"Yes."

"You always tell it like it is."

"I try to."

I pull the blanket behind me off the couch with effort and wrap myself in it. It's not cold in here, but I want to feel warm anyway. "There must be something I can do."

"To be at peace?"

"Yes. That's what I want."

"My best advice at this point is to try to let go as best you can."

"Let go of what?"

"Whatever you can. Whatever is tethering you to the past."

I look out the window. It's dusty and there's a spiderweb in the corner, glinting in the sunlight. If I weren't dying, I'd appreciate this unusual weather. Endless sunny days, the lawn drying out, rain and fog and cold a faint memory. "Jake?"

The corner of his mouth turns up. "I think letting go of Jake is too much to ask since we haven't been able to accomplish that in the last two years. But perhaps you could begin by forgiving yourself."

"You've said that before."

"I have."

My eyes swarm with tears. "I can't."

"You must. If you truly want peace, you should. Stop punishing yourself and try to enjoy what you can. Your daughters. Your grand-children. Take good memories with you."

"They're all terribly mad at me."

"Why?"

I push the blanket down, feeling hot. "Because I wouldn't let the poisoning go. I . . . I've done some stupid things in the last few weeks."

"Such as?"

"How much time do you have?"

He shakes his head. I have an hour, just like every time.

"What do you want to tell me, Jennifer?"

"Oh, the details don't matter, but the girls know. They know that I didn't have cancer, that I was in a mental institution, that I aban-doned them, that I lied."

"That's a lot."

"Yes, and it's not even everything. They don't know the worst of it."

Paul taps his pencil against his notepad. "Perhaps you should tell them."

"They'd hate me."

He nods slowly. "They might, yes."

I'm filled with dread. "I can't take that risk. They're mad enough at me already, between that and Andrew . . ."

"I've lost the thread here."

I close my eyes and lean back. It's an effort to sit upright. "An-drew and I broke up, and I didn't tell the girls, but Miranda contacted Andrew to tell him I was sick, and he came over to the house the other night when the girls and I were trying to figure out what hap-pened to me together and . . ."

"Breathe, Jennifer."

I take in and release a deep breath. Then another.

"Sorry, a lot has been going on."

"I understand. Why don't you walk me through it?"

I pull the blanket up to my shoulders. I was hot a minute ago and now I'm cold. I seem to be losing the ability to regulate my own temperature. Another symptom. Another sign.

I roll my head to the side and open my eyes. Paul is watching me. Waiting. "I asked Aline to look into the lead levels in my blood. To make sure there wasn't some innocent explanation for it."

"And?"

"She didn't find anything. The water in my house is clean."

"There must be other ways to be exposed? Natural ways. Accidental ways."

"Yes. But I've been looking for those, too, and none came up. None of the products that can cause problems—no lead paint, no kohl products, I didn't eat anything I haven't eaten a thousand times. And also, it went away. I don't have it in my blood anymore. So it's something I was exposed to, but the exposure stopped."

Paul frowns. "You're still thinking that someone poisoned you."

"Yes."

"Jake."

"That's what I was working on with the girls when Andrew came back. We were going through the timeline. Setting it all out to see if he could have done it."

"And?"

It hurts to admit this, but I do it anyway. "It doesn't work. I've been staring at the board where we wrote all the clues down off and on all week. The pieces don't fit together. Something is missing."

"Or it wasn't Jake."

"Not Jake?"

Paul hesitates. "I only meant that the missing piece, the most likely answer, is that you were exposed to it by another means, or the test results were wrong, that there's an innocent explanation."

"Yes, that's what I think as well."

Paul's surprised. It's not an expression I've seen from him often. And how sad is that? To be so predictable even when revealing your biggest secrets. "Are you sure?"

"Yes," I say, almost certain. "Even if I'm wrong, what's the point? I'm never going to be able to prove anything. I want to reconcile with my girls and make it right between us. For me, and for them."

"That's good, Jennifer."

"Is it?"

"Yes. It's a good step. It's a good plan."

"So how do I do it? How do I get them to speak to me again?"

"I think you know the answer."

"I do?"

He smiles gently. "Ask them to forgive you and tell them you forgive them too."

"Will that work?"

"I can't promise you that. But I do know one thing for certain."

"Don't ask, don't get?"

"Yes," Paul says. "Yes."

Chapter 30

NO ONE TALKS TO ANYONE, ANYMORE

Miranda

Miranda had problems that even hitting a thousand tennis balls wasn't going to fix. That's why she was sitting in a restaurant, waiting for her father to show up for their Sunday brunch date.

Life was full of shapes and echoes. The shape of her waiting was a rectangle, her body rigid in the chair, her arms straight by her sides. The echo was the fact that Aline had done the same thing a few days ago, waiting for her father to meet her, a conversation they both felt the need to have. They'd made their plans independently, only realizing they'd done the same thing—reach out to Jake—after Miranda brought it up with Aline.

No more lies, she'd texted Aline on Saturday morning. She'd been staying at Aline's apartment for almost a week, a refugee from

Jennifer's. She'd packed a bag when she left, but not with enough things. She'd have to find a way to go back. Whether she snuck in or let her mother know she was coming was something she hadn't decided yet.

Ha! Aline had texted back, quickly for Aline. Miranda always suspected that she checked her phone religiously but had the self-control, or the petulance, to leave others hanging for her responses.

I mean it. I need to talk to Dad. Then I'll explain everything.

When are you talking to him?

We're meeting for brunch tomorrow.

I saw him on Thursday, Aline wrote. At his office.

Miranda was surprised. As far as she knew, Aline hadn't been alone with Jake since the separation. And, yet, maybe that's why Miranda had felt such a strong pull to ask for the meeting with Jake in the first place—because Aline had. Shapes and echoes. Strings and repeats. That was her and Aline whether they wanted it or not.

How did that go? Miranda wrote.

About how you'd expect. He's such a dick.

I know.

And yet, he paid YOU off.

That stung, but the truth did sometimes. Aline was mad. Jealous. Probably both. Miranda didn't blame her. She'd be the same if the situation were reversed. When she'd asked Jake for money, she knew that he'd already said no to Aline, Aline's indignation at the refusal still fresh in her mind. Somehow, she knew instinctively that he would say yes to her. She just didn't know the price he'd exact.

You're right, Miranda wrote.

You admit it?

Yes. I'm sorry.

Whatever.

No, not whatever. I want things to be okay between us, A. I mean it.

We'll get over it. Not sure Mom will tho.

I know.

You should be talking to her. Not Dad.

Miranda knew that was true also. But she had to do things in her own order.

I'll let you know how it goes.

Okay. We owe Mom a better Sunday night dinner.

Agreed.

They owed their mother a lot of things, but she owed them something too. Miranda knew there was more to the story than what Jennifer had served up on the bristol board.

She pulled out her phone to check the time. Jake was twenty minutes late. He was doing it on purpose, probably. He wasn't ever late for court.

She dialed Aline.

"He's late," Aline said by way of greeting.

Miranda almost laughed. "How did you know?"

"It doesn't take a psychic connection to figure that out."

"He's punishing me."

"Probably. But for what?"

"I'll explain," Miranda said. "I promise."

"You keep saying that and, yet, no explanation."

Miranda sensed her father before she saw him. A shadow behind her, a cautious step. Jake used to always stride into everything, but all of this seemed to have diminished him somehow. Miranda felt small and sad when he sat across from her at the table. Her rectangle collapsed as her shoulders drooped.

"I've got to go," Miranda said to Aline, then put her phone facedown on the table. "Hi, Dad."

Jake acknowledged her. "Miranda." His voice was clipped, his phone in his hand. He was making it clear that he wasn't going to be there for long. He was wearing pressed chinos and a golf shirt. Maybe he'd been playing golf? Miranda hadn't asked about his schedule because Jake always talked about what he was doing without prompting. How busy he was and, by implication, how important. Words they mostly ignored growing up because who cared where the grown-ups were so long as there was food in the fridge and their laundry got done?

"Thanks for meeting me," Miranda said. She rested her palms on the table. They felt slick with sweat, which matched the nervous beat of her heart.

"Do you have something to report?"

"You don't have to talk to me like I'm one of your employees."

"No?"

"Dad, come on."

Jake put his phone down on the table and leaned back. "What do you want from me, Miranda?"

"I'm trying to keep up my end of the bargain, okay?"

"I don't think you've managed that, from my perspective."

"You're talking about the break-in?"

"Among other things. Kim was terrified."

Miranda controlled her eye roll. Who gave a shit about Kim? Her dad, okay sure. But was she supposed to care? Did he expect that? After everything?

"She wasn't going to hurt Kim, come on."

"You're certain of that, are you?"

Miranda looked away. The restaurant was busy, the bustle of servers and forks clinking on plates mixed in with the Top 40 radio. She wished she were sitting at one of the other tables, the ones where the people were simply eating brunch, lazing away their Sunday.

"I didn't know Mom was going to do that."

Jake shifted in his chair. "But that's the problem, isn't it? You're supposed to be giving me a heads-up. And you haven't been doing that. Not since your mother got sick."

"It's complicated, Dad. This is not what I signed up for."

"Not from my perspective."

Miranda wished he'd stop saying that, wished she were somewhere else. That she'd never struck any sort of bargain with Jake. She'd taken the easy way out, or what had seemed that way at the time. Doing that was one of her major flaws.

"She thinks that you poisoned her."

"What?"

"Mom. She thinks that you poisoned her."

"That's ridiculous." Jake paled. "Why haven't you told me about this until now?"

That was a good question without a good answer. She should have told Jake from the beginning, but if she was being honest with herself, she assumed it would just go away. Ignoring problems was another one of her specialties. And though there was usually a price to pay eventually, putting it off for as long as possible was always easier than confronting things head-on.

"I didn't think she was serious. I thought she'd let it go."

"And has she?"

"I don't think so. She has . . . she has these test results from last spring. She had a lot of lead in her blood."

Jake drummed his fingers on the table. "Is there something you want to ask me, Miranda?"

"I'm trying to tell you. She felt sick last May. Right after the boys' birthday."

"And?"

"When you were talking to her. When you gave her something to drink."

Jake waggled his fingers dismissively. "That was vodka."

"Which would be hard to prove now, right?"

"Why am I going to have to prove anything?"

Frustration was building in Miranda. It started in her stomach and crept up her chest. "I've tried to dissuade her. We all have, we've all been trying to convince her that there isn't anything for her to worry about."

"You haven't convinced her?"

"I'm not sure. Maybe we have."

"Try harder."

"You don't understand. It's not that easy."

"No, I don't understand, clearly."

Miranda looked down at the table. Her phone, her father's phone, the sticky menu, the container full of napkins. She tried to find a pattern, a shape. But there wasn't anything she could think of. She didn't know how to get her point across, and she wasn't even entirely sure what it was she was trying to say.

"I've done what I could. And I haven't told her."

"About what?"

Miranda hated Jake for making her say it out loud. "Why you wanted the divorce."

"I don't see how that's relevant."

"Dad, come on. Don't you get how guilty you look?"

"I don't see it that way at all."

How could that be? Jake was the one who had taught her how to approach things rationally. How to lay everything out in a way that made sense. But that had never applied to his own behavior, of course. How could it?

Miranda stared at him as coldly as she could. "You need me to spell it out for you? Fine. Remember when we made our little deal? The reason you were so desperate to get something on Mom? Well, that's when she got sick. She's not an idiot, Dad. It's not that hard to put two and two together."

"Who else knows about this?"

"All of it? Only you and me. But the pieces are all there. Mom knows you paid off my debt. I told her."

Jake looked uncertain for the first time. "Why?"

"Because she's dying, Dad? You don't know what it's like. You're not there. She wants to know what's happening to her and I can't lie to her face, okay? I'm not going to do that."

Miranda watched the emotions play across Jake's face. When he'd picked her up at the airport last year, she'd never thought they'd end up here. She thought she was making an easy bargain. But everything had a hidden cost. She should've thought about that. She should have learned that lesson by now.

"So you had no issue lying to her for over a year, but now that's over?"

Jake was using his litigator's voice, the one Miranda used to hear when she went to visit him in court when she was a teenager and she was flirting with becoming a lawyer herself. That plan got cast aside like so many others.

"I never should have agreed to any of it in the first place."

Jake leaned forward. He had a look that Miranda couldn't read, but it scared her. "But you did. And once I make a bargain, I expect people to keep it. You see this through to the end, and then you'll have your freedom. That's what you wanted, wasn't it?"

Shame flooded through Miranda. That is what she'd wanted. A fresh start without the yoke of debt her indecision had given her.

"Yes."

"But?"

"I didn't know what I was getting into."

"That's not my concern."

Miranda leaned back in her chair, hit by the blow of his indifference. "You don't give a shit about any of us, do you?"

"That's not true."

"It is. You only care about *her.*"

"Oh, grow up, Miranda. I was there for you and your sisters for your entire life. Everything you have, everything you've done, everything you were able to do, I financed that. I was there. Don't you try to change history and say I wasn't a good father. I'm not responsible for all those mistakes you made. I offered you a way out of them. If you don't like where that's brought you, that's on you. Not me."

"What about Mom?"

"What about her?"

"She's dying, Dad. Has that even sunk in yet?"

Jake's face fell for a moment, then the mask was back in place. "I didn't want that."

"It's happening though."

"What do you expect me to do?"

Miranda looked away from her father, her eyes traveling over the restaurant until something pulled her focus to the entrance. "I thought that—shit. Oh, no."

"What, Miranda?"

Miranda lifted her hand and pointed toward the back retreating through the door. "That was Mom."

Chapter 31

BURY ME

Jennifer

On Sunday morning Emily picks me up to take me to our appointment at the funeral home.

Oh, the places you will go.

It's in a nondescript cream building set back from the road behind large iron gates. There's pan flute music playing in reception, a built-in waterfall, and the air smells like flowers. Everything about the place is hushed. The ring of the phone. The volume at which the receptionist speaks. The thickness of the carpet, which sucks at my shoes. The whole place feels sleepy, like the room you might expect to wake up in before you're ushered into the afterworld on the show that Miranda likes so much.

Everything is going to be fine, the décor suggests. It's supposed to be calming, but all it does is make me want to close my eyes and leave all the decisions to Emily. So I do. Emily listens to the young woman in a dress with a Peter Pan collar as she explains the process while I stare out the window and try my best to stay awake. When she's done with her spiel, she pushes a brochure with a series of options toward me.

A casket. Plain, not much more than a box, because who cares what I end up in.

Sure, I nod.

A simple service.

Again, it's fine.

Do I want a thumbprint to leave to my grandchildren? On a tasteful piece of jewelry, perhaps?

"Do I?" I ask Emily.

Emily smiles awkwardly. "It might be nice."

I turn away from the young woman. Her name is Mary.

"You don't think it's a bit . . . tacky?"

"It's something that lives on."

"It's access to my iPhone."

Emily turns back to Mary and says with a forced smile. "No thumbprint locket, I don't think."

"Very well, ma'am. Shall I ring all this up for you?"

"Please."

She leaves, her steps hushed by the same carpet that tried to swallow us as we walked in. Such a strange place. I've never been in a funeral home before. My organized father had prepaid for his funeral before he died, and so I'd only gone to the service. I hadn't had to deal with the choices, or marvel at the things people wanted to bring with them into the ground.

"Sorry if this is weird," I say to Emily.

"No, it's fine. The least I could do."

"Are you still mad about the other night? Andrew? The cancer? Or the not-cancer, I should say."

Emily glances at me, then looks away. She's wearing slacks today instead of a summer dress, black ones with a white sleeveless blouse tucked in. Small diamonds in her ears that we gave her when she graduated from university. She looks put together, efficient. She looks like Emily.

"I'm not sure, Mom. It's a lot to take in."

"I know. But I was talking to my therapist, Paul, and I wanted to ask you to forgive me."

"Forgive what, exactly?"

"The lies. You can't imagine how differently I would've done so many things if I could. But life doesn't work like that. You're only given the one chance to do it right."

"You can learn, though. You can change."

"Would things have been any different if I'd told you about my illness?"

Emily looks at me blankly. "Why didn't you?"

"I didn't think I needed to. I didn't even think you remembered it. It was never anything that came up."

"We never talked about anything in our house."

"That's not true."

"Oh, sure. What was on TV, or in the headlines. Debating Dad at the dinner table about his cases or the latest legal issue that had caught his attention. We did all those things. But us? Our family? What was really going on? No."

Is this true? I don't recall any specific conversations, but that doesn't mean they didn't happen. Besides, what family sits around and discusses their flaws on a regular basis? It wasn't something I'd ever experienced growing up. Bea's house was a house of secrets. Don't bring anyone over, because who knew if Mom was having a good or a bad day. Don't tell anyone about the late-night disturbances, because what if they came and took Bea away? What if they came and took me away?

"Were there things to talk about?"

"Of course there were."

I sigh. This isn't what I wanted from this conversation. But Paul warned me that it might not go the way I want, and I went ahead anyway.

"I didn't mean it like that. I meant were there things that happened that you felt you couldn't discuss? Was I not available to you if you needed me?"

Emily frowns. "It was up to me to bring it up?"

"How was I supposed to know if something was wrong?" I regret the words as they leave me. I don't want to fight. I want to leave the fight behind.

"By paying attention."

"I was, though. Maybe I even paid too much attention."

Emily played with one of her earrings. "I'm not talking about whether we had a fever or the chicken pox, or any of the other things you thought we had."

"What, then?"

"I don't know . . . Take all that acting stuff."

"You mean the stuff you did as kids?"

"Yeah. We hated that."

"You did?"

"We were being paraded around like a freak show. And for what?"

That stings. When the girls were three months old, Jake and I had spent hours discussing whether we should go ahead with the first commercial after we'd been approached to do a national campaign. The offer—a year's supply of diapers and formula and five hundred dollars a day for each girl—had been too good to pass up. We were living in a two-bedroom apartment. Jake was studying for the bar, and we had no income other than the part-time money he was getting working at a sleazy divorce lawyer's firm when he could in between classes.

SIX WEEKS TO LIVE 249

"Honestly? We needed the money."

"What? Why didn't you ask Grandma and Grandpa for help?"

"We did, sometimes. When we had to. But you don't understand—anything we got from them came with strings. Maybe you never saw that side of Grandpa Norman because Grandma Bea takes up so much room, but he was very difficult about money. We took as little as possible because we didn't want to be beholden to him. The only time we deviated from that was for the house."

"I didn't know that."

"It wasn't for you to know. But that's why we agreed when we were approached. We thought, what could it hurt?"

Emily looks away. "It did hurt us. All that attention, then it just went away. That wasn't good for anyone."

"Ah, here we are," Mary says, walking into the room. We didn't hear her coming, but that's the point of this entire place. To lull you into a sleepy state so you're much more likely to say yes to things a dead person doesn't need.

Mary puts a sheet down in front of us. The total makes my eyes water.

"That's a lot," Emily says.

"It's fine. You take Visa, right?"

Mary nods and scurries over to a sideboard to get the machine to charge me for my burial. As I put in my pin, I have the fleeting thought that I won't be around to pay this bill. But my estate will, the thing that lives on after me, the money I inherited from my father, who finally opened his purse strings to me once he was dead.

What he left me was much more than I expected. We'd lived a modest life, growing up. My father ran every car he ever owned into the ground. The biggest purchases he'd made were his house and mine, and we'd paid him back every penny. When the will had been read and I'd been told that my 50 percent was worth more than my house and our savings combined, I'd been shocked. Jake had been, too, and we'd agreed to put it aside for our retirement and pay for something nice for each of the girls—their wedding, or their first house. Something a bit later in life, when they needed a boost. But we wanted them to struggle a bit. We wanted them to have to work to get somewhere, as we had. To clear part of the driveway, but not all of it. Because of that, I would've told Miranda no if she'd asked me to pay off her debts. I didn't want to pay her way home from Africa, either. Let her tough the year out, was my position. Let her learn.

Jake didn't keep our bargain, another broken promise.

"I want to pay for the rest of med school," I say to Emily as we leave the funeral home. We're twenty paces past the entrance. I close my eyes and breathe in deeply, clearing my lungs of the cloying scent of flowers that's seeped into me, steadying myself for the walk to the car. "For you to complete it."

"What?"

"I should have offered before."

"Mom, no, it's fine."

"Are you, though?"

"Yes."

"Why won't you let me help you?"

Emily looks down at the cracked pavement. "I think you're angry."

"Oh, you're thinking of the will? Your sisters?"

"You always said you wanted to treat us as equally as possible. No favorites, right?"

She's right, that was my motto. Especially because of the fraternal/identical split. It was easy for Emily to feel left out and I wanted her to know that in her family, at least, she was the same as her sisters.

"But I want to give this to you."

"Leave it, Mom. Okay?"

A month ago, if you'd asked me whether I thought I knew my

daughters, I would've given an emphatic yes. But now, as the layers peel away like discarded clothes after a long day, it turns out that I don't know them at all. I can't predict their reactions. I don't know what to say or how to act. I'm a stranger in my own family.

"Okay, I will."

"Where to next?"

I want to crawl back into bed, but this might also be the last time I can be out like this with Emily. I should savor it. Hold on to it for as long as I can. If I take another pain pill, I think I can make it through lunch.

"I should eat."

Emily checks her phone. "There's a good brunch place not too far from here."

"Sure."

I watch Emily on the short drive. I wish I had the ability to see into her mind, to know what she's thinking. But this is not a movie, and my cancer has not given me magical powers or insight or anything else but pain and grief. All I know is that we are driving together, and at least one of my daughters is still speaking to me.

When we get there, the restaurant is busy. We hover in the entrance, waiting for a server to come take us to a table. That's when I see them. Jake and Miranda, sitting in the corner, deep in conversation.

"We should leave," Emily says.

"Maybe we should go over there."

"No, let's go." Emily grabs my elbow. "Come on, Mom. Let's not do this."

I nod in agreement and follow her. But in the doorway, I find I can't help myself. I turn and stare at Miranda so hard that she looks up as if she feels me.

Our eyes meet for a moment before I turn and hurry away.

Chapter 32

LISTEN UP

Aline

Aline thought she'd seen it all until she walked into her apartment on Sunday afternoon. She was running out of fresh clothes at Nick's, and she didn't feel like doing laundry in the creepy basement in his building.

Aline's usually neat apartment was a mess. Dirty dishes in the sink, empty wine bottles everywhere, a red ring on the white counter that would probably cause a permanent stain. The trash was full, with a swarm of fruit flies around it, and the air smelled like smoke—a mix of cigarettes and weed. To cap everything off, there was a trail of clothes leading to the bedroom, Miranda's and someone else's.

What the fuck was going on?

"Miranda!"

She heard something knock over in the bedroom, and then a giggle. Great, she was going to have to deal with Miranda and a stranger.

Gross. Who had sex in someone else's house in the middle of the afternoon? Her sister, apparently.

Something was going on with her, and Aline didn't like it.

"Hello?" she called again. "Miranda?"

"I'll be out in a minute!"

Aline crossed her arms and started tapping her foot. Then she stopped herself when she realized she was giving a perfect impression of her mother. This was not how she wanted this to go.

"Hurry up, I have shit to do."

"I'm coming, hold your horses."

Aline's bedroom door opened, and Miranda appeared. Her hair was wild, and Aline could smell the booze and cigarettes and sex that was pouring off her.

"What the hell? Is Devon in there?"

At least Miranda still had the ability to look embarrassed. "No, it's Cassandra."

"Who's that?"

Miranda shrugged. "We met at the bar."

"The bar? What bar?"

"That Irish place we went to last Sunday?"

Her bar. Where Aline hung out. Where everyone must've been super confused about her leaving with a woman. Not that she cared what anyone thought, but it was rude. Thoughtless. Not like Miranda. None of this was like Miranda.

"You picked up a woman in my bar?"

"Yeah, so?"

"What the fuck is wrong with you?"

"Nothing."

Miranda wandered past Aline into the kitchen and opened the fridge. There was an old coffee to-go cup in there and nothing else, though the fridge had been half-full when Aline last checked. Miranda picked up the cup and put it in the microwave.

"Nothing, huh? Right. Sure." The microwave beeped. "Are you going to get that?"

Miranda scowled at her and took her cup out of the microwave. The coffee smelled off, or maybe it was the milk, but Miranda took a sip anyway, then made a face and poured it down the drain.

"Well?" Aline said, her rage simmering. "Are you going to say anything?"

"What do you want from me, Aline?"

"I already told you. I want to know what's going on with you. You hide shit from us, like vital shit about Dad, you're fucking randos and my castoffs from high school. Do I need to arrange an intervention?"

"Ha. That's rich coming from you."

"What's that supposed to mean?"

"You never told me about Nick." Miranda walked to the recycling bin and kicked it. The glass inside rattled. "And this thing is full of empty bottles. And unless you had a party you didn't invite me to, which I highly forking doubt, that's a lotta booze you've been drinking."

Aline felt her cheeks go hot. "We're not talking about me. I don't have anything to explain."

"Oh, no? Sure, okay. Cool, cool. Blameless Aline, right? You never told me why you had to ask Dad for money. What was that about?"

"Hypocrite."

"Maybe. But at least I can explain myself."

"Really? I heard you," Aline said. "I heard your conversation with Dad today."

"What? How?"

"You didn't hang up our call. Remember? We were speaking when he arrived."

Miranda looked off into space. "You listened in?"

"I wanted to hear what Dad had to say for himself."

"You shouldn't have done that."

"Really, Miranda? That's what you're going with? I find out that you and Dad are in some sort of plot together and that you were what, warning him about what Mom thought, and you think the worst thing that happened was I listened in on your phone call?"

"It's not what you think."

"You and Dad don't have some secret plan together?"

Miranda looked away. "No, we did, but not . . . I didn't try to kill Mom."

"Did Dad?"

"I—"

"Um, excuse me?" A short woman with dark brown hair was standing in the doorway to the bedroom, her body half in and half out of the room. She was covered in a sheet. Cassandra, Miranda had said her name was. "Sorry to interrupt, but my clothes are out here? And I have to get to a yoga class I'm teaching?"

"Come on out and join us," Aline said. "Why the fuck not."

The woman scurried into the room, the sheet trailing behind her. She picked up her scattered things, mixing them with Miranda's. She looked up at Aline. "Oh, you guys are twins?"

"No. We're triplets."

Chapter 33

I GIVE UP

Jennifer

"It's not what you think, Mom," Emily says to me after we get home from our aborted brunch. I'd asked her to drive around for a while, to just drive around Surrey and let the radio sing to me, something gentle and sad. She put on Tom Waits, and I watched the trees and the houses and the roads flash by, and now my head feels like that Indigo Girls song, like my head is on a board, cloudier than I'd been before, but there isn't any clarity for me to seek, no prophet to visit or mountain to climb or . . .

"What's not what she thinks?" Bea says, floating into the hall from the kitchen with a glass of chardonnay in one hand. She didn't explain where she'd gone when she came back a few days ago. She'd just kissed me on the forehead and insisted on changing the sheets on my bed.

She's marking time here, waiting for the moment when she can leave for good and go back to her life and live out the tragedy of losing a daughter before her. Maybe that's uncharitable, but it's what I know is true.

"It doesn't matter."

I push past them and head to the kitchen. A drink is what I want, a million drinks. Maybe I'll ask someone to move the wine fridge up to my bedroom and drink myself into oblivion until the end. I should've called that number on the bottom of the palliative care options while I had the chance. It feels too late now. I have to ride this out to the end whether I want to or not.

"Mom, come on. Talk to me."

I open the fridge and pull out the bottle my mother's drunk half of already, or maybe it was left over from one of the girls. Who cares. I pour the rest of the wine into a water glass, almost full to the rim.

"There's nothing to talk about."

"I'm sure there's some perfectly good reason why Miranda was meeting Dad."

I take a large gulp of the wine and set the glass down on the counter. My hands are shaking, but my mind is blank. I'm sick of thinking about this, talking about this, trying to convince those who are supposed to love me that I'm worth listening to.

I'm out. I'm done. Fuck it, as Aline would say. *Fork it.*

"I just want this to be over."

Emily pales. "Don't say that."

"Why not? Who cares?"

"I care," Bea says, tears streaking down her face. She looks so old, standing there, her features sinking under the weight of the alcohol. That's why she needed a break. Not because she's bad, but because this is hard. I've done this to her. I'm the reason all of this is happening.

Shit. *Shit.* I'm screwing up dying just like I screwed up everything in my life.

"I'm sorry, Mom. It's been a tough day."

Bea reaches for a tissue and dabs at her face. "It's all right, dear. Please don't give up yet."

Emotions race through me. I don't know what she wants from me. Does she think that if I'm around for a few more weeks, we're going to have some big moment where we clear everything up?

Even though it's what I've been hoping for with my own girls, life doesn't work like that. I knew that before and I definitely know that now.

"I won't."

"Thank you."

I take another gulp of wine. It's cold and tart and sparks a nudge of hunger in my belly. I never did get lunch, and now it's almost dinnertime. The fridge is full of casseroles brought by the neighbors.

"Can you heat something up?" I ask Emily.

"Oh, sure. What would you like?"

"I don't know. Whatever looks best."

Emily nods and I take my glass of wine to the living room. The headache that comes and goes but mostly comes is building like a wave.

The doorbell rings.

"Come in!" I yell, because I don't feel like going to the door. It's probably another casserole delivery.

"Mom?"

"Aline?"

"Where are you?"

"In the living room."

I sink down into Jake's chair, resting the glass on the table next to it. Aline walks into the room holding two pieces of mail in her hands. She looks agitated, a flush along her cheekbones.

"This was in your mailbox," Aline says, handing the mail to me. "What are we drinking?"

"Whatever's going, I think."

Emily walks in with a plate of casserole. "What are you doing here?"

"Am I not allowed to come to my own mother's house?"

I pick up my wine and drink. "Girls, please. My head is killing me." I put the glass down and look at the mail Aline handed me. I haven't checked the mail in days. One envelope is from the phone company. The other is from my doctor's office. My hands are fluttering.

"Mom?" Emily says.

"Yes?"

"What's going on?"

"Just give me a minute."

I rip open the first envelope. It's the test results from the hair-and-nails tests I took at Dr. Parent's office. The ones I fast-tracked. And there it is in black and white. The traces of lead are still in me, buried in my hair follicles. *Acute lead poisoning*, it says across the bottom. Confirmed.

I hand the paper to Emily. She reads it as I rip open the second envelope. It's the phone records I asked for.

"Can you bring me my purse?" I say to Aline. "I left it in the hall."

She leaves and brings it back. I take out my phone and pull up the number of my doctor's office. Then I scan through the list of called numbers from my home phone. It's there—a call lasting two minutes from June of last year that I do not remember making.

"What was the date of the call to the doctors?" I ask Emily. "The one that noted that I was seeking a second opinion?"

"I don't remember. Early June?"

I'm about to say that they can check the board in the living room, where we wrote it all down. But I'd put it away a few days ago after staring at it for too long. I should have this information memorized, though, and the fact that I don't, that fact scares me more than anything.

I close my eyes. I can see the paper Dr. Parent gave me upstairs in my bedroom, but the details are fuzzy. But I know as deep as the cancer is in me, that when I check it the dates will match. Someone did call the doctor and wave them off.

And the call came from inside the house.

"What's going on?" Aline asks.

"I did have lead poisoning. And someone called my doctor's office from the house."

"Not you?"

"No, not me."

Aline looks at her hands.

"What is it, Aline?"

"Are you 100 percent sure you didn't forget?"

"If the doctor had asked me to get more tests, I would have. My brain was working fine back then." It's a struggle to say these words, my tongue thick in my mouth, but I know it's true.

"Okay, well, I went back and looked through all the articles I had on lead poisoning, and how contamination could happen. There's a long list of products that can do it: lead paint and kohl products and shooting on firing ranges, none of which seem to apply to you. But the thing that jumped out is that accidental lead poisoning usually happens to kids, when they swallow a lead-based toy. But even then, one-time poisonings are rare. It's usually a buildup over time. I don't think that it could have been Dad."

"He was in the house more than once."

"But not enough times, right? It would have to be a lot. A slow buildup over several months."

I want to fight her, but I know she's right. It was the same conclusion I'd arrived at. The pieces didn't fit. It wasn't Jake.

"Was the call to the doctor when Miranda was living here? It was, right?"

"Yes. Why are you asking?"

Aline looks miserable. "I know something about Miranda. Miranda and Dad, something more than him paying off her debts."

I look at Emily. "We saw them. We saw them together today."

"You did? Where?"

"At a restaurant. Why? What does that have to do with what's happening to me?"

Aline clucks her tongue. "I heard their conversation. I was on the phone with Miranda right before Dad got there and she didn't hang up properly. I listened in."

"What did you hear?"

"I heard them talking about some plan they had. Some deal."

The wine I've chugged starts to rise. I clasp my hand over my mouth.

"Mom, are you okay? Are you going to be sick?"

I gasp for air, breathing in through my nose. My heart jackrabbits in my chest. "No, it's okay. Go on. What was it?"

"He paid off her debts, and in exchange she had to move in here."

"Move in here to do what?"

"To spy on you, basically. To help get him information so you'd divorce him."

I feel sick again, my vision closing in, but I manage to get the words out. "The divorce. The divorce. I was worth killing for a divorce?"

"She didn't say that, Mom," Emily says.

"Isn't that what this is about? Why did he care so damn much about the divorce? Enough to spy on me? Jesus."

Aline looks at Emily. Emily shakes her head.

"Tell me," I say.

"Mom, I don't think—"

"Please. Enough secrets, okay?"

"I agree," Aline says. "We should have told you a year ago."

"Told me what?"

Aline looks grim. "Kim was pregnant. That's why Dad was pestering you for the divorce. She was obsessed with getting married before the baby was born. He told us at the boys' birthday party."

I reach up and touch my head, that reflexive movement from the first day at the doctor's office. Back then, when I tapped it, the pain went away. But now, no matter how hard I hit it, my head feels as if it's being split in two and my vision is closing in faster than I can stop it.

I was right.

I was right.

Only it's so much worse than I thought.

Chapter 34

TO THE BEAT OF OUR NOISY HEARTS
Aline

Aline felt sick to her stomach. She'd felt that way too often recently, but as she watched her mother react to the news that she'd been right all along, that someone had tried to kill her, and that this person might be one of her daughters, well, she couldn't help but think that she should've kept everything to herself. But she'd been so angry with Miranda when she'd found out what was going on, she'd marched right over to their mother's. She didn't have a plan, and she didn't take the time to stop and formulate one. She only knew she had to tell—if she could work up the courage to take her mother's side against Miranda's.

What the hell had happened to them?

"Aline!" Emily shouted, breaking her out of her state of shock.

"What?"

"Call an ambulance."

"Why?"

Aline focused. Emily had a hand to Jennifer's neck, another on her wrist. Jennifer wasn't sitting up straight and she looked as if she was having trouble breathing.

"Something's wrong with Mom. Call now!"

Aline pulled out her phone and dialed 911 with shaking fingers. Fuck. Fuck. She should have kept her fucking mouth shut.

"Nine-One-One. Please state the nature of your emergency."

Hours later, in the hospital waiting room, Aline tried to think back to when this all started. What was the precipitating event? When did Jennifer become the enemy that needed to be destroyed? Was it Jake's affair and the fallout from that? No. Aline didn't blame her mother for that, and she couldn't believe that Miranda did either, though Aline wished sometimes that Jennifer had taken it better. That there was some way the family could have remained intact, even if it was only for the holidays Aline was surprisingly sentimental about.

No. It went back much further than that.

She should be able to figure this out. She and Miranda were the same person in so many ways; there wasn't anyone Aline knew better, not even Emily. She knew Emily felt left out sometimes. But she and Miranda were a unit. One group of cells, one set of DNA. What had happened in their life to make it possible for Aline to believe that Miranda could have done this?

Aline rested her head against the hard wall behind her, trying to get some rest. The hospital had been renovated, and it was such a change from the hospital she was used to growing up that it seemed like it came from the future. The walls were bright white, the waiting room had comfortable seats, even the vending machine offerings seemed healthy in comparison. But it was still a hospital, and Jennifer was in one of those cubicles behind the emergency intake desk,

hooked up to machines, with worried doctors swarming around trying to determine what was going on with her.

The tumor, they said after they'd completed their first assess-
ment within minutes of arriving in the ambulance. They never knew
exactly how it was going to proceed, and proceed it had. But Aline
knew better. The tumor was the excuse they were all using to paper
over what they were doing: suffocating their mother with the past,
holding it over her like a weighted blanket, until she couldn't breathe,
until she couldn't think, until she ended up here weeks before she
should have.

"I shouldn't have told her about the baby," Aline said to Emily,
who was sitting next to her, looking at her phone. "I mean, the baby
that wasn't. The embryo, whatever."

Emily didn't look up, just shook her head aggressively. Her hair
was in a high ponytail, and her shirt was rumpled. She looked extra
pale under the fluorescent lights. "I told you not to. I thought we'd
agreed."

"Yeah, we did." Another shot of guilt flooded through Aline.

"Why did you?"

"I was probably trying to punish her, to be honest."

Emily started and raised her head. Her eyes were bloodshot, as
if Emily were the one who'd been drinking too much, not sleeping
enough. Maybe she was—what did Aline know? What did any of
them know? "Punish her? That's not what I thought you were going
to say."

"You thought I was going to go on some rant about truth?"

"Yes."

"Yeah, well, that would be a lie. I mean, sure, in the moment,
that's probably what I was thinking, but it's deeper than that. It's always deeper than that with Mom."

"Why do you hate her so much?" Emily asked.

"Why don't you hate her at all?"

"Why should I?"

Aline felt sick again. She needed a drink. She needed to leave. She needed to scream. None of these was an option. The past was calling to her, and where she'd always looked away before, she was staring straight at it now.

"Don't you remember what it was like before she got sick? Don't you remember what she was like?"

"I don't know what you're talking about."

"Em . . ."

"Yeah, okay, sure, she was being a bit weird. Like that time she forgot to pick us up from school. But we know why now, right? She was depressed. Or manic? Was she manic?"

Aline was confused. She knew they never talked about it; it was one of the unwritten rules of their house. Discuss nothing bad, pretend we're all amazing and happy all the time. She'd always hated that, and eventually it had driven her away. But did her family have collective amnesia? Did Emily truly not remember? Or was it just the fact that when you were a kid, you didn't always know what was normal and it was only later that you could figure it out?

No, that wasn't right. Aline knew her mother wasn't normal when it was happening. Aline hadn't understood it then, not that or the myriad other things that had occurred before their mother went away and came back as someone who looked like their mother but acted like someone else. She'd never entirely forgotten, and it had come back to her with a wallop when she'd started college. She'd been in the lab, doing her first experiment in organic chemistry with her new partner, recording cell growth and how it was affected by various reagents. She'd been noting the changes on an hourly basis in a notebook and had been hit with an enormous sense of déjà vu.

She'd seen these very notations before. Only they weren't about a bunch of cells, they were about her and her sisters. When her classes moved on to rat experiments later in her education, she'd become certain. What they were doing to the rats, well, she'd been the rat.

"Forget it," Aline said. "I don't want to argue."

"So why did you tell Mom about the baby?"

"What?" Miranda said, coming around the corner with her phone in her hand as if she were using it to navigate through the complicated set of hallways. "You what?"

Aline looked at Miranda. Her hair was in a tidy side braid but she was in sweatpants—Aline's, actually—and was wearing a pair of flip-flops. At least she looked like she'd had a shower.

"I told Mom that Dad and Kim were going to have a baby."

Miranda's face fell. "Why? Why would you do that?"

"Because I thought she had a right to know."

"We agreed, though. We said we wouldn't tell her."

"Yeah, well, that was before I found out that you were living with Mom in order to spy on her for Dad and God knows what else."

Miranda sank into a chair. "I didn't, though. I didn't tell Dad anything."

"I find that hard to believe."

"There wasn't anything to tell him. Mom's life is super boring."

Emily put her phone away. "I think you need to explain yourself, Miranda. Because it doesn't look good."

"What's that supposed to mean?"

"What do you think?" Aline said. She bunched her fists in frustration. She hated it when Miranda acted dumb. It was like being that way herself, a feeling she tried to avoid as often as possible.

"Enlighten me."

Aline growled. "Mom *was* poisoned—she got the additional test results back and her phone records too, which show that someone called her doctor from the house—and you were living there under false pretenses, trying to dig up dirt on her for Dad so he could get his divorce in time to marry his little hussy before she popped out a baby."

"Little hussy?" Emily said. "Really?"

"Whatever."

Miranda looked like someone had knocked the wind out of her. "You're not saying that you think I . . . What?"

"It doesn't matter what we think," Emily said. "It's what Mom thinks."

"Mom thinks I poisoned her?"

"Well, did you?" Aline asked.

"No. I forking swear—"

"If you say fork one more time, I am going to end you right here."

"Hey, now. Hey," Emily said, putting her hand on Aline's arm and squeezing gently. "Come on."

Aline breathed in slowly, but it didn't diminish her rage. This whole conversation was ridiculous, but she couldn't see any way around it. Because her mother had been poisoned, and unless Jennifer did it to herself, then the prime suspects were pretty obvious.

"Did you poison Mom?" Aline asked Miranda.

"No. I swear, Aline. There's no way I would do that. No fucking way."

Aline almost smiled at Miranda's use of real language. She wanted to believe her, she did believe her, because believing her was like believing herself, and she knew that she hadn't done it. "What about Dad? Did he do it? Did he tell you that's what he was doing?"

"No. Of course not."

"That doesn't mean he didn't."

"But why would he have me move in if he'd done that?"

"Because it didn't work?"

Miranda twisted her fingers into her braid. "That doesn't make any sense. Dad didn't want her dead. He wanted the divorce. He was even concerned about her. I know you won't believe this, okay, but he isn't all bad. He asked after her. He wanted to make sure she was okay. He was happy she was dating someone."

"Because he thought that would make her agree to the divorce," Emily said wearily.

"Yeah, okay, that's possible. In fact, that's probably true. But guys, come on. I don't know how Mom got sick, but it wasn't Dad. It wasn't."

Aline thought about what Miranda was saying. What did the facts show? Jennifer had acute lead poisoning. It came from long-term exposure, not a one-time event. Jake couldn't have done that. He didn't have enough access despite his occasional visits to the house, or the motivation. Kim hadn't been pregnant for long if that was the motivator, and it wasn't his way. He wasn't subtle. He badgered. He asked for what he wanted and then he pushed and pushed until he got it. The fact that he'd sent Miranda in undercover was the most subtle thing he'd ever done.

Which brought her back to the one thing she hadn't considered until now but was the only thing that made sense.

It was her mom.

Her mom had done this to herself.

Two Weeks to Live . . .

Chapter 35

SHALLOW

Miranda

If there was one thing Miranda knew, it was that time wasn't meted out in equal parts. The most amazing things in your life could feel as if they were taking forever to pass, and something terrible could flash by in an instant. That wasn't the common wisdom, but it was her experience. Time was an uneven beat in an uneven world.

When Miranda had realized she was stuck in Namibia, that she'd made the stupidest decision in her life following Bonnie into the Peace Corps and signing away several years of her life to a job she hated from the first day, she'd felt lost. Kidnapped. Someone had stolen her life, only she'd agreed to go. She'd walked right in and signed on the dotted line. It was probably how you felt after you joined Scientology and found out about Xenu and the spaceships. That you'd been sold one thing and swallowed another.

Whatever metaphor she tried to employ, the fact remained. She was stuck there for the next two years without any means to get home. And even if she did go home, there was a shitstorm of debt waiting for her. Her mother, pissed that she was leaving, pissed in general at the world since Jake left her, had told Miranda that it was on her if she went. Jennifer wasn't going to bail her out. "Not again," she'd said in a definitive voice. A voice Miranda knew well from all the times Jennifer had used it when they were growing up. Jake had always been the softie—giving in with little persuasion. They each knew it and took advantage of it.

Miranda had been cavalier in the face of that *not again*. She'd told her mother that she was fine, that she had to go *live her own life*. She'd implied Jennifer should do the same and then she'd used up the last bit of credit some company was stupid enough to give her to buy her plane ticket out of there.

She was stuck. So she hatched a plan. Her dad had told her he felt isolated from the family. She also knew that though everyone thought Aline and Miranda were both on Jake's team, she was his favorite. Being the youngest in a family of triplets was an easy role to assume, and she used it to her advantage. It hadn't taken much for Jake to agree, but there were going to be conditions attached, he'd said, if he sent her the money. They'd talk about it when she got home.

She'd agreed without much thought and hopped on the next transport without even telling Bonnie goodbye. Bonnie wouldn't care. Or maybe she would, but that wasn't Miranda's problem. It was one of the reasons Miranda never stayed with anyone too long. Miranda didn't do attached. Following Bonnie to Africa had made that clear to her. It had been a moment of weakness, after she'd lost the restaurant and knew she needed something to distract herself.

She liked to float, to chill, to keep things easy and light. Too bad most of the people who liked to be chill were also assholes like Devon. And Bonnie, who'd seen Miranda bounce out of relationships a bunch of times, should've known what was coming.

God, that made her the asshole, didn't it?

"Then what happened?" Emily asked. It was after midnight, and they'd moved to the cafeteria once the doctors told them that Jennifer was sleeping and would likely be out for several hours. It was Emily who'd asked if she was in a *medically induced coma*, but no, *not yet*, they'd said. She was simply resting, catching up on all the sleep she should've been getting these last few weeks.

That *yet* was devastating.

"I came home before the boys' birthday, remember?"

Emily picked at the rim of her paper coffee cup. It was the middle of the night and the cafeteria was a ghost town, the lights turned down low. The cafeteria lanes were shuttered and the only thing available were the vending machines.

"I remember. You were jet lagged."

"Right. That trampoline place gave me the worst headache."

"Try living with two three-year-olds."

"Can we get on with it?" Aline growled. Miranda looked at her, her twin, her copy. Aline's hair was in her typical ballet knot, though it had been ten years since they'd stopped dancing. As always, Miranda only saw the differences between them, Aline's slightly longer nose, her skin paler from working inside, the frown line between their identical eyes. Miranda still couldn't believe Aline had told on her to Jennifer, but she supposed she deserved it.

"I'm getting there," Miranda said, taking a sip of her coffee. It wasn't half-bad. "Anyway, we were at the party and Mom left and then Dad told us his news."

"That Kim was pregnant?" Emily said.

"Yes. Remember how happy he was?"

"I thought he looked more stressed, actually," Aline said.

"I agree," Emily said.

And there it was again. They could never agree on anything

about the past, the three of them. How many times in their lives had it happened? What was the remedy? Notes? Videotaping everything? The differences didn't usually matter, but today they were critical.

"No, he was happy. He wanted another chance, another kid."

Aline made a face. "A redo? Yuck."

"He wasn't a bad dad."

"That's not . . . Ah, what's the point?" Miranda unwrapped the sandwich she'd bought. They refreshed the egg salad in the vending machines once a day, right? Not that she should even be eating this, but there weren't any vegan options and she was starving. She took a bite and closed her eyes to savor it. Why had she given up eating eggs, exactly? Oh, right. Because Aline had become convinced that their eating habits were destroying the world and it was easier to go along with her than to stand up on her own. Like so many things. "Anyway, Kim lost the baby a few days later."

"And?"

"You don't feel bad for her at all?"

"No, Miranda," Aline said, her arms crossed, her expression set. "I do not."

"That's cold."

"Did she give a shit about Mom when she slept with Dad? I don't think so."

"Is this the point?" Emily said. "She lost the baby. What does that have to do with anything?"

"Well, it was the reason Dad was pushing so hard for the divorce, and then it went away. The immediacy, anyway. But he, um, he told me they were going to start trying again as soon as Kim was able, and he still needed the divorce."

"So you made a trade?" Aline asked, eyeing Miranda's sandwich with disdain.

Miranda took another large bite, meeting Aline's eyes as she did so. "This is good."

Emily leaned forward. "Miranda."

"Right, so, yeah, they were trying to have a baby. Dad still wanted the divorce. He asked me to help him with that."

"How?"

"By moving into Mom's and seeing if I could get information on her that would give him leverage."

"What kind of leverage could he possibly think you could find?"

Miranda sat back in her chair. "He was never clear on that, actually. He just said to report on what was going on in the house, if she did anything suspicious."

"And in exchange?"

"I asked him to pay off my loans."

"And he agreed."

"Yes, I already told you."

Aline narrowed her eyes. "How did you convince Mom to let you move in?"

"I asked."

"That simple?"

Miranda scrunched the cellophane from her sandwich in her hand. "There may have been some groveling."

Miranda thought back to the conversation she'd had with her mother when she'd asked to move in. How she'd told her over and over that she was right, and *it wouldn't happen again*. When Jennifer had continued to be reluctant, Miranda used her nuclear weapon: *Wouldn't it be so much better to have someone else in the house?* Miranda knew Jennifer was lonely—how could she not be after living with Jake for so long? It had worked. It had come with cautions and promises and time limits, but Jennifer had let her in.

A wolf in her daughter's clothing.

"You told her what she wanted to hear, right?" Emily said. "That Dad was a jerk and you weren't ever going to speak to him again. That you were on her side, unconditionally."

Miranda felt caught. She'd said all those things too. It wasn't a proud moment. None of it was. "That's right."

"That's pretty terrible," Aline said.

"Well, it was mostly true."

"Sure. Mostly. Because that's what Mom needed. Another person lying to her living under her roof."

"Oh, fuck off, Aline. At least I'm nice to Mom. I don't act like she ruined my life or anything."

"Your mistake."

"Meaning?"

"We'll get there. What did you tell Dad?"

A group of young doctors walked in, laughing at something, then stopped short when they saw they weren't alone. Emily watched them approach the vending machines, nudging each other in the ribs as they made their selections.

"Do you miss being in the hospital?" Miranda asked Emily.

"What? No. It's fine."

"What did you tell Dad?" Aline asked again.

"Nothing important. I'd email him once a week about what she was up to. He wanted to know everything. What she ate. How she was feeling. All about Andrew. How often she saw the boys. It was weird, but harmless."

"Doesn't sound so harmless, given everything."

"Well, no, not now that I know . . ."

Emily continued to watch the doctors. "Did he ever react to what you sent him?"

"Not really. I mean, he was concerned when I told him she was recovering from something when I first moved in. But after a while, I wasn't even sure he was reading my emails anymore."

"But you kept on doing it."

"I'd agreed. I'd agreed to do it for a year."

"And yet, you're still there."

Miranda looked at her hands. "I told Dad I'd stay on for the summer and then that was it."

"So he still wanted you there?"

"I think Kim might be pregnant again."

"Fucking hell," Aline said.

"Are you sure?" Emily asked.

"No, it's just a vibe I got. I was going to move out in June, but he asked me to stay. Said he'd pay for the club, give me a chance to save up some money so I could get my own place."

"Which you've totally been doing," Aline said.

"I'm going to say 'fork' if you don't leave it alone."

"Do what you want. You know the consequences."

"I didn't though. Not when I agreed. I didn't know what was going to happen to Mom. And Dad didn't either. I swear."

"He thought something, though," Emily said. "Why else would he be asking how she felt? How *you* felt?"

"I agree," Aline said. "And I have an idea about that, but we need more information."

Miranda furrowed her brow. "What? Why?"

"Because someone did poison Mom, and I think Dad can tell us who."

Chapter 36

BLANK SPACE

Emily

Emily stood in the hospital parking lot watching the sun rise. The day was already warm, July rolling into the Pacific Northwest like a cresting wave. It almost made her long for the wetter months to come, even though the endless gray days between October and March often left her feeling low.

She'd stepped out of the hospital to call Chris and check in on the kids. She felt disconnected from him and the boys. With them in camp all day, they came home exhausted, their demands less than usual. They fell half asleep in their nightly baths and tumbled into bed without even demanding a story. She couldn't think of the last time she and Chris had had any time alone together. Their nighttime conversations where she caught him up on the continuing drama with her mother didn't feel like they counted.

She texted him to see if he was up, and he responded by calling.

"Did I wake you?"

"Nah. Ethan threw up a few hours ago."

"Why didn't you call?"

"Because you've got enough to handle, and I can deal with it." There was an edge to Chris's voice. This wasn't how he imagined this summer, she knew. Before Jennifer got sick, they'd meant to take a long family trip through the States, meandering from town to town, camping wherever the day took them. The school year took a lot out of him and he needed the break, needed the outdoors. Camp had been as much for him as for her, she knew, giving him time to train for a marathon, his long runs taking him from one edge of Surrey to the other.

"Sorry," Emily said.

"No, I'm sorry. Just tired."

"I know."

"I miss you."

"Same. This will all be over soon."

"Did something happen?"

Emily's throat felt tight at Chris's concern. "Nothing new. She never had much time. They said it wouldn't be long now. A week or two."

"I'm so sorry."

"I know."

"You want me to come there?"

Emily wiped away her tears. "Could you keep the boys home from camp today and bring them over?"

"Do you think that's a good idea?"

"I don't know, Chris. But she wanted to say goodbye, and we haven't managed it yet. I think they're strong. I think they'll be okay."

"And you?"

Was she strong enough to watch her kids say goodbye to the

grandmother that they had no reason *not* to love? "I have to go do something with Aline. Miranda will be here."

There was silence on the line. The reality was it would be easier for Chris to do it. He loved Jennifer, sure, but she wasn't his mother. It was a big ask, though.

"Why don't you bring them by around ten?" Emily said. "I'll be back then."

"Where are you going?"

"Aline and I are going to talk to my dad."

"Why?"

"I'll explain tonight, okay?"

"Okay." Chris sounded troubled.

"Look, don't make it a big deal for the boys, all right? Don't dress them up or anything. They know Grandma is sick. Just tell them she wants to see them, and that they should be brave."

"And you'll be there?"

"Yes, I promise."

She hung up the call with those words on her lips. So many promises.

It wasn't possible to keep all of them.

Emily hadn't been inside her dad's new house since he moved in, though she'd driven by out of curiosity after he built it. Was the lack of a visit a conscious decision? She wasn't sure. She only knew that when it was time to have their Christmas lunch, she'd asked that it take place in a restaurant, somewhere where the family didn't have any memories.

While the house was in the neighborhood they'd grown up in, she didn't like the look of it. She'd felt that way when she'd done her drive-by, too. Their house—Jennifer's house—was all soft surfaces and comfort, but this house was modern, cold. That was the look their father was giving them in the kitchen, too, her and Aline. It was "early for a visit" he'd said when he'd answered Emily's text, even though he was up. He was always up at six. It used to be to work, and now it was to work out. He had a young partner now, Emily supposed. He had to take off the belly fat and get active to keep up with her.

Emily shivered. She was sitting on a hard stool at the marbled kitchen island. Aline was next to her on a matching one. Miranda had been left behind to look after Jennifer as her *punishment*, Aline had said. Emily hadn't put up a fight. They all needed to be punished in one way or another. And who was to say visiting her dad wasn't punishment?

"To what do I owe the pleasure, girls?" Jake said. He was using his formal voice, the one he used at parties and when he was trying to woo clients. Emily had heard it enough times the summers she'd worked in his office growing up. It wasn't a voice she liked. And if she was honest, Jake wasn't a man she liked very much. Had she always felt that way? Or was it everything that had happened in the last few years that had turned her thoughts about him dark?

"We have some questions," Aline said.

"About?" Jake ran his hands through his hair. It was still thick, and the weight he'd lost made him look younger than he had before. But he was still their dad. Too old for a girl who was only a few years older than them.

"Mom."

"Is she all right?"

"No, obviously not."

Jake looked pained. "I'm sorry. That wasn't what I meant."

"What did you mean?"

"Why so hostile, Aline?"

"Because we're sick of the bullshit and we want some answers."

Jake raised his coffee cup to his lips. He'd offered, but they'd both declined. Emily felt as if she'd drunk enough coffee for a week. She was keyed up and frazzled. She needed sleep. Time to think. Time to recover.

"About?"

"We know about your deal with Miranda."

Jake lowered his mug. "Is that why she's not here?"

"She's with Mom," Emily said. "Mom's in the hospital."

"I'm sorry to hear that."

"I find that hard to believe," Aline said.

"It's true."

"That's why you sent in Miranda to spy on her in her own house. Or worse."

Jack placed his hands on the counter as his face reddened. "Not this again. For the love of God, I didn't do anything to hurt your mother."

"That's not true. You hurt her a lot."

"I only meant . . . I'm not responsible for what's happening to her now." Jake rested his elbows on the counter. It was white, like the one in their own kitchen, but without the gray marbling that warmed it up. "Can we stop this?"

"Stop what?" Aline asked.

"Talking in circles. You obviously have something you want to ask me, so do it."

"And you'll be honest with us?"

"Yes."

Aline huffed, but went ahead anyway. "Did you poison Mom last year?"

"No, absolutely not." Jake looked at Aline for a moment, then at Emily. To prove his sincerity, Emily guessed, but she didn't know anything about detecting when someone was lying. He sounded sincere and more like himself.

"But you had some plan for her, right?" Emily said. "That's why you had Miranda in the house?"

"Yes. As you know, Kim was pregnant."

"And is again, I heard."

Jake's face lit up. "Yes. We'll find out the sex next week."

"Ugh," Aline said. "I hope it's a boy."

"Whoever he or she is, they won't replace you."

"Oh really?" Aline looked around the kitchen and at the glistening new appliances. The house looked like a show home, nothing lived-in about it. "Isn't that what this is all about? A replacement life? A replacement family? Don't like the old one, so just wipe it all away and start over?"

That hit close to the bone, Emily could tell.

"That's not what I wanted."

Emily put her hand on Aline's arm. "We didn't come here for this."

"Right, okay. So what was the plan, then, Dad? Why send Miranda in?"

Jake's head drooped. "I'm not proud of this."

"We know you wanted her to dig up dirt on Mom for the divorce," Emily said. "And by the way, that's gross. But what we don't understand is why you thought there'd be any dirt to find."

Jake slumped down on his arms. "I was under a lot of pressure."

"Okay."

"I didn't see it. Or if I did, I didn't understand it."

"Dad, what the fuck are you talking about?"

Jake looked up. "How much do you remember about when your mother was sick when you were kids?"

"We know she didn't have cancer and that she went to a psychiatric facility," Emily said. "Bea told us recently, and Mom confirmed it. Is that what you wanted to use over her? I don't get it. You already knew that."

"No, I . . . How much do you remember about before she went away?"

Aline nodded as if she knew this was where the conversation was going. "I remember some things, I think."

Emily turned to look at Aline. Her face was set in anger. "What, Aline? What do you remember?"

Aline kept looking at Jake. "I remember all those times Mom used to give us medicine, but it never made us feel better, only worse. How often we went to the hospital and the doctor. I think that Mom was making us sick. Doing it on purpose. Is that right, Dad? Is that why she went away?"

Jake's hands started to shake on the counter, but he looked at them steadily. "I didn't know it at the time, but . . . yes."

Chapter 37

WHY CAN'T I SAY GOODNIGHT?

Jennifer

"**H**ey, can we come in?"

A soft rap at the door. It's Chris, and before I can nod yes, Ethan and Noah barrel into the room.

"Boys! Careful."

They stop short at the edge of my hospital bed, their eyes wide, their energy palpable. Ethan's wearing a seersucker jacket and khaki shorts. Noah's in a T-shirt and soccer shorts. Ethan's always cared about what he's wearing, ever since he could voice an opinion. Noah couldn't care less.

"Hello, little men," I say, the way I always greet them.

"Hi, Ganma!" Ethan bellows.

I push myself up and try to straighten my hair. I wish I had a bit of warning that the boys were coming. They look like they've grown a few inches in the last month, though that can't be the case. It hits me that the reason they're here now is that the end is nigh. I know this—my body is screaming it at me every minute—but it's still so hard to sink in.

"Can I have a hug?"

"Sure!" Ethan says, then tugs on Noah's arm. Noah looks hesitant, put off by the surroundings.

I open my arms and they walk into them, climbing up on the bed so they're on either side. I breathe in their little-boy smell, and feel their soft skin pressing into me. They are the opposite of me, boys who have their whole lives ahead of them instead of the few short weeks or days left to me.

I can't believe I'm not going to be there to see them grow up.

I'm angry about a lot of things, but I'm angry about that most of all.

"Have you seen Emily?" Chris asks. He's hanging by the entrance, wearing a polo and khaki shorts. His arms and face are tanned, and his dark hair could use a cut.

"She had to do some errands I think."

Chris nods, then sits in the visitor's chair. He looks like everyone who talks to me does these days. Sad, worried, tired. It will be a relief when I'm gone, though Chris and I have always gotten along. He's a better man than Jake, I think, though up to now they've been confronted with the same problems and made the same choices. Keep the babies, get married, settle down. Is he going to break Emily's heart in twenty years and leave her for some new teacher at his school? Finally, something I don't want to know.

"I want Emily to finish her degree this year. Make sure that happens, all right?"

Chris shakes his head. "I don't think that's up to me."

"Sure it is. I know you're supportive, but she needs a push. She worries about being away from the boys, working too hard . . . But it's what she was meant to be."

"Have you talked to Emily about this?"

"I offered to pay her tuition, but she pushed me off. But there'll be enough money, just so you know. You'll have enough to get help, too."

Chris runs his hand over his face.

"I like school," Noah says.

I look down at his dark brown eyes. "Do you, sweetheart?"

"We don't go to school," Ethan says. "We go to play!"

I laugh. "That sounds like fun."

"It is fun. So much fun."

"Well, enjoy it while you can, boys. Soon you'll have to be in school like Mommy."

Ethan cocks his head to the side. "Mommy no go to school."

I smile at him. "Sure she does. She goes when you go to play."

"Nuh-uh. She no go." He leans closer to my ear and whispers. "It's a secret."

"Oh?"

"Yeth. Mommy and Daddy yelled."

He pulls away and his eyes are round. The yelling scared him, and the thought of it, the reason, is scaring me. I hug him for a moment to gather my thoughts, then look at Chris. He heard what Noah said, and I can see the truth in his eyes.

"She's stopped going to her med school classes?"

"Yes."

"When?"

"Last spring. But I only found out this year, a few months ago."

"Is Mommy in trouble?" Ethan asks, then plops his thumb in his mouth.

"No, honey, of course not."

I look up at Chris and mouth, *Is she?*

He shrugs his shoulders. "She said she wasn't into it anymore. That when she went back, she'd lost her passion for it."

I place my hands over the kids' ears, pressing them to me. "Because of the depression?"

"Maybe."

"Why did she keep it from you?"

"I guess she was embarrassed."

"You must've been mad when you found out? Her keeping a secret for that long?"

Chris hesitates. It's not any of my business, but I can tell that he wants to talk about it. The relief of a secret released.

"I wasn't happy, that's for sure. Ethan's right. We had a massive argument about it."

"I just don't get it," I say. "What was she doing instead?"

"Not much, as far as I know. Catching up on sleep. Taking care of stuff around the house. Which is fine. She needed a break. I get it. I just wish . . ."

"She'd told you."

"Yeah."

Ethan wiggles around and I take my hands off their ears. The boys are being remarkably good, not punching one another or climbing all over me like they usually do. It's such a comfort to have them next to me. And now my final minutes with them are ticking down.

I close my eyes, feeling as if I'm drifting away.

"You all right?" Chris asks.

"I'm tired. Worn out."

"Do you need the nurse?"

"No, not right now. I think . . . I think I'll go to sleep."

"Do you want me to take the boys?"

I open my eyes and look down again at their silken heads.

Ethan blinks at me. "Don't cry, Ganma."

"Okay, I won't. I love you."

"Love you too."

"Me too!" Noah says. "So much."

"So much," I agree.

My vision is cloudy as I meet Chris's eyes. They're filled with tears too.

"Let them stay until I'm asleep, okay?"

"I will."

"Take care of them."

"Of course. And Emily too."

"Thank you."

I close my eyes and listen to the boys' breathing.

In and out. In and out.

In

And

Out

I open my eyes with regret.

I don't want to be here, in the hospital. I don't want to have to go through whatever tests and concerns are in front of me. I mostly want this all to be over. The suspicion. The regret. The secrets revealed and hidden.

I'm alone in my room and I feel groggy. There's an IV in my arm and a cord with a call button at the end tied around the edge of my bed frame, within reach. I press the button and wait, thinking of how I pressed the panic alarm that day I learned I was dying. Summoning help. Is that what I'm doing this time?

Help doesn't come.

Instead, it's Jake.

"Hi," he says shyly. He looks as ragged as I feel, the first time in a long time that I've seen him anything less than entirely put together. I don't want him seeing me like this, though. Worn down and helpless.

"What are you doing here?"

"The girls came to see me."

I look past him, expecting to see their familiar faces fill up the entrance to my room, but it's empty.

My throat is scratchy, and it hurts to swallow. I reach for my water cup. Jake hands it to me and I take a sip from the straw. The water burns, but also brings relief.

"Why?"

Jake runs his hand over his close-cropped head. "Do you mind if I sit?"

"I guess not."

But I do mind. This man is dangerous. I grip the call button in my hand. If he tries anything, help is close by.

He pulls the one chair in the room away from the wall until it's close to my bed and sits in it. I feel vulnerable and exhausted as I sip water. Here he is. Jake. The man I've been so convinced tried to kill me. Only, now that he's here, he's just Jake, a man I've known so long I can easily paint him into moments he was never ever a part of.

"Where are the girls?"

"They wanted to give us some time alone."

"Why?"

Jake rubs his head again. A sure sign of stalling. Anger rises in my chest. Goddamn it. I know so much about him, but I have no idea whether my pre-knowledge is something that makes it easier to know him or less. My mind is all confused. Part of me still loves him even while the rest of me hates him.

And he knows it.

He knows it and he'll use it against me if he can.

"They had some questions. They wanted to know . . . I owe you some explanations."

"About?"

"Why I wanted the divorce so badly."

I look away. "I heard."

He makes a noise in his throat. It sounds like grief. "Will you let me explain?"

I raise my shoulders slightly in surrender. What choice do I have? Where can I go? "You wanted the divorce because Kim was pregnant."

"Yes. In part."

"And the other part?"

"I think I wanted to punish you."

I realize I've been clenching my hands against the sheets. I let go. "Why?"

"Because you wouldn't give me what I wanted."

"To let you walk away without a fuss?"

"Yes."

"Why would you expect me to do that?"

Jake shrugs. "Because you always have in the past."

He's right. I wasn't the aggressor in our marriage. Usually, if he wanted something badly enough, I'd give in. But this . . . Did he truly think I'd shrug the way he did just now and accept that he was leaving me after more than twenty years together? That I'd understand the affair? That I'd forgive him?

"Jake. Seriously?"

He looks at me again, tired, sad, a bit shocked at himself. "Yes, I know. But you know how I am once I get an idea into my head. I thought one thing and you did another, and I was angry."

"You wanted to win."

"I like to win."

"You can't win in divorce." But I thought I could. I thought I was winning. Stupid me.

"I know that now, but it took me an awful long time to get there. I'm sorry."

I wait. "Can I ask you something? Did you change a section of pipe in the basement? The one in the storage room."

Jake thinks for a moment. "Yes, I did. Maybe six months before I moved out. Why?"

"It doesn't matter. And Miranda?"

Now he looks ashamed. It might be real, it might be how he's truly feeling, but it also might be fake. Jake is good at faking emotions. It's one of the reasons he's so good in court, his power to emote whatever he needs to convince a judge. I've seen him do it. Go from scoffing at his clients' concerns to me privately to turning in a performance that would make you think his clients' troubles were his own.

So maybe he is ashamed, or maybe he wants me to think he is.

"When you wouldn't give in, I thought Miranda could help me."

"How, exactly?"

"By letting me know if you were doing anything that could be used as a pressure point."

"Spying on me."

"Yes."

I turn away from him and face the wall. There are so many things that are wrong with what he's saying, my mind can't focus. I am all mixed-up emotions. Sad, angry, confused.

"Why, Jake? What made you think there was something to find?"

He clears his throat. "It was when you texted me last year that you'd taken the boys to the hospital."

I turn my head back with effort. The headache's building again despite the relief dripping into my arm. I squeeze the call button. I could press it over and over and end this conversation right here and now.

I should.

"You didn't come to the hospital," I say.

"No, I didn't."

"So?"

"I was worried. It had me worried. About the boys. About you."

Bile rises up my throat. No. No, no, no, no, no.

"I would never hurt the boys," I whisper. "Jake, come on."

"I want to believe that."

"But you can't? Why?"

"You know why."

I feel like I'm falling right through the bed. Or that might be a wish.

"You knew?" I say eventually, my voice barely audible.

Jake nods, then stops. "I didn't know for sure. I suspected, when you said you needed help. And then, over the years, I put two and two together."

Three and three, he means. Three girls. We have three.

"You never asked me about it."

"How was I supposed to bring that up? You didn't tell me."

"I couldn't. I couldn't lose everything."

I'd kept my secrets. But they were back with a vengeance now.

"Why didn't you just tell me you knew, to get the divorce?"

He shakes his head. "I didn't have any proof. And I'd be implicating myself if you fought me. Because I never called child services. I let you come home and take care of the girls."

"I never did anything to them again. Never."

"I know."

I close my eyes. I am so tired I can barely make my mouth move. "So that's why you sent Miranda in? To see if I was . . . if I'd relapsed?"

"Yes."

"If I had, you'd use that to get the divorce."

"Yes."

"Did you tell Miranda? Is that why she did it? Does she know?"

"No."

I feel relieved, but only for a moment. If Miranda knew what I'd done, then this would all make more sense. The fact that she went along with Jake's plan without knowing. I don't know what to do with that.

"But they know now," he says.

"What?"

"The girls. Aline and Emily, anyway. I told them this morning."

Oh no, no, no.

Chapter 38

THE WORLD SPINS MADLY ON

Aline

When Aline was six, she and her sisters went to Disney World with their parents. It was an all-expenses-paid trip because Disney was promoting some new version of *The Parent Trap* that involved triplets and not twins. It was weird, their triplet fame. Usually multiples had to come in fives and sixes to get anyone's attention. But something about them drew people in. The oddness of being a set of identical twins inside triplets. The fact that they didn't even look related. Their beauty, even then. Their very different personalities. It had a snowball effect. One local photo shoot led to a local TV appearance that led to a regional one and on up to the *Today* show.

And then Disney World. Aline and her sisters were beside themselves with excitement. They had the run of the park with the eight other sets of triplets and a camera crew. All the others were dressed identically and spoke as if they'd learned a script. Only the Gagnon girls were free to be themselves, it seemed, each of them dressed differently, though everyone got Aline and Miranda confused anyway.

It was the first time they'd roamed free without their parents. They were there, but with the minders and the other triplets and the crew, they took a back seat. It was so much fun to fly around the park, the sun on their skin, their special park bracelets letting them on ride after ride. They ate and rode and laughed themselves sick.

It all came crashing to a halt when Aline decided to do dares with another triplet rebel, Chasten. It started out with small stuff. Skipping stones into the lake, trying to get past the age gate on one of the rides. It finally ended with them jumping stairs, going up one, two, and then three until Aline crashed to the ground, her wrist limp beneath her.

Tears. Someone screaming for her mother. Worried frowns among the camera crew who'd watched them doing their feats with bemused expressions on their faces. Then her mother was there, and Aline was being assessed by a doctor. Her wrist was broken and needed to be set. It hurt, and her tears were dried on her face. She wanted an ice cream.

She got one.

The rest of the day was spent with Jennifer at the hospital, waiting for X-rays, Aline getting her arm encased in a hard plaster with a pink coating to it, even though she told the doctor that she hated pink. Everyone fussed over her and Jennifer. The camera crew even followed them around, intent on building her accident into the story line if possible.

Looking back on it now, Aline wondered if she sensed her mother's weird energy at the time. Jennifer was comforting, she always was, but there was something else. *I love hospitals*, Aline remembered her saying, one of those statements that clings to memory. *Did you know I was supposed to be a doctor?* That was the first time she'd told Aline that. Her mother pooh-poohed any suggestion that it was the triplets' fault that she wasn't the one putting the cast on. The nurses were in her thrall. She told them how she had kept at her coursework through her pregnancy and gave up the dream only when the three babies arrived. *Maybe I'll go back one day*, she mused.

They signed Aline's cast and discharged her with instructions about when to go back to the doctor once they were home to get it off. In the van back to Disney, Jennifer held Aline's good hand and looked out the window, her toe tapping to the country music twanging through the radio. When they arrived back at their hotel, Jennifer helped her out of the van and pulled her into a tight hug.

"Wasn't that an amazing adventure?" Jennifer asked, her eyes sparkling with delight.

Even at six, Aline knew that wasn't right.

"Did you know?" Emily asked Aline in the car on the way back to the hospital.

They were driving in Aline's old beater, the same car she'd had since she was eighteen, when Bea had given up driving and passed on her fifteen-year-old car to her. Aline's hands were gripping the wheel tightly; she was scared about what she might do if she let go.

"I remembered some stuff."

"Like?"

"How often we went to the hospital when we were six, seven, eight. None of my other friends lived in the ER like us."

"Mom's a hypochondriac."

"I don't think so. Besides, it stopped when she came back from treatment. I think she has that disease where you make people sick to get attention."

"Munchausen by proxy?"

"Yes."

They passed a stand of trees. Aline wished she could roll down the window and breathe in their scent, but it was sweltering outside, her air-conditioning barely keeping up.

"You don't remember?" Aline asked.

"No, I didn't," Emily said quietly. "You think this means that Mom did this to herself?"

"Stands to reason, doesn't it? I mean, I don't know much about Munchausen's or whatever the fuck she has, but it's attention-seeking behavior, right?"

"I don't know."

"Google it, then."

Emily pulled out her phone. "Oh shit. I'm in trouble."

"What? Why?"

"I was supposed to be at the hospital by ten so I could be there when Chris brought the boys in to see Mom."

Aline checked the clock on the dashboard. It was ten thirty. They'd been longer with Jake than they realized, going over the past with him until he spilled every detail he could remember, and explained why he kept it to himself all these years.

"Chris is pissed."

"He'll get over it. What does Google say?"

Emily tapped at her phone. "It's a 'mental health problem in which a caregiver makes up or causes an illness or injury in a person under his or her care, such as a child, an elderly adult, or a person who has a disability. Because vulnerable people are the victims, MBP is a form of child abuse or elder abuse.'"

"What causes it?"

"Apparently, the cause is unknown. But risk factors include having complications in pregnancy, or a mother who was abused herself as a child, or was also a victim of 'factitious disorder.'"

"What's that?"

"What they call MBP now I guess."

"But she got treatment for that, right? And it seemed to work. I don't remember anything ever happening since then. Do you?"

"No."

"What prompted it to start up again? Assuming that's what happened?"

"Dad, obviously."

Aline clicked on her turn indicator, following the road signs for the hospital. "Okay, sure, stress, that makes sense. But why tell everyone about it? Why not make a big deal last year when she got sick?"

"Maybe she had second thoughts."

Aline frowned. Something about this was off. "No, let's think this through. The separation was super hard on Mom, we all know that. So, based on what you read to me before, it makes sense that this kind of trauma could cause a relapse. And since we were all grown up—Oh."

"What?"

"Something Dad said before . . . Do you think she hurt the boys?"

"No!"

"Okay, okay, calm down. But what about that thing he mentioned, when Ethan hurt himself?"

"Ethan fell in the park. Mom didn't have anything to do with that."

"No, but . . . stay with me here. Remember when we went to Disney World?"

"Sure."

"I broke my wrist."

Emily gave a thin smile. "You had that terrible cast that you hated in all the footage. It was the only way they could tell you and Miranda apart."

"Right. And Mom came with me to the hospital."

"So?"

"I think it was some kind of trigger for her. She was excited to be there, you know? She thought it was an adventure that we'd gone on. That's what she said."

"Come on, Aline. You were six."

"I remember, okay?"

Aline took her next left and pulled into the short-term parking lot. She rolled down her window to grab a ticket from the dispenser, then shoved it onto her dashboard. The heat rolled in like a punch.

"This weather is the worst." Aline closed her window. "Anyway, that's what happened. And based on other stuff I remember and what Dad said, I think that's when it started. I think that's when she started doing stuff on purpose to us."

"Stuff like?"

"Remember when we all had terrible food poisoning when we were seven?"

Emily shuddered. "That was bad."

"Maybe it was just poisoning."

Emily looked out the window. "What does that have to do with the boys?"

"Well, what about if when Ethan got hurt that day, it brought it all back. She felt that same charge or energy or whatever it is that being the center of attention in a hospital gave her, but she didn't have kids anymore. And if she hurt Ethan and Noah . . . I mean, I'm sure she didn't want to hurt them."

"So, she hurt herself instead?"

"Yeah," Aline said. "I think so."

"But she went to the doctor. She had those tests."

Aline rolled through the parking lot slowly, looking for a space. "Right, but that makes sense. She gave herself something, maybe more than once. It would have to be, to match the test results. Not sure what her initial plan was, but maybe she took too much. Made herself too sick. That must've put her off the whole thing."

"So why go to the doctor?"

"She must've been worried that she'd done some permanent damage."

"But she didn't do the follow-up tests."

"She was feeling better, right? And if she'd done the follow-ups, she would have been discovered, potentially. Lead poisoning is rare. A doctor would want to get to the bottom of it. So she called the doctor and told him she was getting a second opinion."

Aline found a parking space and eased the car into it. She left the engine running, environment be damned. The heat was unbearable. Anyone who didn't believe in climate change was an idiot.

Emily undid her seat belt, letting it slap back into the car's wall. "So, she was the one who called her doctor and said she was getting a second opinion elsewhere?"

"Stands to reason, doesn't it? The call came from the house. Who else is supposed to have done that?"

"It was right around when Miranda moved in, wasn't it?"

Aline met Emily's eyes, wishing she could peer into her brain. "You think Miranda did it?"

"No, of course not. I'm just trying to understand what your theory is."

"Okay."

Emily turned away. "*You* thought Miranda did it."

Aline's hands slipped off the steering wheel into her lap. "I thought it was possible, for sure. She's such a liar. Who knew?"

"Everyone's a liar."

"What's that supposed to mean?"

"We all lie in little ways, big ways. That's how you get through life."

"Are you talking about something specific?"

"It's a general observation."

"I didn't peg you for a cynic."

Emily shrugged. "What do we do now?"

"You think we should confront Mom?"

"No."

"Why not?"

"Because she's being punished enough, don't you think?" Emily opened her car door. "I need to get in there, or Chris is going to freak out."

"What should I do?"

"I can't tell you that, Aline. But my advice is to let it go. Mom doesn't have much time left." Emily scrambled out. She shut the door behind her firmly and walked toward the hospital entrance without looking back.

Aline watched her walk away, her mind full of questions. Was her theory right? Had Jennifer moved from hurting others to hurting herself? Did it matter? Emily had a point. If she was the one responsible, she was paying the ultimate price.

Who was Aline to try to make her pay more than that?

Chapter 39

THE END OF THE LINE

Jennifer

Days pass in a haze. I think it's Thursday. Then the nurse in the hospice that I've been moved to tells me no, it's Friday. That means I've lost three days. Three days of a dozen left. That's a lot.

But today I feel clearer. I feel hungry. I wake up alert, feeling as if I don't belong in this warehouse for the dying. I take myself to the bathroom, weak from having eaten so little. I drag my IV line with me, wishing I could rip it out. I suppose I could. There's no law keeping me here. I could ask them to take me to my house and never be seen again. Would that be fair? Who cares? Who is there left to be fair to?

Instead, when the nurse comes in looking concerned, I insist on taking a shower and changing into fresh pajamas that were left by one of the girls, probably Emily. They've all been in and out of here—this much I know—their expectation hanging in the air in the brief conversations I managed. Except for my mother. She came the first day—Tuesday, I guess it was—her teary self back in place, hugged me hard enough for me to feel it through the haze, told me she loved me and then left. I haven't seen her since.

I don't answer the girls' questions about what I did to them exactly. How I could do anything to harm them. Why I didn't get help earlier. I don't owe them answers. After I got well, I did right by them. I did what I could. I don't have the energy to convince them otherwise.

The hospice isn't much different than the hospital, only quieter, less beeping and coming and going. I'm in a room by myself, but the showers are down the hall, a communal room, like in college. I have it all to myself today, though, just me and the nurse.

The water is hot and courses over my body like a balm. I stand in it as long as I can, then change into my pajamas with only a little assistance from the nurse. I comb out my hair and braid it loosely. I feel more human than I have in a while.

I shuffle slowly down the hall, holding on to the nurse's arm. This place is so quiet compared to the hospital. Everything seems to happen in slow motion. Is this where it's all going to end? And how? Me alone, the consequence of things I did so long ago?

"Hey, friend."

"Oh, Suzie!" She's standing next to my bed, sun-kissed in a loose cotton dress I know she wears when she feels like she's been eating too much. She looks shy and nervous, and I'm so glad she is here. "I'm so happy to see you," I say, falling into her arms as emotions rip through me.

She holds me tight against her. She smells like the ocean. "Oh God, Jenn. I came as soon as I got home. I never should have gone on that trip."

"It's okay. I told you to."

"I shouldn't have listened."

"You're right."

She lets me go as she laughs. She knows I'm mostly joking and that the rest doesn't matter.

"I brought you lunch."

"Pasta?"

"Oh yes."

"Thank you."

She puts the bed into an upright position and helps me back into it, then swings the meal tray toward me. The most delicious smells are coming from the brown bag sitting on the end of the bed, and I know what's inside before she hands it to me. Pappardelle Bolognese and Dungeness crab arancini from my favorite—our favorite—Italian restaurant, Pasta Vino.

"Is there wine, too?"

She grins guiltily and reaches into her purse. She pulls out a half bottle of a red we've shared a million times.

"Close the door."

She laughs again in conspiracy and does as I ask. Then she cracks open the twist top on the bottle. I don't know if we're breaking the rules and I don't care. What are they going to do? Kick me out of hospice?

Suzie dishes out two servings onto the plates that came with the order and fills up two plastic cups with wine. It takes an act of will not to eat like an animal, not to groan in pleasure when I take a bite of the pasta, and drink the wine, each mouthful satisfying me in a way I haven't been in a while. When I'm done, I lie back in the bed, my hands on my belly like I used to do when I was pregnant. I'm pregnant with food, I guess, and the glow of a good red wine.

"Better?" Suzie asks. She has a ring of sauce around her mouth and I hand her a napkin so she can clean herself up. Suzie's always been a messy eater—it's one of her endearing qualities.

"Yes, thank you." I feel drowsy from the food and the alcohol, but I do feel better. I feel almost normal. An illusion, surely.

"Sorry, again, for leaving."

"You're here now."

"I am."

Silence unfolds. Then Suzie clears away our plates and refills our cups with the last of the wine.

"Where are the girls?"

"Not sure. They've been . . . Things are not good."

"Why? I mean, besides the obvious."

I close my eyes, the cup resting on my belly. "Some stuff has come out. Stuff from the past."

"Like what?"

"Things from when they were kids. Before you knew me." Suzie and I met when we moved into the new house after I got back from treatment. One day she was the friendly neighbor who brought me a banana bread. The next she felt indispensable. Some people in your life are like that.

"Is this connected to what you wanted me to look for after . . ."

I open my eyes. The room is blurry, like I need glasses, which I don't usually. My vision is getting worse each day. Remarkably, I don't seem to care that much. This might be the grace note of dying—being able to finally let go.

"No, I don't think so. I mean there is all of that, but this is something else."

"All of what?"

"I thought Jake was trying to kill me."

Suzie chokes on her wine. "What?"

"Last year. But I didn't suspect it until I was diagnosed."

"What?"

"I was poisoned."

Suzie looks around her, as if she's hoping for someone to come and rescue her.

"I'm not crazy."

"I didn't say that."

"Your eyes did though."

Suzie's shoulders come down from where they'd shot up around her ears. "I'm sorry, I didn't mean . . . Tell me what's been happening."

I close my eyes again and fill her in. The illness last year, the doctor's visit, the tests, how the symptoms receded. How they came back, but a hundredfold. The lead in my blood, the phone logs, my finger-pointing at Jake.

"I can't believe you've kept all this from me."

"I'm sorry."

"No," Suzie says. "I'm proud of you. A couple of years ago . . ."

"I wouldn't have been able to go through this alone?"

"Frankly, no."

I nod because Suzie is right. Two years ago, I was weak as a kitten. But despite everything, I'm stronger now. Fat good it will do me.

"I can't believe Miranda was spying on you."

"I know."

"Do you think she's involved in all of this?"

"I don't know. Maybe I've imagined it."

Suzie puts her empty cup down. I wish she'd brought a full bottle and I bet she does too. "Those tests aren't imagined. The calls either."

"Yeah."

"Do you have the papers here?"

"No, they're at home."

"Somewhere safe?"

A sliver of fear pricks through the fog. "Why? You think I'm right?"

"I don't know. It is all suspicious."

"The girls think I'm nuts."

"I'm sorry."

"They're right though."

Suzie crosses her arms over her chest. "We've talked about this. You are not nuts."

"You don't know. There are so many secrets in my family. So many things I never told you. Things I couldn't tell you." I'd wanted to tell her at some point over the years, but how do you start that conversation? *I used to harm my children. Did you want some more wine?*

"Like what?"

I try to form the words, then stop myself. Suzie has stuck by me through everything; I can't lose her too. "Emily dropped out of med school."

"What? When?"

"Last spring, apparently. But no one knew. Not even Chris."

"Why did she hide it?"

"I haven't had a chance to ask. Chris thinks she was embarrassed. But I think it's just the way things are with us. We don't share what's going on in our lives. We keep it to ourselves."

"I never thought that about you guys."

"Me either. But it's obviously true."

Suzie stares off into space for a moment. She does this when she's puzzling out a problem.

"Suze?"

"Yeah?"

"You still with us?"

"Sorry about that. I was just thinking about Emily. Keeping that secret. What was she doing with all that time if she wasn't in class?"

"Chris said not much. Catching up on sleep, mostly."

"I guess that's why she was around your place so much. I didn't think of it then."

"She was?"

"I saw her car in your driveway sometimes on my eleven o'clock walk. I just assumed she was visiting you."

"I guess she was." I pause and take a couple of breaths. "I didn't notice her coming over more than usual . . ."

Suzie frowns. "You look like you need some rest. Should I come again tomorrow?"

"How about Sunday?"

"Any particular reason?"

"Because then I know I'll make it there."

A sob escapes Suzie. I didn't mean to make her cry. I need something to keep me going. A reason to get up in the morning. A reason to stick around a while longer. At least until I resolve things with the girls.

That's what I need tomorrow for.

Suzie leans down and hugs me. "I'm so sorry about all of this."

"Me too."

"I love you."

"Don't say goodbye," I say. "Come on Sunday."

"I will."

She squeezes me tightly once again, and then she's gone.

Chapter 40

WATER IS WIDE

Miranda

Miranda felt more lost than she ever had in her life. She'd felt that way on and off since she'd gotten back from Namibia, but now, with her mother dying and all the ugliness that had been unearthed as a result, she felt as if she had no foundation at all. Nothing she'd thought was true actually was, and everything she thought could never happen, had. Her life was shapeless; even her basic static shape—that she was a triangle, a triplet, always part of something—didn't seem true anymore.

Take Aline. They weren't talking. That had never happened before. Not in their whole life. She'd never stopped talking to Emily before, either, but that felt less core-shaking to Miranda. Yes, they were triplets. Yes, they were sisters. But Aline was *her*, the same person inside out. It just felt different, no matter what anyone said.

Today they were going to have it all out. Jennifer had asked them to visit her at the hospice together, instead of for the individual short visits they'd been making since she'd been moved there on Tuesday. They hadn't discussed it, but it wasn't something they could say no to, like that first call to dinner they'd received the day Jennifer was diagnosed.

So there they all were, midday on a Saturday, gathered around their mother at a picnic table in the backyard of the facility.

This Last Stop, as Miranda thought of it, sat on ten acres in a corner of Surrey that Miranda had never been to before. The streets around it were twisty and not intuitive, so she had to let the GPS on her phone guide her there. She had a bagful of sandwiches that she'd made at the house. She'd moved back in there once her mother had gone into the hospice. Aline hadn't asked her to leave the apartment; she hadn't had to.

She was the last to arrive, even though she was only a few minutes late. It was another scorcher, but the picnic table their mother had asked them to meet at was in a shady spot. As Miranda approached, she caught the fresh smell of the woods that surrounded it. Earth and pine, and behind that a hint of salt from the ocean a few miles away.

Jennifer was wearing a sweatshirt and sweatpants, but she looked better than Miranda had seen her look in a while. Her hair was washed and braided, which made her look young and vulnerable. She'd even put on a bit of makeup. Miranda felt a beat of hope at the color in Jennifer's cheeks. Did the doctors make a mistake? Is that why she had called them there?

"Mom, you look great," Miranda said, moving into the shade. She'd played a hard match at the club that morning in the women's round-robin tournament. Though she'd showered and changed afterward, she still felt heated, and her hair was wet against the back of her neck. Amazingly, she'd been able to focus during her match and had pulled out a win.

"The final rally," Jennifer said, and she probably wasn't referring to tennis.

"What does that mean?"

"It's something that happens, apparently. When things are nearing the end."

Miranda's bubble of hope burst. "Oh. I thought—"

"That you were going to get away with it?"

"Mom!" That was Emily. She was sitting next to Aline on the other side of the picnic table. In contrast to Jennifer, her hair looked limp and as if she hadn't washed it in a couple of days. Her face was free of makeup, and the summer dress she was wearing had a stain above her left breast. She also had dark circles under her eyes, like she had when the boys were first born. It was weird to see put-together Emily like that. It made Miranda nervous.

"Sorry," Jennifer said, but she didn't sound sorry.

"Take a seat, Miranda," Aline said. She was the only one of them who looked normal, with her hair in its pristine ballet bun, and her short-sleeved white blouse crisp and clean despite the heat. But her tone was off, like she was giving commands.

Miranda did as she was asked, sitting next to her mother. "Is this what this is going to be like? Us all making accusations and hating on one another? Because if so, then I'm out."

"No," Emily said. "That's not the point of this. I don't think. Right, Mom?"

Jennifer let out a deep breath. "No. Not the point at all. I'm sorry for what I said earlier, Miranda. That was . . . well, not uncalled for exactly, but unnecessary."

"Okay."

"I wanted . . ." Jennifer laid her hands on the picnic table, turning them over so her palms were up. "I wanted to give us all an opportunity to clear the air, once and for all. I don't think I have much time left, and though I know it's not possible to leave without any regrets, I didn't want to leave you with questions."

"Questions about?" Miranda asked.

"How she made us sick when we were kids," Aline said.

"Wait. What?"

"She doesn't know," Emily said. "Right? You didn't tell her?"

"You made us sick?" Miranda asked Jennifer. "On purpose?"

"I did."

Miranda shifted uncomfortably on the bench. What was going on? She thought that she was coming here to have a make-up lunch with her sisters and her mom, and now, what . . . What? "What the fork is happening?"

Aline clenched her jaw, but Miranda didn't care. They all seemed to know something they were keeping from the others.

"How did you know this? Aline? Emily?"

Aline looked at her, then away. "I remembered some stuff from when we were kids. And then Dad confirmed it when we went to see him when Mom was in the hospital."

Miranda nearly fell off her seat. Her brain felt as if it was on a tilt, one of those rides they loved as a kid when you were suspended at an impossible angle, and gravity pulled at you in a way that felt uncomfortable and scary. How was she supposed to absorb this information?

"Why didn't you tell me?"

Jennifer reached out and touched her arm. "Don't be mad at them. It was me."

Miranda turned toward her mother. "What did you do?"

"Remember how we talked about me suffering from depression? Me having a breakdown?"

"Yes."

"Well, that wasn't the whole truth. I was depressed, I'd probably been depressed for several years, but it was more than that. I had . . . God, this is so hard to say, but I had started to make you girls sick on purpose."

"Why would you do that?"

"It's called Munchausen by proxy."

Emily pulled at the end of her hair. "The technical term now is factitious disorder."

"Is that helpful, Emily?" Aline snapped.

"No, sorry."

"You were hurting us to get attention?" Miranda said. "That's what that is, right?"

Jennifer looked sad. "It's more complicated than that. But yes, I was . . . giving you things that made you need medical attention."

"Things like what?"

"I gave you too much medicine at first, when you had a cold or a cough. Then it progressed into giving you medicine you didn't need. And worse."

Miranda felt a flash of memory. *Open up, Miranda bear. This will taste awful, but it works.*

"You were poisoning us? That's what happened?"

Jennifer's shoulders drooped. "In a way, yes. Until I realized I had a problem."

"You realized?" Aline said in that same bitter tone. "Or you were caught?"

Jennifer looked stricken. "What do you mean?"

"When we saw Dad, he told us how he realized what you were doing. That time that Emily had to go to the hospital because she couldn't stop throwing up. You'd said that she had gotten into the Drano, but the doctors were asking questions. They were about to figure it out, he thinks. So you faked an illness and ran away to rehab or whatever and sent us to live with Bea."

"That's not how it happened."

"So tell us, then."

Jennifer raised her palms up and down on the table as if she were patting it down. "You make it seem as if I knew what I was doing. That I had control over it."

"You did."

"No, it wasn't like that. Just give me a moment and I'll try to explain."

Miranda nodded, then Emily, then Aline, like dominoes.

"You don't know what it was like with the three of you. Maybe you, Emily, have some idea, but I wanted to be a doctor since I was a girl. I studied so hard, you have no idea. I didn't even have a boyfriend in high school because it would get in my way. I took extra classes, tutoring, summer school. Whatever I needed to get perfect GPA and MCAT scores."

Jennifer lifted her head defiantly. "And I made it. I made it in. But that was just the beginning of the hard work. I almost failed my first semester of med school. I couldn't let my dream slip away. So I worked harder. I got my grades up. I made it through.

"But I also met your dad studying in the library one night. He asked me out and I said no. He pursued me. I'd never had anyone be like that with me before. I gave in. I fell in love with him, hard. And he was super supportive of my dreams. He was proud that I wanted to be a doctor. Then I got pregnant. I was so upset. We'd been careful. I considered getting an abortion, but your dad was against it. His Catholic upbringing. But also, I wanted a baby. Maybe not then, but it felt wrong to give up the chance. Jake promised that it would be one year off and then we'd find a solution so I could go back.

"We got married. Then I found out I was having triplets. I walked around in a fog for a month after that. It seemed like a joke. One baby would be manageable, but three? Your dad got me through it. We'd get help, he'd accelerate his law classes so he could graduate early and get a job.

"You guys were born, and I fell in love with each of you. You were perfect. But I also suffered from postpartum depression. It wasn't as talked about then, and it took me a while to figure out what was going on. Eventually I saw a doctor and got on medication, and it helped. At the same time, we'd been approached about doing all that public stuff with you guys. We needed the money and we didn't think it would hurt, so we agreed. And I know, now, that maybe you girls didn't love it, but I did. It got me out of the house and into the world again. It gave me a purpose other than being your mom. It also gave us some financial freedom so that I could get help and have some time to myself again.

"You guys were doing well. I started thinking about going back to school. I asked and they said that if I took a class and did well, they'd let me back in. I was going to start when we got back from Disney World."

"What happened?" Emily asked.

"Aline broke her wrist."

"That doesn't explain anything."

"It was the start, you see? I was back in the hospital and I liked it."

"You liked the fact that I was hurt?" Aline asked.

"No, of course not, honey. I don't understand everything about this disease, okay? But it triggered something in me. Maybe if I'd been able to go back to school it wouldn't have come to anything, but that didn't work out."

"Why not?"

"When we got back from Florida, your dad got a massive case. One that would require him to basically live at the office for the next six months. And then the babysitter we'd lined up decided to move away."

"Why not find another one?"

"I tried. But you can't leave three six-year-olds with just anyone. And while I was looking, we found out that we weren't getting a commercial spot we'd hoped to book. That you weren't getting it, I mean."

"I remember that Disney trip was the last thing we did," Miranda said.

"Yeah, well, you were getting older, and there was a set of quintuplets that were born, made up of two sets of identical twins and a fraternal sibling, and next thing we knew, you weren't the flavor of the month anymore."

"So you didn't have the money?" Emily asked.

"That was part of it. Everything seemed to be happening at once. Your dad was working all the time. We had less money coming in."

"You got depressed again?"

"Yeah, I did. And again, I didn't see the warning signs. Then Miranda got the flu and we ended up back in the hospital."

"On purpose?"

"No, not that time, but I felt that . . . thrill, I guess you'd call it? Everyone was so concerned. You might not remember, Miranda, but you were very sick."

"This is sick," Miranda said.

"It is. I agree. And honestly, I'm not sure how it goes from there to my sickening you deliberately. I found myself doing it once. Giving you too much Tylenol when you had a fever, making you vomit, so I took you into the ER and then . . ."

A bird landed on the tree behind Emily. It was small, with a red beak. "You did it again."

"Yes."

"How many times?" Aline asked.

"I couldn't tell you now. But back then I kept a . . . log. So I'd remember what I'd done and make sure not to do it again."

"You did it so you didn't get caught."

"Yes."

"You knew it was wrong." The bird pecked at the tree bark. Was it looking for a worm? Miranda felt like one. Filled with dirt and ready to be consumed.

"Yes, on some level. But I didn't think . . . I know this sounds crazy, and I was crazy—I was—but I didn't think it was doing you any permanent harm."

Emily looked incredulous. "Then what happened?"

"I took it too far. I don't even remember what I gave you, Emily, but it was too much. They were asking a lot of questions at the hospital, about how it had happened. I said you'd gotten into the Drano, but I didn't think this one nurse believed me. I was scared she was going to report me. She didn't, but it didn't matter. I was scared about what I'd done. I wanted to stop. I'd tried, but I couldn't."

"Where was Dad in all of this?" Miranda asked.

"He didn't know."

"He figured it out after, though," Aline said.

Jennifer looked exhausted, like she might keel over right then and there. "He never said anything. He told me that he didn't know how to bring it up. Maybe he didn't want to know. Didn't want the responsibility. But it's not his fault, it's mine."

"You went to treatment, though," Miranda said.

"Yes, once Emily left the hospital, I told your dad I was struggling, that the depression was back and that I needed to check in to an inpatient facility. I told him I was worried I might hurt myself, and that was true. I convinced him to let my parents take you."

Miranda turned her attention back to the bird. It was easier than looking at her mother. "Why?"

"Because I didn't know if it would work. And I thought maybe, if it didn't—"

"That you'd give them custody of us?" Emily guessed.

"Yes."

"This is a forking nightmare."

Jennifer patted Miranda's leg gently. "I know, honey. I'm so sorry you have to know about any of this. But I went to treatment. I got help. I got you girls back and I was okay. I never did anything like that again."

Aline made a growling noise in her throat. "Till the twins were born."

"No. I swear, I never, ever hurt them. Not once. I didn't even think about it. I went to therapy for years to make sure it never happened again. I took medication and I did the work and I got better. I went off meds years ago, and I didn't need regular therapy anymore until your dad left. You girls didn't even remember what happened. And you're all fine. Good."

"I did remember, though," Aline said. "Not all of it. Not completely, but I knew that something wasn't right."

Jennifer looked at her hands lying flat on the table. "Is that why you were so angry with me all the time?"

"Yes."

"Why didn't you say anything?"

"Why was it my job to say anything? You were the mom."

Jennifer looked around at each of them. "I failed you. I'm so, so sorry."

"This is a lot to take in," Miranda said.

"I know it is. But I hope you can understand. Or even if not . . . I'm here to answer any questions you might have. Whatever you want to know, I'll tell you."

Aline bit her lip. "I have a question. When did it stop being Munchausen by proxy and flip to just Munchausen's?"

"I don't know what you mean."

"Come on, Mom. We know you poisoned yourself. Just like with Emily, right? You went too far this time?"

"No. No, I didn't do that."

"You expect us to believe you? After everything?"

"I swear, I didn't do it. I didn't do anything."

Aline reached down beneath the table. Her hand reappeared a minute later with a bottle, one of those ones used for a household cleaner. "I found this under your sink the other day. And I tested it. It's a lead solution. I bet if it was added bit by bit to your food, you wouldn't even notice the taste. So how do you explain that, Mom?"

Miranda got up, walked to the other side of the table, and stood behind her sisters. Emily's arms were splayed out in front of her. Aline reached out with her own arms and touched her.

And just like that they were a triangle again, pointing at the guilty party.

One Week to Live . . .

Chapter 41

SAY SOMETHING

Jennifer

For the next two days, my daughters' questions circle my brain like vultures. I denied it and denied it, and eventually they agreed to leave it alone, but I cannot.

Am I responsible for my fate and I don't remember it? Did I suppress it or simply forget, the cancer hiding my sins from me?

I have to agree with the girls that it's possible. Munchausen's can migrate. I was there. The poison was in my body and in my house. I'd seen that bottle of cleaner before. I noticed it again when I searched the house weeks ago for the source of my illness. I'd never thought to test it or any of the other cleaners. Was that a product of my broken brain? An oversight? Or a sign of something more?

The calls were made to me and the doctor's office says I returned them. I had the means and opportunity.

But what's the motive?

Attention I did not seek? Medical interventions I avoided?

Maybe I chickened out. Had regrets. Decided it wasn't worth the pain.

Whose attention was I trying to attract?

Jake's? Andrew's? No, that's silly. And Jake was lost to me; I knew that from the moment he told me about Kim. Jake doesn't admit mistakes. He doesn't revisit decisions, even if it's to spite himself.

Besides, did I even want Jake back? If he'd come crawling to me on his knees, full of apologies, telling me it had been the worst mistake of his life, would I have acquiesced? Was I that tied to this man who did not want me?

No. The girls were raised, I had my own money, I did not need him. I did not need to be the woman who forgave.

I only wanted to be the woman who forgot. Who got to a place where I did not cringe in his company, where I did not want to run in the other direction when we had to be together. I wanted everyone else to forget, too. Forget that he had humiliated me, that I'd been replaced.

Did I do it?

Are my daughters right?

I remember that day at the park with the boys. How Ethan was dragging Noah around, wanting to go on every apparatus whether it scared me or not. I never understood why society built high castles for children to climb when they were so fragile. But the boys didn't listen to me; they ran around with abandon and delighted whoops. Ethan was proud that he'd climbed to the top of the jungle gym. He yelled at me to look, his small arms windmilling, and then he fell.

My heart felt like it stopped as I ran to where he lay on the ground, his arm at a bad angle. I examined him myself, that old knowledge coming back. He was crying and in pain, and Noah started crying too because he felt it like it was his own pain.

I called Emily from the car as I drove them to the hospital. I thought she was in school, but now I know she wasn't. Where was she that day? She showed up at the hospital pale and wearing an outfit meant for a yoga class. Not her usual way of dressing. I didn't notice it; we were all so worried about Ethan. He was calmer by then, the professionals taking over, their voices soothing and cool. He was going to be fine, *Grandma*. That's what everyone called me, resting their hands on my arm, reassuring both of us that accidents happen, and he wouldn't even remember his cast after it was off.

It was the first time I'd been in a hospital since the girls were teenagers. When I left the mental health facility, I avoided being the one to take them to the doctor whenever I could. I told Jake that I found it too depressing and begged him to do it instead. I was trying to keep from being triggered, and I thought he believed my cover story. Looking back, I guess he didn't. But after a few years, I tested the waters. Aline had pneumonia and I went with her. I used my coping skills and had some extra therapy sessions and I was okay. The same when Miranda had a ruptured cyst a year later. I may have continued to catalog any signs or symptoms they had at home, but that was as a bulwark against me harming them. Keeping them healthy became my new passion—so much so that they thought I was a hypochondriac. Better that than the truth.

But there I was with the boys in the hospital and I can admit I felt that old thrill tugging at me. The wonderful concern, the touch, the soft voices. It had been a long time since I'd felt anything similar. I liked it. I did.

That scared me.

I should've left that hospital and gone right to Paul's office, and waited outside until he had time to see me.

I didn't do that.

Instead I stayed at the hospital as long as the boys were there, and I reveled in that feeling like an alcoholic does in their first drink after a relapse.

Just one drink, you think.

But it never stops there.

My rally is still holding.

It's such a strange thing. If I didn't know better, I'd think I was cured. That the cancer had given up the ghost and I could return to my shattered life.

But I do know better. I made that suggestion to the doctor yesterday, and he crushed my hopes. I'm getting these last days and I should cherish them. But there will not be any clemency for me.

The girls continue to visit separately. None of them stay for very long and none look me in the eye. Is it a sense of duty that brings them? Or do they think I'll confess? If they catch me sleeping, maybe I'll reveal the truth in my dreams, speaking it out loud.

That doesn't happen. Instead we pretend there are no accusations between us, and we talk of mundane things. Aline's work at the lab, her new focus and passion for investigating a true connection between heavy-metal exposure and brain cancer. Miranda's updates about her job search. She's decided she wants to be a tennis pro, probably teaching kids like she's been doing this summer. Tennis is the only thing she's stuck with her whole life, so I approve of this choice. With that and her inheritance, she can make a good life for herself catering to the rich and their children, and play in tournaments on the weekends. When she gets a couple of years of experience under her belt, she thinks she might move to California. She can play all year round there, and the coast is dotted with communities looking for someone like her—someone who fits right into the country club and looks as if she might've played pro.

Emily comes with the boys. Their last visit was supposed to be the goodbye, but since I'm doing better, she sneaks them out of day camp and lets them run around the property for an hour to amuse me. When they get cranky, she takes them away, asking only that I let her know each morning if it's safe to bring them. I know she means that I'm still in this state, not deteriorating. She doesn't want the boys to see me like that, and I can't blame her.

Suzie comes too, bringing dinner and wine most nights. We go through photo albums and talk about trips we took together. It is better to remember-when than to focus on what is to come. Only once does she bring up the photo montage she's working on, a presentation she'll play at my memorial service. She lets me approve the pictures and the music, Death Cab for Cutie's "I Will Follow You into the Dark," which I've always loved, even though it's maudlin, and seems fitting in the circumstances.

One day more, two, three. And now it's Thursday of what might be the last week of my life. My skin is tanned from sitting outside, but I've lost weight despite the dinners with Suzie, because I don't have much of an appetite for anything else.

There isn't much time left now. They can't say how much—they won't—but I can feel it. I feel thin, and not in a good way. Stretched out, transparent. As if I'm already a ghost haunting myself.

The sun has continued bright and sunny and hot. The grass is parched and the trees are starting to look limp. I'm sitting outside on a lounger they've brought out here for me. I'm reading a book, an Agatha Christie that I've read before. I can't help wondering if this is the last book I'll ever read. If it is, I'm good with that. Agatha, you were amazing.

"Hello, Jennifer."

I shade my eyes. My therapist, Paul, is standing there. He's wearing shorts and a T-shirt, which is disconcerting. But he's not a surprise. I asked him to come. To help me figure out whether I truly could have done this to myself without any memory of it.

I sit up and pull my sweater close to my body. I'm always chilled now, despite the heat.

"Thank you for coming. We could go to the picnic table over there in the shade?"

"That'd be great."

He helps me to stand and holds my arm to steady me while we walk slowly across the lawn. Paul wipes at his brow. It's strange to see him out here in the world. The only other time I saw him outside his office was when I ran into him and his wife once in the grocery store. I was friendly and chatted with him, but he looked stressed. It was the bonds of confidentiality, he explained to me later. He never spoke to a patient outside his practice unless the patient approached him first.

We sit down where I sat with the girls before, me on one side, him on the other. The table is sun-parched.

"How are you?" Paul asks.

"I'm hanging in."

"You look remarkably well, I must say."

"It's deceiving, isn't it?"

"Are they certain . . ."

"I asked. This is the calm before the storm, and I'm trying to enjoy it while I can."

"That's good."

I pick at a small piece of wood sticking up from the table. "I told the girls everything. About the Munchausen's. All of it."

"How did that go?"

"About how you'd expect."

"Which means?"

"I don't want to relive it. But suffice it to say, it did not lead to a round of forgiveness, not overtly anyway."

"I'm sorry to hear that. It's a very difficult thing for others to understand."

"I don't even understand it. And well, I guess I'm paying for it now. Irony of ironies and all that. The poisoner gets poisoned. Only, the girls think I did it to myself."

Paul takes in a sharp breath. "Did you?"

I raise my head slowly and look him directly in the eye. Sudden movements are not a good idea. "It looks bad. It looks like something I would do, and I had the best chance of doing it." I hold his gaze for a moment, then look off into the trees. "Sometimes I can almost see myself doing it. But then I think . . . how could I forget that? Is it possible?"

Paul goes quiet. I can feel him watching me, probably assessing if I'm telling him the truth. But I have no reason to lie to him, even if I had a reason to lie to the girls.

"We do sometimes repress trauma."

"But something this big? Me poisoning myself?"

"It's unlikely."

"Could it be the cancer?"

"The cancer can't delete specific memories. It doesn't work like that."

"Yeah, I didn't think so. It fits the facts, me being responsible. Some of them anyway. Enough for the girls."

"I'm sorry, Jennifer."

"Thanks."

Paul rubs at his beard. He's sweating slightly, even though we're in the shade. "What was it, though, truly, that made you think you might have done this to yourself?"

"Munchausen's can migrate, can't it? From by proxy to simple Munchausen's?"

"Yes, rarely, but—"

"When I told you about what happened with Emily's children last year, were you concerned?"

"A little, of course. Relapse is always possible. I'd have a duty to report if I thought you were responsible for anything that happened to them."

I turn toward him slowly. "Did you think about reporting me?"

"I noted what you told me and then I observed you closely. If I had seen any signs of relapse, any signs at all, yes—I would have alerted the authorities, and your daughter."

"I was so careful, though. I made sure I didn't fall apart again. And Emily made it easier for me—she didn't leave me alone again with the boys after that."

"She didn't?"

"You think that's odd?"

"Why would she do that if you weren't at fault?"

I thought it over. Back then I'd chalked it up to her being a nervous mother and, given my own state of mind at the time, I was relieved. It was better for me not to be alone with the boys so I couldn't be tempted. I could still see them regularly, but it didn't have to be alone.

Then I started seeing Andrew more frequently, and I had other concerns. The desire for that kind of attention drained away as quickly as it had come back. I felt free.

But now that information feels like a clue I missed.

"Emily and Miranda said that they didn't remember anything about what happened to them as kids."

"But Aline did?"

"Some, she said, but not enough to put it all together."

"Memory is something that is not truly understood."

"But the girls were old enough to remember, right? They could have."

"Yes, of course."

"And memories can come back suddenly, yes? If they're triggered by something?"

"That happens. It's not as simplistic as that, but yes. Sometimes we suppress something for years and then an event occurs that raises the memories to the surface."

I stare off into the trees. My mind is whirring at a thousand rpms—what does this mean, *what does this mean, what does this mean?*

"None of this means that anyone knew about the Munchausen's before you told them."

"True," I say, but I don't believe it. Because the dominoes are falling one after another now, click, click, click.

Chapter 42

CAN'T STOP

Jennifer

I'm reeling. There is no other way to put it than that. My brain is doing cartwheels. I don't know what to do. Did Emily know about the Munchausen's and just didn't say anything? And if that's true, what does it mean? I have to think about this methodically, though I can barely put two thoughts together. I need to slow down. Think.

Think.

Motive. Means. Opportunity.

I get the motive—I do. Even if it sickens me like I sickened her. If she knew, or found out somehow (*how?*), about the Munchausen's. If she thought I hurt her son on purpose.

Opportunity—All the girls have keys to the house, the password to the lock. Emily has come and gone like they all have over the years. My daughter. My heart. She would have had lots of extra time on her hands if she wasn't in school. And oh—Suzie mentioned she'd seen

Emily hanging around more than usual last year. So yes, she had the opportunity.

It's the means I'm stuck on.

No, I'm stuck on all of it but I'm trying to cling to something I can analyze. How did she do it? That bottle containing lead that Aline found under the sink in my house. She could have used that to slowly contaminate my food and beverages over time.

How did the bottle get there? She brought it? But where did it go? Who has it now?

I lie back in my bed and close my eyes. I try not to collapse under the weight of my own thoughts. My rally is an illusion now, but I need it to stay with me for a bit longer.

The bottle. It was Aline who found it. Aline who had it analyzed.

I take out my phone and text her. I don't think I can trust myself on the phone.

A—can you send me a photo of that bottle that had the lead solution?

I wait impatiently for an answer. She's usually slow to respond to my texts, when she does at all. But this time the answer comes quickly.

Why?

I want to see it.

You know what it looks like, Mom. You saw it at our lunch. It was yours.

I know you think that, honey, but it wasn't, and I need to see it again. Can you please indulge me?

There's a silence that's filled with Aline's grudging thoughts. But then my phone dings and there's a photo. A bottle of an environmental brand that I've never used in my life. The girls used to bug me about it. No, not the girls. A girl. Emily.

Emily has these products in her house, I'm almost sure of it.

But how can I check? How can I know for sure?

Can you please bring that to the house this afternoon?

Why?

Please, Aline? Just do as I ask.

Fine, okay, whatever.

Thank you.

I hold the phone in my hands and think for a minute. How can I check that this is the product she uses without going to Emily's? I dial a number.

"Jennifer?"

"Hi, Chris."

"Is everything okay?"

I breathe in and out slowly, trying to keep my voice normal. "I'm fine. But, um, Suzie is going to be clearing out some stuff at the house later today and I wanted to know, do you guys still use those environmental cleaning products? I have a bunch that someone gave me, and I don't want them to go to waste."

Chris hesitates, then chuckles. "Emily won't use anything else. But you don't need to be thinking about that now."

"I know, but that's what I thought." My voice is rising to an unnatural pitch. "I'll ask Suzie to set those aside for her then."

"Why did you call to ask me that?"

"Oh, I tried Emily and she didn't pick up."

"Okay."

"I . . . I also wanted to say goodbye. And thank you. For taking such great care of Emily. She's going to need you and—" My voice breaks and I stop myself. What the hell am I saying, anyway? I do love Chris, and I do want him to be kind to my grandchildren and to Emily, but I might be in the middle of destroying his life. Is that what I want to do? "I guess I wanted to say I love you."

"I love you too."

"Thank you. If I don't see you . . ."

Chris clears his throat. "You will, okay? I'll bring the boys by later."

"I'd like that."

I hang up before I start to cry. Nothing about this is fair. Nothing about this is easy. I don't know if I want to be the one making the decision about any of this. But I created this mess. I am the cause and I can be the solution.

I know what I have to do.

The Uber drops me off in front of my house. I snuck out of the hospice because I didn't want to have an argument about whether someone needed to come with me. I let myself in with the code, grateful for once for something Jake did, because I have no idea where my keys are. I'm wearing pajamas, a T-shirt, and flip-flops. I look destitute. But this is my house. I feel relief as I walk through the door and close it behind me, slipping to the floor to catch my breath. I breathe in the scent of home, that smell that lets me know this is my place. I lean against the door and listen. There's complete stillness. I'm alone.

When I can muster the strength, I climb the stairs slowly to my room. Someone has changed the sheets on my bed and made it, but everything else is as it was. I open the blinds to let the sunlight in. After I'm finished, I think I'll stay here. I don't want to go back to that anonymous place, even though everyone there is very nice. It won't be long now, anyway. Of this, I am certain.

I shuffle across the room and search through the papers on my desk. I find the test results and the phone records. I pick up a highlighter and I mark the initial results, then the secondary ones, pointing out the important facts. I highlight the numbers on the call log from the doctor's office and the ones on my phone bill. I check my calendar again. I realize that the call from my house occurred when I was doing my weekly stretching classes. Two hours every Thursday for years. I print my calendar up too and add it to the pile. Then I sit at my computer and write an explanation of everything to Suzie. I lay out the whole timeline. What I did back when the girls were kids. The dates I was in the mental health facility, so they can confirm the records. The dates I started feeling unwell. The cleaning solution with lead that must have been used on my food, slowly over time.

That Emily might have found out what I had done. That she might be behind it all.

My head is pounding fiercely as I go over what I wrote. Am I doing this? Accusing my daughter of this? Accusing *Emily*? We've always been the closest. Because we look alike. Because we are alike. But if she did this, something is broken between us. Did I break it? Am I responsible? Of course I am. If I'd had better control of myself. If I hadn't felt the need to play out what was missing in my own life in theirs. If I'd run from the first feeling of wanting to hurt them, none of this would be happening.

I print out the text I've written and place it in an envelope with the other documents. I sit there at the desk, looking out at the sunlight in my backyard. It's peaceful. So many memories hang in the trees. The girls' shouts as they ran around playing games. The family time barbecuing and drinking wine with friends. The sound of a ball being kicked. The crackle of the fire in the firepit. My life is flashing through my mind like a highlight reel. All the bad parts have been edited out.

When I can, I go downstairs and step out into the backyard. I walk to the firepit, the one I sat around so many nights in the last couple of years with Suzie while I cried and drank Jake away. The place where we used to stash our wine—my papers and the cleaning solution bottle will fit in here perfectly, and then Suzie can decide what to do.

I move the loose rock out of the way. There's a lighter in there, one of those fire-starter ones that has a long nozzle on it. It's pink, a gift from Suzie. Oh, Suzie, thank you. Thank you for holding me up after Jake left. I couldn't have made it through without you. I told you, but I should tell you again.

Suzie doesn't deserve this. She doesn't deserve to make a decision that I'm too afraid to make. That would be one more instance of me putting the hard choices onto someone else. A selfish decision.

No.

I can control this. I can decide what to do. I can make the right choice for once.

I put the envelope into the firepit and flick the lighter. The edge hesitates for a moment, the wax coating resisting the flame. Then it catches and the decision is made.

I replace the rock, making sure it looks undisturbed. I watch the flames. The envelope is a dancing yellow light.

And then a massive shock of pain feels like it's splitting me in two.

I fall to my knees, gripping my head.

I am alone out here.

I cannot call for help; I cannot even make a sound.

I roll into a ball on the grass. It feels wet and smells like the earth I'll be lowered into soon.

The pain is enormous.

The pain is everything.

And if I'm not dying right now, I want to be.

Chapter 43

HOME

Aline

Aline didn't know what to make of her mother's latest request.

When she'd found the bottle of cleaner under the sink a few days before their picnic, it had jumped out at her. She hadn't gone to the house for that reason—to look for evidence against her mother. At least, she didn't think she had. She'd thought she was going there to make up with Miranda. Being on the outs with her felt off, as if part of her was missing. She needed it back. And Nick, who was revealing depths she didn't know he had, had encouraged her. "Don't let this fester," he'd said. "You'll regret it."

She had enough regrets, so she'd gone to the house. She hadn't told Miranda she was coming; she didn't want to be dissuaded. But then Miranda wasn't there. Maybe she was at the hospice. More likely she was playing tennis. Aline felt lost. Lost in the house she grew up in, the place she knew best, wandering from room to room, in search of she knew not what. She'd ended up in the kitchen and had started going through the cupboards. Instinct had made her look under the sink. Instinct, too, made her reach for the bottle of cleaner to test it with one of the lead kits she'd bought that was still in her bag. It had tested positive.

Coupled with the information about what her mother had done to them as children, the answer seemed obvious. Jennifer had added a few drops of the liquid to her food or drink for long enough to give herself acute lead poisoning. Her mother was sick, so much sicker than Aline thought possible. She'd done this to herself and made them all suffer for it. Not that Jennifer wasn't suffering. Her cancer was probably a by-product of her stupid and reckless actions.

So that was it. Her mother had hurt herself, and soon this would all be over. Nothing would be resolved, and Jennifer would be gone, and they'd be left with their questions and regrets.

Questions. Aline's scientist brain couldn't turn those off. She had more of them than she could count, but the one that kept coming back was *why*?

If she'd done it, why would her mother tell anyone about the lead poisoning? She'd been diagnosed with cancer; she was getting plenty of medical attention. Plenty of attention from the girls without adding in a poisoning.

Why would she blame Jake? What was the point? It wasn't as if any of them were so close to Jake now. Their contact with him was minimal, even Miranda's. What Jake did might not have brought them closer to their mother, but it did drag them away from their dad.

What was Jennifer trying to achieve? Was it her illness? Was it beyond her control?

Why, why, why?

Try as she might, Aline couldn't figure it out, and the questions kept circling like water disappearing down a drain. Even as she drove over to her mother's house with the bottle on the seat next to her, she couldn't decide if she wanted to confront Jennifer with it again. Maybe alone, maybe without the others, they could come to an understanding.

She pulled into the driveway. Her mother's car was there, but when she knocked on the front door, there wasn't any answer. Of course, her mother didn't have her car at the hospice. Was she even there? Had Aline misunderstood?

Aline used the code to get in the house and was met with silence. "Mom?"

Her voice echoed through the first floor. She put the bottle down on the entryway table.

"Mom?"

Aline walked upstairs, past all the photos of her childhood. It was like a prototype of social media. Everything looked perfect, but behind the white-teethed smiles there was something rotten.

"Mom?"

It was silent upstairs too. She wandered through the rooms like she had the other day. The one that used to belong to her. Miranda's. Emily's. The personality of each remained, though their things had mostly gone. Then her parents' bedroom, all evidence of Jake stripped away. The house smelled stale, and as she reached the guest room, Aline realized that she hadn't seen Bea in a few days, not since Jennifer had been taken to the hospice. How had she not noticed until now? Were they all that self-involved?

The obvious answer was yes.

There was an envelope sitting on Bea's bed, a card, Aline realized when she got closer. It was a note, explaining that Bea was slipping out because she couldn't be there anymore. She had to *take care of herself*. Aline wasn't surprised. Bea always looked out for number one. Some people would resent her, but Aline never did. Then again, it was easier to forgive an absent grandmother than an absent mother.

Not that Jennifer had been absent. She'd been right there next to them the whole time, but the past felt like a screen. A film that coated everything and kept her from being close to the girls. Aline, anyway.

Aline threw the card down. Why had her mother asked her to come here? What did she want with the bottle in the first place? To retest it? To destroy it?

Why did she do what Jennifer asked? She wasn't someone who tended to do that. Part of her wanted all of this to end. But that was awful, wasn't it? She was awful.

She went back downstairs, ready to leave. She heard a sound from the kitchen and walked in. The door to the backyard was open, and there was something—someone—on the ground . . .

"Shit!" Aline ran outside, her feet pounding to the rhythm of her heart. Jennifer was lying in a ball, groaning next to the firepit. The air was acrid. "Mom. Mom. Are you okay?"

Jennifer's eyes fluttered but didn't open. "Emm . . ."

"What is it, Mom?"

Aline pulled her phone from her hip and dialed 911.

"Emmm . . ." Jennifer said again.

"Emily? No, it's Aline. I'm here, Mom. Right here."

"What is the nature of your emergency?"

"Please send an ambulance to 45187 Stanford immediately. My mom has cancer and I think she's had some kind of stroke."

"Emmm . . ."

"I'm right here, Mom. I'm here." Emily pushed past a startled Aline and dropped to the ground. She put her hand to Jennifer's neck and checked her pulse. "Pulse is thready."

"Did you hear that?" Aline said into the phone. "How long will it take?"

"The ambulance is on its way, ma'am."

Aline threw the phone down onto the grass and moved over to where Emily was cradling Jennifer. "What's wrong with her?"

"I don't know. Stroke, maybe. Stay calm, Mom. It will be okay."

Jennifer's eyes opened again, and her head lolled to the side. Her mother's eyes were full of panic.

"Emily," she said again, but instead of a plea, this time it sounded like forgiveness.

Chapter 44

FINIS

Jennifer

I open my eyes and it's the middle of the night. Finally, I can tell the time. The quiet glow of the clock on the wall says it's three a.m. The space around me is eerily quiet, a silence that makes its presence known. But there's someone standing in the room. A form in the corner.

Is this death? Has it come for me at last?

The form advances, its face in shadow. It's wearing a white coat, like the doctors.

It's a doctor.

It takes another step, turns its face and catches some light from the hall. It's my daughter.

"Emily?"

I whisper the words because that's all I can do. I feel afraid, but it's a fleeting feeling. The drip into my arm absorbs my emotions and floats them away.

"Yes," she says, moving closer. "It's me."

"What . . ." I cannot get more words out, but these seem to be enough.

"I came to see you one last time."

My mouth is dry and it's hard to form words, almost impossible. "You . . . were . . . here . . . before?"

"Ever since you were brought into the hospital two days ago."

Two days. That's how many notches there are in reality. I have been in and out of it. Mostly out. But where was she?

"I . . . did . . . not . . . see . . . you . . ."

She nods. "That was deliberate."

"I . . . don't . . ."

"You don't understand? I don't think that's true. I saw what you wrote on your computer to Suzie about what's happening to you. About me."

"The computer?"

"I installed a program on it a while back. So I could read what you wrote."

"Why?"

Emily walks away and closes the door. Then she's back by my side.

"Don't pretend. I know who you are. And now you know who I am too."

I stare at her. My daughter. She has my face. We look so much alike. And now we are exactly alike. No, not exactly. I acted without thinking of the consequences. Not Emily. The cleaning solution. The calls to the doctor's office. The visits to the house. That was deliberate.

She meant to kill me.

"I don't . . ."

Emily's face twists. "No, Mom. No more lies. You know what I did and why I did it."

"The . . . cleaner . . ."

"Yes, that's right. When I realized what you did to us when we were kids, I was livid. I couldn't believe what you put us through. And all for what? Attention? There's no one here, Mom. No one's paying you any mind."

"I . . . sorry . . ."

Emily leans closer to me. Her breath is sour, and I can smell her sweat. I'm filled with terror but there's nothing I can do.

"Sure, right. You know what, Mom? I don't think so. If you knew everything I've gone through . . . Because of your lies . . ."

Emily's thoughts are as scattered as my own. I can't follow what she's saying, but I can feel the pain.

"I . . . didn't . . ."

"You didn't want to know. You wanted to pretend it didn't happen. You wanted to forget. But I couldn't."

She reaches into her coat pocket and takes something out. A needle.

"Please . . . I won't tell . . ."

"No, that's right. You won't."

"Please . . . Emily . . ."

She leans over me again. Her breath is hot against mine. "I gave you a taste of your own medicine. Did you like it?"

I can't say anything. The force of her hate pushes me back into the bed. There is nowhere to go.

This is my fault.

I deserve this.

I don't say anything as she reaches for my IV line and inserts the needle. I close my eyes as she pushes the plunger. I don't know what she gave me, but I know it will be over soon.

Soon.

Soon.

I'm so sorry, Emily. So sorry for everything.

After . . .

Chapter 45

AIN'T NO LOVE

Miranda

The rain that had been missing the last six weeks showed up for the funeral. A row of black umbrellas made a shape Miranda didn't know the name of. Perhaps its name should be grief.

It flooded through Miranda like the water gushing through the streets, falling too fast to be absorbed by the ground or the sewer system. She was surprised by its force, though she shouldn't have been. Her mother was the center of their family, whether they acknowledged it or not. Without her, even the bonds between her and her sisters seemed to have failed.

It didn't look that way. On the outside, they were the picture-perfect portrait of grief. Jennifer's death was reported in the local press and someone made the connection back to the family they were during their brief stint of fame. They wanted to conduct an interview. Miranda and Aline hadn't wanted to do it, but Emily said that she would, and so all three of them agreed, putting on identical black dresses and sitting in front of a camera for a remote. They spoke well of their mother, talking about how she coped with triplets. They each came up with a funny story and then it was over.

It was the same thing at the funeral. None of them wanted to speak, yet they all did. The church was full. All of those people behind the casseroles, the mothers and fathers of their friends growing up. Everyone on their street. Suzie, inconsolable. Bea, stoic, self-medicated. Devon, who looked sheepish and gave Miranda an awkward hug.

Jake stayed away at their request.

The rain pelted at the stained glass windows, then their umbrellas at the graveside. They buried the casket their mother picked out. They buried her secrets, but they were still a wedge between them.

If you'd asked Miranda before her mother's diagnosis if tragedy would bring her and her sisters together or tear them apart, she would've said the former. And then she would've said, *but we were together in the first place. We couldn't be closer if we tried.* She believed that with every fiber of her being, but it turned out she was wrong.

All the suspicion, the lies, it had ripped them apart, maybe forever.

If only the rain could wash away the past six weeks and all the secrets it leached out.

After the funeral, they gathered at the house. There were more casseroles, more people filling it up. Hands pressed on arms offering kind words. Everyone was sorry, so sorry. It was what Jennifer had said to them too. Was it a confession? Or was she simply apologizing for all the hurt from the past, all the damage she'd caused?

Miranda didn't know, and it didn't feel as if there was anyone she could ask.

The house felt oppressive, humid and full. Miranda followed Aline's lead and drank too much to cope with it, because leaving your mother's funeral to hit a thousand tennis balls was something that would be frowned on. Slowly, slowly, the people left one by one until the only ones left were Miranda, Aline, and Emily and Bea.

But Bea wanted to leave too. She needed to, she said, and because she looked so diminished and small, they hugged her close, then helped her into the car of the man who'd brought her to the funeral. Bea had introduced him only as Hector, and he'd smiled sadly and shook their hands. Another understated man who was happy to let Bea take center stage, Miranda diagnosed, then forgot about it.

They cleaned the kitchen in silence, no radio on, no remember-whens. Maybe those times would come again, but for right then, they had a job to do and it was almost over.

Emily's phone buzzed on the counter. She'd been jumpy all day, and she snatched it up quickly.

"It's Chris. He's waiting outside." Chris had left earlier to relieve the babysitter. "He's got the boys."

"Go ahead," Aline said. "We can finish up here."

"Okay."

"Let's meet next week to decide what to do."

"Decide?" Emily wiped her hands on a dishcloth.

"About the house. All her stuff . . ."

"Right, okay. Yes. Next week."

Emily hurried out and Aline watched her go. "What's up with her?"

"What's up with any of us?" Miranda answered. "Shall we finish?"

"Yep."

Miranda rolled up her sleeves and dug her hands into the sink. "Who knew so many dishes could be produced in one day?"

"Not even a whole day."

"Right?"

The doorbell rang. "I'll get it," Miranda said.

She rinsed her hands off and walked to the front door. It was Suzie. She looked wrung out and tired, her eyes red-rimmed. "Can I come in?"

"Of course. Did you forget something?"

"No, I . . ."

"Do you need a drink?"

"Sure, if there's anything left."

Suzie stepped into the house. She was wearing a raincoat, and the water dripped off her and pooled on the floor. "I should take this off."

"Don't worry about it."

Miranda turned and Suzie followed her into the kitchen. "Suzie's here."

Aline was loading the dishwasher. "Hi, Suzie, what's up?"

"I know this might sound weird, but I need to check something in the backyard."

"Why?"

"Your mom asked me to look for something there after she died."

Miranda and Aline shared a look. "She told you?" Aline said. "That she thought she was poisoned?"

Suzie turned paler. "Was she?"

"Who knows. There's a lot . . . There's a lot about her that you probably don't know."

"I know she loved you girls. I know she was my best friend. And if someone did something to her, then I'd want to know."

Miranda was tired. She thought all this was over. Now her mother was still bringing it up again from beyond the grave. "Did she say where she'd leave it?"

"In our hiding place."

"You had a hiding place?"

Suzie laughed nervously. "It wasn't like that. It was a joke be-tween us. There's an empty space out in the firepit. It was to keep wine cold."

"She never told us that," Miranda said. "More lies."

Aline nodded her head. "I guess that's innocent. Not that she was."

"What do you mean?" Suzie asked.

"She wasn't poisoned. Or if she was, she did it to herself."

"I highly doubt that."

Aline leaned against the counter. "You don't know what we do."

"Why would she tell me about it if she was responsible? Why would she hide something for me to find?"

Miranda had to admit, Suzie made a good point. One that didn't seem entirely foreign to Aline.

"The poison was right there under her sink," Miranda said. "Aline found it, and had it tested."

"Shit."

"What?"

"I forgot it here. The day she . . . when I found her in the back-yard. Hold on." Aline left the room and returned quickly. "Did you see it?"

"What?"

"The bottle. The one I found, it's not where I left it in the front hall."

"Maybe it got put away. There were a lot of people in here today."

Aline walked to the sink and looked under it. "Not here."

"I'm sure it will turn up."

Aline stood up slowly. "Where's this hiding place again?"

"In the firepit."

"Let's go look."

"Now?" Miranda said. "It's pouring out."

"No time like the present."

Aline grabbed an umbrella from the stand by the back door and opened it. They walked together through the unrelenting rain, the grass sucking at their shoes.

"I found her here," Aline said, pointing to a spot a few feet from the firepit. "That day she collapsed."

"Did she have anything with her?" Suzie asked.

"No." Aline walked to the pit. It was filled with water and ash. "But something had been burned in it. I could smell it . . . some papers maybe? Where is this hiding place?"

Suzie crouched down. She pulled back a loose stone, revealing a crevice underneath it.

Aline reached her hand in, then pulled it out, empty. "There's nothing in here."

"Oh," Suzie said. "I thought . . ."

"More drama," Aline said bitterly.

"No, Aline, I'm sure . . ."

Aline stalked back to the house. Miranda stood there with Suzie, both of them looking at the black space in the ground.

"Maybe she didn't have time to get here," Suzie said. "Or she burned it for some reason?" Suzie poked her finger into the firepit. "There's some paper . . . It's all burnt."

"Maybe there was nothing to put in there."

"Do you believe that?"

"I don't know anymore. Some things are better left buried, you know?"

"I'm sorry," Suzie said, putting her arm around Miranda's shoulders.

"She said that too."

"I know she meant it. Whatever she did. Whatever happened

in the past. She loved you girls, more than anything. You can't fake that."

Miranda knew at once that it was true. Jennifer had loved them, perhaps too much. But the love had been there the whole time. It was still there, waiting to be uncovered once they wiped the past away.

It was going to take time and work, but for once, Miranda wasn't afraid of that. She and her sisters; she always had that, and she still had them.

They would get through this together.

She'd fight for that.

She had to.

Chapter 46

FUNERAL SONG

Emily

This is what I said at my mother's funeral.

I said that my mother had given up her dreams for us. That was true.

I said that we were her whole world. That was true too.

I said that I'd had so much admiration for the way she got through my dad's betrayal. That she'd come through the other side of something terrible and had rebuilt her life in a way that we could all model. She'd shown courage. She'd shown grace.

The wine had helped too. That got a laugh.

I told this story: When I was five, I took a test that said I was advanced. They wanted to skip me, to put me in a different grade than my sisters. I didn't want to do it. I thought I was a freak.

"No, honey, your brain is just different." She'd leaned her head close to mine and whispered, "Want to know a secret?"

I nodded the way kids do, eager to share something with my mom.

"My brain is different too."

Then she'd kissed me on the forehead and tucked me into bed, and the next day she asked me whether I wanted to skip ahead or stay with my sisters. It was my choice, 100 percent, she'd said, and whatever I chose, she'd support it. And she did. I skipped, and when I got picked on by the other kids, she was there to make me feel better, to defend me, to remind me that I was special. My brain was different, but that was okay. Because her brain was different too.

Telling this story made me cry, and I wasn't the only one.

I fought through the tears as I said: *I have a dozen stories like that. Stories about my mother's selflessness and sacrifice. She beat just about everything life threw at her the same way: planning, effort, work. Cancer was the foe she couldn't beat.*

Then I rushed into Chris's arms before I lost it completely. He led me back to my chair and held me until the shuddering tears stopped. Chris. My Chris. I could not live without him.

But here's another story. One I couldn't tell at the funeral.

It starts with a confession. Something I've never told anyone.

I didn't get pregnant by accident in med school. I got pregnant on purpose.

I've wanted to be a mother for as long as I could remember. I don't know why. Was it an absence in my own mother that I wanted to fill? One I didn't even notice? Who knows, who cares, the need was just there.

It grew when I met Chris. I knew he was my guy from the beginning. But he was a reluctant lover at first. I'd been in relationships before where I was the one who cared less. I knew how it felt. This was like that. Chris liked me, sure. But love? Undying passion? I wasn't sure. I was scared all the time. That I'd lose him, push him away. I had to keep my love hidden so I didn't scare him away, when all I wanted to do was to shout it out loud.

We started to drift when I went to med school. I had so much less time to devote to him, and he was young. Other girls were interested. He wanted to explore his options. Panic set in, but the solution came quickly. I had a template in my own life, after all. If I got pregnant, I knew Chris would do what my dad had done. He'd stand by me. He'd lean into our life together.

I could get everything I always wanted.

Only I couldn't get pregnant. It seemed like a joke at first. All my worrying about birth control. I was only twenty-one! My mother was so fecund, she'd had natural triplets. I went one month, two, three. I was running out of time. Chris was slipping further away.

I went to see a doctor.

That's when I found out about the fertility problems. I'd always had unpredictable periods but had never thought much about it. Now a doctor was telling me that I had abnormal hormone levels and a natural pregnancy was unlikely. I cried for two days, and then I made a plan.

I raided my college fund and signed up for IVF treatments. I told the private clinic that my partner wanted to do his sperm "donations" at home. Do I need to spell out the rest of it? I got Chris's sperm the old-fashioned way and collected it carefully to bring into the clinic. We ended up with five viable embryos, two of which were implanted in me.

It worked the first time.

I told Chris tearfully eight weeks later when I was sure they were safe.

He did the right thing.

He became loving and attentive. He became everything I wanted.

I got everything I wanted.

But something was niggling me.

Why couldn't I get pregnant naturally? What was the cause of my infertility? When I could, I spent time researching. There were several possibilities—lead exposure was one.

I put that aside. It didn't seem likely.

I tried to let it go. I tried to move on.

I had the boys. I was joyous. Chris was fantastic—everything I'd dreamed he'd be. I settled into motherhood, till the postpartum hit. I don't like to think about that, but I felt defective. Couldn't get pregnant and then once I did, I was unhappy. I know it's common, but it didn't feel that way to me.

I did what the doctor ordered: medication and therapy. I got better, I went back to school, but things weren't right. I couldn't focus. The passion I'd had for medicine seemed to have leaked out of me. I was ashamed, so I kept that to myself too. I didn't register for the next semester, but I couldn't find a way to tell Chris. Instead, I spent my days aimlessly, dropping the kids at day care, then picking them up again hours later. Sometimes, when I knew she'd be out, I hung out at my mother's house. I'd lie on my old bed, listening to songs on my phone or reading a book.

I was lost.

Then I got the call from my mother that she was at the hospital. Ethan was hurt. I rushed there in a panic, feeling guilty. The only reason Ethan was even with my mom was because I was being selfish. Not taking care of my own children.

Ethan was fine, but I was not. I was sitting in the hall, crying with relief, when a nurse stopped to see if I was okay. She told me some stupid story to calm me, and I found myself telling her about the time when I was eight and I'd drunk Drano by accident. I hadn't thought about that in years, maybe not since shortly after it had happened, but now I was remembering. Too much. Why would I get into the

Drano? I was a smart kid. A rule follower. At eight I was too old to do something like that, something I didn't remember doing. And what about all the other times I'd been sick? All the hospital visits and school days missed? When had those stopped? When my mother went away.

I went to the records department and asked to see my medical file. When I got them a week later, I pored over the pages as if I were studying for my medical boards. And there it was: the pattern of visits. The stomach ailments and undiagnosable symptoms that had brought me over and over again to the hospital. And the blood tests. The ones that showed the elevated levels of lead. I was supposed to have been brought in for chelation therapy. Instead, we'd gone to live with Bea.

I had my answer, then. All the questions that I carried with me. I knew without a doubt that the cause was my mother. My dad never cared about medical things and let her take care of all of it, popping in for visits to lift our spirits. Now our going to live with Grandma Bea made sense. Mom didn't have cancer, she was in a mental institution. That proved easy enough to verify. I called the nearest one, pretending to be my mother's therapist, and they confirmed the information readily enough.

My rage was a flame. It burned inside me so hot it was hard to think of anything else. I could've confronted her, but to what end?

No, no, I wanted something more visceral. More fitting.

I wanted to give her a taste of her own medicine, and I did.

But like her, I went too far. She got so sick I stopped. I couldn't have her going to a doctor and finding out she'd been poisoned. She went anyway, though, and I fretted. When she mentioned that she was waiting on test results, I knew I had to act quickly. I called the doctor's office, pretending to be her, making sure they had the right number—her home phone—and that they didn't use her cell. Then I redirected her landline to my phone. When they called a second time, I called back from my mother's and said I was going elsewhere for a second opinion. I thanked them for their concern. Then I left a message for my mother on her voice mail using a computer program I found online to modify my voice, telling her that her results had come back negative.

I watched her carefully as she got better.

I thought I was in the clear.

My rage simmered, then burned out. I concentrated on my family and stopped wandering aimlessly through the day.

Then that call from the hospital saying my mother had been admitted. The questions my mother was asking. The conclusion she was jumping to.

I felt sick with worry. I needed to hide what I had done. I did what I could to convince her to leave all this alone.

When she didn't, I had to act. I stayed as close as I could. So long as her suspicions fell on my dad, I knew I was safe. When they shifted to Miranda, I felt myself coming apart. I had been so careful, I thought, but mistakes I'd made kept surfacing. Like that bottle I'd used to slowly poison her food. I'd forgotten to remove it from the house. I'd meant to go back and get it, but it had always slipped my mind.

I have it now, though. When Chris texted me that my mother was asking what brand of cleaner we used, I knew what that meant. I went to the hospice and followed her back to the house. I watched what she typed on her computer on my phone, using the program I'd installed to track her. I'd meant to go into the house and stop her from sending what she wrote to Suzie. But instead, she turned off her computer, came down the stairs, and headed toward the backyard. I followed her out there and watched as she went to the firepit and lit something on fire. What was she doing? I was about to ask when she suddenly crumpled to the ground.

Finally, something was going right.

Then a car pulled up. I snuck around the side of the house to see who it was. Aline, bottle in hand. I hid in the house while Aline yelled for our mom, and when she went outside, I put the bottle in my purse. My mother was still there on the ground, the firepit smoking behind her, Aline yelling for help. I showed myself so I could control the situation.

I watched and waited for two days. She was close to death, but not dead. She might still regain consciousness. I needed to be ready for that. I stayed alert and gathered my supplies. A medical coat stolen out of one of the offices. A syringe full of morphine plucked from a distracted nurse. It would be a release for her, I reasoned. All that lay ahead was pain and confusion.

There's been enough of that already.

And this, this is my release. A trick my own therapist taught me. *Write it all down*, she used to say, *and release it.*

So I have. I poured the poison out of me onto these pages and now I have only one thing left to do—burn them like my mother did. The papers that were missing from her room after she died, the test results and phone records, all the clues I'd left in my wake. That's what she was doing at the firepit.

She'd decided to let me off the hook, it seems, and so I will too.

Sorry, Mom.

ACKNOWLEDGMENTS

This book was a strange journey for me, not the least of which was because I finished the first draft in early March 2020. I wrote it in one world, and it's going to be published in another. I wondered if I should update it to reflect that but decided to leave it as the time capsule it is.

As always, each book takes a village. I'd like to especially thank my new team at Atria—Kaitlin Olson in particular, who has been a joy to work with. To the Simon & Schuster Canada team, thank you for signing on again, and to Laurie Grassi for her great suggestions on this manuscript. A special shout-out to Kevin Hanson for being there when I needed him. Thanks to my agent, Abigail Koons, for always championing me no matter what. To my film and television team at Gotham—Dillon and Ellen, you keep knocking it out of the park.

To my friends and family, I cherish you always. A special shout-out to Tasha, Christie, Sarah, and Candice, who made quarantine fun and always make me laugh.

My husband, David. We made it through months of quarantine together without a homicide, which is pretty amazing.

To my writer tribe, thank you for having my back, especially Liz Fenton, Carol Mason, Therese Walsh, Kim Roosevelt, and Shawn Klomparens. And to Elyssa Friedland—what would I do each day without you?

To the Rings: Scott, Cam, Owen, Liam, Bill, Sean, Quinn, Cora, and Noah—Wilma was a special person who meant so much to so many, but most of all to you. This book made me think of her every day I was writing it.

Lastly, to you, dear reader. This eleventh (!) novel wouldn't exist without you.

ABOUT THE AUTHOR

CATHERINE McKENZIE is the bestselling author of ten novels and has sold over a million books worldwide. She practiced law in Montreal for twenty years before retiring to write full-time. Her most recent novel, *You Can't Catch Me*, has been optioned for a television series by Paramount TV. An avid runner, skier, and amateur tennis player, Catherine lives and writes in Montreal, Canada. Visit her at **www.catherine mckenzie.com** or follow her on Twitter **@CEMcKenzie1** or Instagram **@catherinemckenzieauthor**.